maggie's ruse

a novel

by

Anne Leigh Parrish

To John, Bob, Lauren, and Lacey

Contents

maggie's ruse

a novel

by

Anne Leigh Parrish

chapter one

The floor creaked whenever Maggie shifted her weight. The Jimmy Choo stiletto pumps were killing her. Their cherry red leather called her name in the SoHo shoe boutique only an hour before, just after Kyle's text message urged her to get her lovely butt out the door and down to the gallery for the opening of Luther Galt's exhibition. That Kyle was gay didn't lessen her appreciation for his compliment. Kyle knew a good butt when he saw one. At the moment he was across the room, checking out what was on offer.

Luther Galt, on the other hand, hadn't checked her out once. Her usual gambit, "You've been such an inspiration for my own work," was received with a blank stare. Then he cleared his throat. He was shorter than Maggie by about two inches, another reason she despaired of the shoe choice. Only the other day her mother had complained over the phone that heels had just gotten too high. Maggie didn't like talking to her mother and did so only to keep the money flowing.

The corner of Galt's right eye was crusted. His face was acne scarred and littered with broken blood vessels. His nose dripped. Not a prime specimen by any means, and Maggie abandoned her plans to seduce him. She was a poor seducer, truth be told, though she was pretty, thin, and shapely, all things men usually liked, though not as much as they liked it in her twin sister, Marta. Marta was sassy because she was an actress. Or she was an actress because she was sassy. Either way, her muse was louder than Maggie's, and had pushed her further along the glittery road to success, though she'd appeared in only two plays the whole time they'd been in New York—almost three years. Yet she spoke of herself as a seasoned veteran of the stage in a way that sometimes made Maggie admire her confidence, and other times made her want to scream.

Maggie looped her free arm through Galt's—in her other hand was a glass of champagne—and begged him to show her his favorite piece.

The Dawn of Time, a muddy mess of brown and green, was at the far end of the gallery, and by the time Galt had escorted her there, the little toe of her right foot was screaming. She reclaimed her arm, removed her shoes, and put them in her huge purple leather purse, after asking Galt to hold her glass for her. He must have assumed she was offering it to him, because he drank it down in one go. The alcohol caused him to flush immediately. He looked at her keenly.

"You strike me as a perceptive young woman. Tell me what you're devoted to. Artistically, I mean," he said.

Maggie pulled out the little album she always had with her. She photographed every finished piece, labeled the photos, and put them in chronological order. As she looked over Galt's shoulder while he flipped slowly through, she realized a sorting by color and subject might have made more sense. Maggie was obsessed with two things—doorframes and empty bottles—which appeared over and over in greater or lesser degrees of abstraction, imbued most often with blues and grays, but sometimes with warmer tones, and even a touch of hot pink now and then. She saw now that the current arrangement was jumbled and didn't lead the viewer through any progressive understanding. Galt paused over one, a leaning doorframe with exposed hinges, and asked her if the bullseyes she'd included meant she had an interest in Victorian architecture.

"Not really," she said.

"Pity. In many ways, it represented the pinnacle of design."

"Ah."

He gave her back the album, then the empty glass, and turned away as his name was called by a tall, white-haired man in a tuxedo with a red scarf thrown rakishly over his shoulder.

Maggie put the glass on the floor and padded her way across the room to find Kyle. He was sitting on a wide windowsill, looking at his phone, and sulking. As she approached, he said, "Darling, you've gone native."

"They don't fit."

"Take them back."

"I will."

Maggie joined him on the sill. She told him about showing Galt her album, and his lukewarm response.

"You've got to get him into your studio," Kyle said.

"I left, remember?"

She'd been working in a large co-op studio in Chelsea with two other artists. Her assigned part of it was next to a glorious bank of tall, filthy windows. It was a great arrangement. She dropped by a couple of days a week, painted for an hour or two, then went on her way in a state of energized fulfillment. Sometimes Kyle came with one of his flamboyant friends to look at her most recent work and act impressed. Once she brought a gallery owner she'd bought an expensive dinner for. The owner—a tiny women in her sixties with a heavy silver necklace, peered over her bifocals at two canvases depicting empty bottles, all of which were tipped over, and asked if she had a particular fondness for bowling. Maggie took her question in stride, which was made a little easier by the woman really loving her rendition of one doorway within another.

"Have you named it?" the woman—Giselle—asked.

"No."

"Call it *Inner Child*. I might find a place for it."

Giselle's gallery on Twenty-Third Street had just been renovated into a modern split-level, light-filled space with cable railings, and a painted concrete floor. The floor color, a pale green, would go perfectly with the aqua hues in Maggie's painting. The crowd that gathered to admire it would be stylishly dressed, but it was the adoring gaze of one man, standing apart, that she craved most. He'd be tall and unkempt, with a haunted look in his green eyes. His unshaven cheeks gave him a rough air that his passion for art belied. First, he would be her patron, then her lover.

In the end, Giselle had to pass. She'd just arranged a solo exhibit for a French printmaker. Later, if she put together a show that complemented Maggie's style, she'd be in touch. So much for the spellbound crowd and finding the love of her life.

Not long after, a new artist joined the co-op. Leah was serious, and couldn't tolerate the music Maggie and the other artist, Luis, like to play when they worked. She said it made it hard for her to concentrate. Maggie and Luis complained. They liked a happy atmosphere. Sometimes they laughed and kidded around. What was the harm? Leah called them a couple of idiots. They went to the manager of the co-op, who turned out to be Leah's boyfriend, Digger.

Leah was a rare person, he said. Did they realize that? She'd overcome a monstrous childhood by finding a healthy outlet in art. Who were they to compromise her drive for expression? Some people let their demons control them. Leah was confronting hers, and doing pretty damn brilliantly, as far as he could tell. Maggie agreed. Leah was hugely talented. Her abstract pieces blended the wild fury of Pollack with the measured lines of Mondrian.

One night Maggie splattered one of Leah's canvases with black paint. She had given up on her own work for the day—another doorway with a textured frame and glowing half-moons up and down both sides. The can sat open, just where Leah had left it. It stared at her cruelly. The taunt was unmistakable. The way the paint flew from the bristles of her fat brush and landed with a sloshy *thwack* was fantastic. The psychic relief that followed cleaned her from the inside out.

At the same moment, Leah was in the bathroom, losing a fetus she hadn't known she was carrying. Maggie was still holding the paint can when Leah walked gingerly toward her, pale and teary-eyed.

"Call 911," she said.

"Look, we don't need the cops. I did it. You know I did it. I'll write you a check for whatever you think it was worth."

"Medics, moron."

The crotch of Leah's denim overalls was soaked with blood. Maggie instantly felt queasy. She didn't do well with that sort of thing. Yet she managed to punch in the numbers, and then told Leah to lie down right there on the floor. Maggie draped a cloth over her and offered an old sweater as a pillow. Maggie was overcome with the brutality of what she'd done to the canvas. Waiting for the medics, she broke down crying. Leah told her to shut up.

By the time Leah was on her feet again and back in the studio, Maggie had fled. Her paintings were now stacked against the wall in the apartment she shared with Marta. Marta wasn't wild about this arrangement. She was cultivating Josh, an aspiring director, and he dropped in now and then for drinks. He tended to get distracted by whatever canvas Maggie had most recently pulled out to agonize over and didn't listen to Marta's pitch about what plays they could seek investors for, and what role would be best for her. Marta solicited manuscripts on Twitter, to be sent to a PO Box so her address would remain unknown and unavailable to the legions of disappointed playwrights whose work didn't fit. She had only about ninety followers, gleaned mostly from other actors she'd met at auditions, using the hashtags #stage #play #theatre. (The British spelling looked more elegant.) After nearly four weeks, she'd gotten only two submissions. One, *Lana's Tree*, had been sent by a retired machinist living in Vermont. The tree housed the spirit of Lana's late husband. Lana sat beneath it, grieving, reminiscing, and the tree communicated by brushing her gently with a low-hanging branch or sending a shiver through its trunk as she leaned morosely against it. The play struck her as a perfect vehicle for her own developing sense of pathos. It was essentially a solo performance.

The other play was favored by Josh. There, a group of oversexed high school students go on a field trip and run amok through the town, drinking, fighting, forming factions until the strongest takes control, even quoting from *Lord of The Flies*. The last scene had them executing their chaperones in a bloody display. It was poorly written, needed massive editing, and was, predictably, authored by a fifteen-year-old boy in New Jersey whose pen name was Vader. Josh thought Marta could portray the female chaperone perfectly.

She told Maggie to move the paintings into her own room, or to her side of the third bedroom, which they had converted into a giant walk-in closet equipped with an elaborate shelving system. Maggie did neither. She liked the paintings where they were.

One afternoon, she was home alone. She'd just gotten off the phone with another gallery that had passed on *Inner Child* and four other paintings, all with bottles, one where they were arranged in a circle, as if collectively mourning their empty state. She was twenty-seven years old and going nowhere fast. The keening Irish ballad on the iPod heightened her malaise, and tears welled.

Someone buzzed the intercom. Maggie pressed the button that opened the building's entry door. She didn't ask who it was. She didn't care. This corner of the West Village was fairly safe. A caller might distract her, if only for a few minutes.

She stared at herself in the small mirror in her apartment's foyer. The mirror was supposed to be a sun, with yellow rays fanning out from its round face. She had pressed colored dots onto some of the rays, making the whole thing seem both childish and innocent. She stuck her tongue out, then relaxed her face, opened her mouth wide, and examined her teeth from several different angles. She and Marta were identical twins, and shared the same features, down to the arrangement of their molars. The lower ones on the right side leaned just a little, but never enough to have warranted braces.

The caller's knock was more like a whimsical tap. Maggie opened the door. The man was on the short side—only a couple of inches taller than Maggie—compactly built, swarthy, with a perfectly trimmed soul patch of black hair. The suede elbow patches on his tweed jacket would have struck her as ridiculous—even pretentious—if he hadn't been gorgeous.

He stepped inside, removed his jacket, and handed it to her.

"You cut your hair," he said.

Maggie's free hand went to the back of her neck and felt the feathery tendrils her stoned stylist had labored over two days before.

"I like it," he said, then walked past her into the living room, where he helped himself to the end of the blue velvet couch she and Marta fought over buying, because Marta had preferred the one in red.

He must be Josh, Marta's director friend. Who else would feel so at home there? Maggie put his jacket on one hook of the wobbly coat rack next to the sunny mirror. Then she went to the couch, and looked down at that incredibly handsome man, willing him to open his arms and invite her in.

"You got a beer around?" he asked. "I'm off the hard stuff for a while."

She went into the kitchen and found green cheese, sour milk, and a carton of eggs months past their sell-by date.

"Sorry," she called out. She returned to find him on his feet studying her canvases, which she'd lined up all around the room.

"Are these new?" he asked.

"I don't know."

"I still say she's pretty good."

"Maybe you just have no taste."

"Don't you like them?"

"I never think about them."

He studied a dark doorway, leading down a mad purple hallway. It was the last one she painted before vacating the studio. She couldn't decide if there were something at the end of the passage, something the viewer could identify, or if it were empty, yet luring one further and further in.

"How come I've never met her, anyway?" he asked.

"Because I want you all to myself."

The surprise in his eyes told her that his relationship with Marta wasn't romantic.

He blushed, then held out his hand. She took it. He looked into her eyes without blinking. Up close he smelled spicy and warm. It was driving her a little nuts.

"Is that why you changed your hair? Because of what I said the other day?" he asked.

"I don't remember what you said."

"That you'd have to wear a wig in *Lana's Tree*. Because the author is insisting on the lead being short-haired. That's how he sees her, and that's how it has to be, assuming we still want the script."

"I still don't follow."

"I said you'd look good that way."

So, he thinks I'm trying to please him!

She leaned in and put her tongue firmly in his mouth. He tensed, but allowed it, then reciprocated. Minutes later, when Marta opened the door, complaining about how long it took her cab to crawl down Madison Avenue, Maggie and Josh were lying on the couch, kissing furiously.

Marta dropped her shopping bags and squawked, "What the *hell*?"

Josh jumped up. He gaped at Maggie.

"You're the *sister*," he said.

"You thought she was me?" Marta asked.

"Well, yeah, I mean, shit, you guys look exactly alike."

Back in high school they used to take one another's place for the fun of playing a trick on any number of exhausted, burned-out teachers, ruined by years of low pay and bratty students. Nothing bad had ever come of it, really. A phone call home once or twice. Being summoned together to the principal's office.

"Why didn't you say something?" Marta asked Maggie, who was now sitting up, pulling her shirt back into place.

"I was going to."

"Before or after?"

Josh's eyes filled with shame.

"I can't handle this right now," he said.

"Josh," Marta said.

"I'm out."

Then he was gone.

Marta sat down on the couch next to Maggie. She put her hand on her forehead. She leaned back and closed her eyes. When she opened them, she ran her hand over the patch of blue velvet beside her.

"You didn't even put a towel down first," she said.

"There wasn't time."

Marta shook her head.

"He likes you," Maggie said.

"Clearly."

"Well, isn't that a good thing?"

Marta sighed.

"Sure. But I like to time my romances for myself. I wasn't ready to jump into anything," she said.

"*He's* ready. Go for it. The guy's lit."

"Did it ever occur to you that he's probably super embarrassed by what just happened?"

"Why should he be?"

Because he'd shown his feelings to the wrong woman. Which was what Maggie had had in mind. She'd wanted to know what it would feel like having sex with a man who thought you were someone else. Hardly a lofty ambition.

Thinking about that now, as more people crowded into the gallery, darkened her mood.

Kyle was still staring gloomily at his cell phone.

"Just call him," she said. She meant Sean, the current boyfriend.

"No way. He's being a bitch."

Sean got jealous easily, and Kyle was overt in his admiration of other men, though he swore never to have acted on it. Maggie thought Kyle deserved the cold shoulder he was getting. Flirty people were hard to be in a relationship with. Not that she knew, exactly. She hadn't had a serious relationship since she was twenty-two, and then it hadn't lasted longer than one long, humid summer when she was assaulted by mosquitoes, as if the preference they normally had for female blood had been heightened by all the longing and passion coursing through her veins.

"We're pathetic," Maggie said.

"Oh, darling. No, we're not. Just . . . unlucky."

Luther Galt approached her, with the most charmingly shy expression.

He changed his mind! He likes my work!

She met his eye with a firm, level gaze. She'd be a cool customer. She'd feign disinterest.

He asked where the restroom was. No one else knew, apparently. Maggie didn't know, either. She suggested he try the coffee house two doors down.

He brought three fingers to his forehead in a teasing salute, then teetered off.

chapter two

Josh faked a lingering outrage over Maggie's ruse. He was a sensitive person, he said. Such base manipulation was unworthy of anyone who claimed to be an artist. Marta sympathized. Her eyes smoldered with fury. He loved her a little for that.

Secretly, he obsessed over the incident. Women came on to him all the time. They had since he was about fourteen. He'd always been able to have his pick. Getting them wasn't the problem, it was keeping them happy. He knew he wasn't patient, or particularly kind. He couldn't bear neediness of any sort, and his natural aloofness created a barrier his girlfriends, sooner or later, tried to breach.

Marta's sister had been so . . . what was the word? Direct. Practical. He couldn't imagine her ever being desperate. She was a woman who went after what she wanted. He wanted to ask Marta if this were true but didn't. Marta was smart, cunning even, and would suspect some developing feeling for her sister if he didn't choose his words very carefully.

To put some distance between herself and Maggie, she'd stayed with Josh for the past three days. On the first night, he made up the couch. She asked why. He didn't understand.

"Well, you thought she was me. So, doesn't that mean. . ."

"Oh, I see. Look, it was one of those heat-of-the-moment things. I never had the faintest idea that you and I would ever . . . you know."

"Good. Because I'd have turned you down."

His apartment had old windows, and street noise began early, ended late, and sometimes never quit at all, only softened a little between three and four in the morning. The bedroom was at the back, and Josh emerged around nine thirty each day looking fresh and rested.

That morning, Marta sat at Josh's tiny kitchen table and poured herself another cup of tea from a lovely hand-painted pot that had belonged to his mother. There was money in his background. He'd grown up comfortably. Maggie and Marta hadn't, not until their mother married Chip Starkhurst. She'd shared that information with Josh. He'd asked what the stepfather did. When Marta said he sold manufactured homes, Josh seemed amused, as if the endeavor were quaint.

Josh watched her stir her tea with a little silver spoon. Her bangs fell over one eye, lending her a sly, seductive air. Marta was a beautiful girl. Maggie was a beautiful girl, too, by definition. He wondered if Marta believed him about never having had any sexual thoughts about her.

"I knew it was her all along," he said.

The spoon stopped.

"Then why have you been acting so upset?"

"I guess I'm just mad at myself for going along with it."

Marta thought that was a load of bull.

A truck blew its horn. The sound cut a hole in the back of her head. She loved the city, but there were times when the quiet of the small town she'd grown up in seemed liked an idyll.

Josh's cell phone trilled on the kitchen counter. He examined the caller's number and silenced it. He did that a lot. Someone was hounding him, maybe even several people were. Another wannabe member of the yet-to-be-formed troupe, wanting to know when they could quit their day job. A woman, probably. Marta suspected Sandra, right out of college, tall, intense, with a shaved head. She had a scary light in her eyes, as if she wanted to devour you and reduce you to atoms.

It could also be Josh's mother, who he said tended to cling. She'd lost Josh's father years before, and since he was an only child, it was just the two of them. He had trouble with the oppressive nature of her dependence on him. Sometimes he complained about her, yet between his words Marta saw a woman who was devoted to her son, and made him believe in himself, perhaps a little too much.

Josh thought he was brilliant, the next great director of those hard-to-find off-Broadway gems. He was sure he had a keen eye for what was likely to engage an audience. The trend for the past few years had been quiet dramas with two or three people; dark sets; lots of monologue and little conversation. Josh's new idea—one he'd unveiled just the evening before—was for a play made up of only two actors portraying lovers who were so intimate they could read each other's minds, finish each other's sentences, even predict the next topic of conversation. Marta said the only people plausible in that situation would have had to live together for decades and be old and uninspiring. He totally disagreed. Couldn't a young man and a young woman be deeply connected? As in soulmates?

He looked at his phone again, then sat down opposite her, causing the tea to slosh in her cup. His black eyes gleamed. His color was high. His inner fire made him dangerously attractive. She pinched the inside of her wrist, something she'd learned to do when she wanted to keep herself still.

"You know that idea for a play? I did some tweaking," he said.

"Yeah?"

"Instead of a couple, how about twins?"

Marta stopped pinching herself. "Female twins, of course," she said.

He nodded. He looked like a teenager, how he must have looked over a decade before.

"And what if only one of them can act?" she asked.

"Would it matter? I mean, she'd just be playing herself, don't you see?"

"And who's going to write this amazing play about these amazing twins?"

"I am."

"Have you ever written a play before?"

"Sure!"

"When?"

"Back in high school."

"And since then?"

Josh stared silently out the grimy window at the fire escape across the street. Marta was supposed to take back her doubts, lavish him with praise, and tell him whatever he penned would sparkle.

Another horn sounded. She thought of the walk back to her place. She would hit up some boutiques in SoHo. A new purse was just what this day needed. She had to stop thinking about Josh and focus on herself for a change.

"I'm going to head out. Don't want to overstay my welcome," she said.

"You're not in the way."

"I know. But I need to see what Maggie's up to."

She didn't like the look that came into Josh's eyes at the mention of Maggie's name. She collected her clothes in the Louis Vuitton backpack her stepfather had gotten her for her last birthday (Maggie had gotten an identical one) and paused at the door.

"Give it a shot. See what you come up with," she said.

Josh turned and looked at her.

"Well, I've got them named, at least," he said.

"The twins?"

He nodded. "Dilly and Dally."

She could see that he was serious. She left before she ruined his moment.

chapter three

Maggie told Kyle what she'd done. He commended her, then told her she had the heart of a slut. She said he was channeling her mother.

"When did your mother ever call you that?" Kyle asked. He was lying on the couch. He'd had the good grace to remove his shoes first. He wore pink and white argyle socks.

"Never," she said. "It's just her whole attitude."

"About what?"

"Me."

"So, basically, she's a bitch."

"Yup."

He sat up and leaned forward, his elbows on his knees. He looked grim.

"Ever notice how parents can destroy you worse than anything?" he asked.

He'd never really talked to her about it before, but after he came out, his father refused to speak to him. He was sixteen at the time. His older brother had encouraged him, saying the truth was better than silence. Yet silence is just what he got, and wasn't that a joke? It didn't end there, of course. Everything he owned was gathered up, packed neatly, and left on the front porch. His key no longer fit the lock.

"Jesus. And where the hell was your mother during all this?" Maggie asked.

"She went along with the whole thing. She never crossed that man once in her whole life."

"But she's in touch. She called you just the other day."

"That was the first time in almost a year. She wanted to let me know that my father isn't doing very well. Some heart problem." Kyle stared at the floor and shook his head. "How can a man with no heart have a heart problem?"

Maggie said in time his father might conveniently croak. Kyle's blue eyes turned even more raw, and she saw that despite what had happened, he still loved him very much.

In the street below voices rose in strife—a furious stream of Spanish in a male register, returned by a volley in a female's higher octave. Maggie went to the window. Her apartment was on the second floor, and her view was clear. The woman stood on the sidewalk, the man in the street. There was a child clutching the woman's pant leg, staring up at her with empty eyes. In his free hand was a stuffed elephant. The man and woman went on yelling, and the boy shifted his gaze from the woman's face to the sidewalk. He let go of her, dropped his toy, and kicked it a few feet one way, then back the other. Maggie figured he was about four. He was wearing green coveralls, much like ones that her younger brother, Foster, had had at that age. Foster was the youngest in the family. At the time, Maggie would only have been five, so she wasn't sure her memory was correct. What was clear—brutal and unavoidable—was that they'd watched their parents fight the way the couple below were fighting now. Their old living room came into focus, a messy place the five children colonized; her parents facing each other; Foster in the middle with something in his hand. Then Foster ran to the tiny bedroom he shared with their older brother, Timothy, who would have been seven, maybe eight. Her parents didn't notice his absence. They were intent only on each other. Maggie left, too, to find Foster on his bed, pulling loose threads from the bedspread, picking at it mechanically. Their mother bought that bedspread, she bought everything for everyone because their father did little but drink. As Maggie got closer, she saw that Foster's face was wet with tears.

The shouting in the street stopped, then resumed, louder than before. Maggie pushed up hard on the reluctant window. She asked Kyle to help her get it open. When they'd raised it about eight inches, Maggie shouted: "Stop that! Stop that at once! You're freaking out the kid!"

Three faces looked up at her. The woman gave her the finger. The boy did nothing. The man yelled something sharp, fast, and hard.

"I'm calling the cops!" Maggie waved her cell phone around.

Kyle told her to get away from the window. She was just making things worse. She withdrew.

"I wonder what it's all about, anyway," she said.

"Maybe one of them got caught."

"Doing what?"

"What do you think?"

"Nah. Probably about money. Or booze."

"I say it's another man."

"She looked sort of plain to me."

"Not her, *him.*"

Kyle thought that inside every straight man was a gay one dying to get out. It annoyed her sometimes. She asked him once if he thought she were actually a lesbian. A shrug had been his answer. She supposed it was their common affection for the male sex that kept their friendship alive. That, and a shared love of fashion. He liked exploring the sisters' closet. Maggie was into boots, Marta was crazy about purses. They shared these freely with each other. They were less free with their clothes because Marta liked spicy perfumes and Maggie preferred floral ones. Whatever scents they wore were permanently impressed into the fabric of their clothes. They hadn't found a dry cleaner yet that could purge the other's smell.

After a few minutes, Maggie returned to the window. The family was gone. Her apartment felt cramped and close. In truth, it was actually spacious, almost eighteen hundred square feet, something her mother noted without fail every month when she paid their rent.

"Let's go out," Maggie said.

"I'm broke."

"You just got paid!"

He patted his thigh to remind her of the designer jeans he recently bought. Kyle had to have the best of everything. He needed a sugar daddy. Maybe that's why he was such a flirt, hoping both a good body and a big bank account would come his way. He was jealous of Maggie's generous allowance. He thought she didn't know about suffering, and that her work needed more agony to be respected. If agony were wanting to be loved, she had plenty of that.

But she didn't paint to find love. She painted because she had so much inside. As long as she could remember, she wanted to capture beauty. And to own it, one must create it. Or something like that. She tried to explain it to Marta once, in one of their closer periods. Marta said she understood; she felt like that, too, but with a character on a stage, in a constructed world. The truth of portrayal was her definition of beauty. The fantasy of drama didn't seem much compared to the reality of colors on canvas, but Maggie didn't get into that.

When she drew bottle after bottle and doorway after doorway, was she capturing beauty? Or something deeper, like the human condition itself? In the last quarter of her two-year community college art program, one of her professors said she must render truth so well a stranger could easily recognize it.

And what exactly was she trying to *say*?

That bottles led to doorways. The story of her own childhood.

chapter four

When they were little girls, Maggie and Marta Dugan were the same person. Not only did looking at the other feel like facing a mirror, an illusion enhanced by their mother dressing them in identical outfits—usually jumpers over long-sleeved turtlenecks—but because they read each other's minds. Always together, it was easy to know the ideas that skipped through their identical brains.

Their parents were the subject of their telepathic conversations. Their father was kind, drunk, and lazy. Their mother was harsh, sober, and industrious. She did everything. He did nothing. In their hearts, they preferred him for his gentleness though they knew that when they needed anything practical—help finding a lost toy; a permission slip signed; a zipper unstuck—she was the one to turn to.

While their older brother and sister, Angie and Timothy, spoke in urgent whispers about the coming split, and little Foster avoided the tension by escaping into his own world of stuffed animals, Maggie and Marta watched, listened, and communicated in silence.

She hates him.

She doesn't really hate him.

I know.

But she's going to leave.

No, she won't.

Yes, she will.

I know.

After the divorce, their mother married her boss. The girls were twelve. Then all five children moved into his huge, ugly house, where footsteps, laughter, even a normal speaking tone, bounced off the tile floor, magnified and horrible.

Maggie and Marta shared a room. When they were fourteen, a rift occurred over a boy at school. Marta had a crush on him; he had a crush on Maggie. Marta moved into a small room at the far end of the hall. She dyed her hair black, got a nose ring, wore heavy makeup. Maggie stayed the same. They didn't look alike anymore, and they didn't think alike.

Gradually, like a river split by rockfall, they came back together. They found their respective artistic drives. Marta was always stronger, surer. It was she who decided they should move to New York; the one who found the apartment; had the idea to convert the extra room into a closet; even picked the studio where Maggie could work. Maggie quietly accepted all this and wondered now if the joke she played on Josh were a way of leveling the field.

Were they still best friends? Maggie's ruse had caused another rift, yet they remained bound together. There was no escape.

Josh assumed the existence of this spiritual enclosure and wanted to capture it in his play *Peas in a Pod,* though he had yet to reveal the title to anyone but his computer.

Setting: The play takes place in a child's bedroom with two twin beds.

<u>*Act 1, Scene 1*</u>

Two little girls sit cross-legged on the floor between their beds, facing each other. Each wears a matching blue jumper over a white blouse with puffed sleeves. They wear white stockings.

Josh realized that he was depicting *Alice in Wonderland.* Was this cliché obvious, or appropriate?

They also wear black shoes. Each has arranged her long blonde hair in a single braid.

Alice wore her hair loose, right? So, this variation was clever.

Between them is a clear pane of glass measuring roughly one foot by two feet. It's held in place by the girls pressing their palms on either side of it as they gaze silently at one another.

That these girls needed the pretense of a mirror to separate them struck him as genius. It was their way of claiming individuality in a world that saw them exactly the same.

His mind wandered then, thinking of Maggie's seduction. He could have slept with Marta when she stayed with him. It was clear she wanted to. Better to make her wait, he thought. When a woman's desire builds to the breaking point, the results were magical.

He wanted them both in bed. Discovering their small differences, how they used their bodies to give him pleasure—the thought of it distracted him from his screen. He unzipped his pants, knowing it wouldn't take long given the state he was in, but before he could touch himself his cell phone rang. Marta's number. Guilt flooded him.

She wanted him to come to dinner on Saturday at her place.

"What should I bring?" he asked.

"A notebook."

"For . . .?"

"Taking notes on the behavior of identical twins."

"That reminds me. I have something to ask you."

"Yeah?"

"Who's older? You or Maggie?"

"Maggie. By all of ninety seconds."

"Ah."

"Ah, yourself."

He wondered if she'd been drinking. She sounded not exactly hostile, but pushy in a way that was unusual, even for her. Her drive had stirred him when they met at the auditions for *The Hearth in Sarah's House*, a lame little play about an old woman trying to keep the fire lit. Josh got a copy of the script from the author because they'd been friends in school. The writing was trite, the dialogue flat, the emotional tension lacking, yet Marta read her lines with a skillfully controlled passion that made the listener assume a fiery spirit. He had been blown away. She didn't get the part; he consoled her by buying her a drink. That was months ago.

Things were different between them now, he realized. Some understanding had been established about what they meant to each other and what they could never mean to each other. He couldn't fall in love with her. He was only able to fall in love with her sister. The question of love never came up before Maggie's ruse. That a woman would try to fool him because she had such a physical desire for him had been constantly on his mind. That kind of hunger is something he could easily relate to.

"What are you making?" he asked. Seafood wasn't his thing. Nor any kind of gross vegetable like artichokes or eggplant. Cauliflower he could stand, but only if it were baked and smothered in cheese.

"Don't know yet. Something lavish."

Lavish? She'd definitely had a few. Would they serve wine? He was trying to get into wine. It looked good to know about vintages and varietals.

"Okay, I'll be there. Count on it," he said.

She made no reply and hung up.

chapter five

It was the same every time. The Metropolitan Museum of Art both restored and discouraged. The noise of the entry hall, all those people milling about and heading up the grand staircase, made her exult, then despair. Maggie supposed you couldn't have one without the other, although this concept always irked. Prevailing wisdom said you couldn't be happy if you'd never been unhappy, but why? Couldn't you just be happy all the time? By that same logic, you couldn't have day without night, but no, that wasn't right either. Those existed because the earth spun in space, not because the human heart needed opposition in order to know truth. Or did it?

Funny, that her mind should have been on the nature of light and dark. She hadn't sought out Rembrandt, she didn't even remember where his work hung, but she found herself there, staring at his portraits, each face illuminated from an unseen source, a strategically placed candle that brightened one side of the face.

She would never have the skill to paint people. The eyes, in particular, would always be the source of failure. Looking into someone's eyes was actually a hard thing to do. She and Marta used to have staring contests, but they could never agree on which of them blinked first. Maybe because they blinked at the same time, and thus couldn't tell?

Her steps across the wood floor were muffled by the cushy flats she wore. No more heels. The idea of shopping for clothes sparked no hunger in her. Marta thought they needed something new for the dinner with Josh. Maggie didn't want to see Josh. Why had she agreed? Because Marta could always talk her into things. There was no avoiding the pressure she applied. Sometimes it was like being joined at the hip, or across the top of their skulls, like those miserable twins that failed to separate.

Marta wanted her to make roasted chicken with rosemary. Alma, their mother's housekeeper, had taught her the recipe. Maggie was the only one of the five children Alma didn't chase out of the kitchen. Alma could be a crab, but she was a good soul, and Maggie sometimes missed her. Alma always loved Maggie's awkward drawings and pinned them to the refrigerator.

A little later, Maggie found herself in the Modern wing. A loud school group followed a woman commanding that all body parts must be kept under complete control *at all times!* The impression as they passed was a mass of waving arms, bouncing feet, and bobbing heads. One boy shoved another one, sending him dangerously close to a fevered Jackson Pollack, all drips and dashes of white, brown, and black, where a quiet uniformed guard gently redirected him. Maggie considered the canvas, letting her mind be pulled by the slim rivers of shiny paint.

Further down the gallery was a wooden bench, and sitting on the bench was Leah, staring intensely at another Pollack. Maggie hadn't seen her since leaving the co-op, though she'd received one text message from her: *Thnx for helping me that night, but you're still an asshole.*

Leah's shoulders rose and fell almost imperceptibly, draped with a blue silk shawl. Her black hair was pulled tightly into a ponytail. Was there something vulnerable about her? Something that hadn't quite recovered?

Maggie took the space on the bench next to her.

Leah turned. "Look who it is."

"How are you?" Maggie asked.

"Spectacular."

"Well, good. That's great!"

Leah's black eyes filled with jagged light. She looked away, back to the Pollack.

Maggie looked at it, too. It reminded her of the way a sheet of ice might crack, revealing inner strengths and weaknesses. Pollack's lines and dots reflected his unique psychic state, a flow of energy from his own soul. Leah, no doubt, understood that.

Maggie said, "Do you have time for coffee? I'll buy."

Leah considered. She looked skeptical.

"Okay," she said.

Leah led the way to the cafeteria on the second floor, never turning back to see if Maggie were still behind her. When they finally arrived, Maggie said she'd get them their coffee and Leah could find a table.

"You still take it black?" Maggie asked.

"Yes."

The acrid smell of their studio's coffee pot, always left on too long, returned, as did Leah's special mug, pale blue with the handle broken off.

The coffee was self-serve. Maggie took hers black, too. She overfilled the cups and they sloshed on the plastic tray she struggled to keep level. She looked over the sea of tables, most of which were occupied. Leah was nowhere. Maggie went down one side of the room, then up the other. A couple got up from their table and Maggie put down her tray. They'd left their plates behind, though the protocol was to remove them, and put them in the plastic bins on metal carts against the wall. When another table opened up nearby, she put the dirty plates there, then returned quickly to the two cooling cups of coffee.

Leah was pretty damn slick to stand her up that way. Maggie checked her phone. There was a message from Marta asking if she'd gone to the grocery store yet, and if not, then to get some toilet paper. Marta wasn't doing anything with herself these days. Why couldn't *she* go to the store?

As she framed a response, Leah pulled out the empty chair and sat down heavily.

"I thought you bailed," Maggie said.

"I was about to."

"What changed your mind?"

"It would have been lame."

Maggie slid one of the cups across the table towards her. Leah stared at it suspiciously.

"There's no paint in it," Maggie said.

"Ha ha."

Maggie became uncomfortable with the silence between them. She focused on the ring Leah wore on her middle finger, a three-sided blue obsidian. It was like a drop of tropical ocean captured in silver. The color evoked peace, an overwhelming sense of well-being at odds with the crushing conflict Maggie had caused that night in the studio.

"Listen," Maggie said, "I wanted to say. . ."

"Don't worry about it. That painting wasn't going anywhere. I'd more or less given up on it."

"Really? So, like, I did you a favor?"

"No. Just because I was going to move on doesn't mean you got to say when."

Leah said that the destroyed canvas haunted her, even though she knew she needed to abandon it. Of course, it didn't help that she'd miscarried at the same time, as if she'd slipped unknowingly into a stream of loss aided by Maggie's own hand. If she'd lost the fetus and not the painting, that would have been one thing. If she'd lost the painting and not the fetus that would have been another, more complicated, thing. She didn't want a baby, then or now, and maybe she never would, certainly not with Digger, though he'd probably be a decent father.

Her hand now sat in her lap, the blue stone concealed. An old man navigating toward an empty table bumped the back of Maggie's chair, causing the cup she held to jerk. A thimbleful of coffee flowed over the rim, down the side, into the empty saucer directly below. Maggie studied the puddle.

"I don't forgive you, don't get me wrong," Leah said. "But I figure you were pretty fucked up in the head about something, and when people get that way, they do bad stuff."

In any case, she'd started a new series called *From Darkness, Light*. Aside from the obvious motifs of life and death, creation and destruction, the colors she'd been so in love with before, all that red, orange, and purple, would now be replaced with lighter tones, a "gentler" palette, for want of a better word.

Maggie nodded. It sounded amazing.

"And you? What are you working on?" Leah asked.

"Nothing. I still don't have a new space."

One side of Leah's mouth drew up. "You live in a three-bedroom apartment with your sister, right? Turn the spare room into an art space."

"Can't. It's our closet."

"What's more important, your work or your wardrobe?"

For a moment Maggie hesitated, not because she was so madly in love with all of her clothes—though she was pretty fond of a couple of outfits, a blue suede jacket and skirt set in particular—but because her painting wasn't important enough to make her claim the space.

Why?

Because:

1) She was on the verge of deciding that she was a talentless hack.
2) Marta would never consent to the loss of the closet.
3) She actually *was* a talentless hack.

Watching her mind spin, Leah told her she could spread a drop cloth in the living room and set up her easel there.

"I don't know . . ." Maggie said.

Marta would complain. She was already ticked off about the sixteen canvases stacked up against the far wall. But were they really such a pain?

Josh had admired them. Maybe he told Marta the same thing, when they were alone, in the days right after Maggie's ruse. Maybe Marta resented the compliment. Marta tended to resent Maggie's successes because she was always competing with her, though they'd each embraced a different métier. Marta resenting that Maggie painted well would be like Maggie resenting a role Marta was chosen to play.

She wanted to be in her own space, without Marta's atoms in the air. They'd never lived apart. Would it feel strange? Thrilling? What would Marta think about it? And more importantly, could she convince their mother to kick in for a second apartment?

"Do you have siblings?" Maggie asked.

"No."

"Wow."

"Wow, what?"

"All that freedom."

Leah's tight expression said freedom hadn't been a factor. Maggie wondered about the nature of the awful childhood Digger had mentioned.

"It's so hard to find decent space in Manhattan," Maggie said.

"That's why I'm moving back upstate."

"I didn't know you were from there."

"Syracuse."

"I'm from Dunston!"

"Just down Route 13."

"Yup."

Leah brought her hand out of hiding to scratch her chin. The blue stone gleamed.

She said she wasn't going back to where she'd grown up—that place was long gone, torn down for a row of townhomes—but over to Sullivan. Her aunt had a dairy farm there, with an old barn Leah could use for a studio. It had been cleaned up, and some insulation had been installed. Her aunt was talking about getting a new door for it and giving it a new coat of paint. It would need a heat source. It was just a matter of rounding up a used wood stove and getting someone to fabricate the metal chimney for it. Come to think of it, Leah knew someone who could do that for her, a guy she went to school with. She hadn't thought of him for a long time.

"And Digger?" Maggie asked.

"When I find an apartment, he says he'll pay the first three months' rent."

"That's super generous."

"He feels guilty, I guess."

"Why?"

Leah shrugged.

"Are you guys still together?" Maggie asked.

"I can't see him living up there."

Maggie's phone buzzed insistently. It was Marta. Maggie declined the call, then told Leah she had to get going, that she had errands to run.

Maggie told Leah stay in touch. Leah said she would. Maggie figured she probably wouldn't.

chapter six

It wasn't Maggie's idea. She wanted that made clear. The matching outfits—two ballerinas with striped stockings (where the hell did Marta find these?)—were stupid enough, but the wigs! Christ! Hers itched like hell.

Marta had come through the door, packages in hand, with an evil glint in her eye. Josh *loved* the fact of their twinship, so why not? She couldn't wait to see him flounder not knowing who was who.

This had always been was a weird side of Marta. She wanted Josh, it was clear. She might even think she was falling in love with him, yet she wanted to make him ill at ease. It was her way of testing him. He needed to prove that he was worth loving.

When Maggie told Marta she also invited Kyle, Marta fumed. She had envisioned some kind of threesome, not necessarily involving any *actual* sex, only the *idea* of sex, the lure of it, the temptation. Kyle's presence would impede that. Maggie said a foursome was more dinner- partyish and would put everyone at ease.

"We'll just be two couples. It doesn't matter that Kyle's gay," Maggie said.

"He's a pain in the ass."

Maggie knew Marta had grown to like Kyle, and thought he was funny. It was just like her to talk him down for no reason.

"He is sometimes, I'll admit," Maggie said. "But then, so are you."

Marta ignored her. She laid out the costumes on the sofa side by side. Then she pulled the wigs from the bottom of the bag. Their short black hair had a distinctly Clara Bow look. When Maggie said so, Marta agreed.

Marta told her to be careful not to stain her outfit, because they wouldn't let her return it otherwise.

"It's rented?"

"Of course."

"And the wigs?"

"Yup."

Maggie didn't like the idea of wearing something that had covered someone else's head. The wig smelled funny.

Marta said it smelled fine. The hair was real human hair. Wasn't that a plus?

Marta gathered up the costumes and wigs and told Maggie it was time to get changed. Maggie followed her into their converted closet. The floor was littered with several silk scarves Marta had tried to create some dramatic effect with the day before.

They dressed in silence. Maggie had trouble with her wig and Marta helped her. As they stood before the full-length mirror, the silence deepened. They felt uneasy, and each knew it was because of the trick they were about to play.

The staccato tone of the buzzer downstairs said Kyle had arrived, thirty minutes early. Both sisters met him at the door. He was wearing a red velvet suit and sky blue leather boots.

"Holy shit," he said.

They curtsied.

"Can you tell us apart?" Maggie asked.

"Not from here."

"Come closer then," Marta said.

He did. He peered at their faces and put his hand on Maggie's chin. He turned her head one way, then the other, then did the same to Marta. He leaned in, eyes closed, and inhaled sharply through his nose.

"Maggie," he said, pointing to Marta.

"It worked!" she said.

"She's wearing my perfume," Maggie said.

"Aren't you the devious duo! But, what's it all about?"

"We're putting on a show for Marta's boyfriend," Maggie said.

"He's not my boyfriend."

"Not yet."

"I'll take him if you don't want him," Kyle said.

Marta accepted the bottle of red wine he pushed into her hand. She put it in the kitchen. When she came back, she told him about Josh's play. The idea gave Kyle a shaking fit of the giggles. He'd had a few on the way over—gin, from the smell of it.

Maggie waved him away. She took the chicken from the oven, put the pan on the stove, and covered it with tin foil. Marta set out a pair of stick-on name cards.

Hello, my name is _______________________

She wrote "Dilly" on one and "Dally" on the other, then told Maggie to come and choose.

"How am I supposed to choose when they're both equally stupid? When this whole thing is stupid?"

"Just close your eyes and point."

Maggie did.

"Dally! Here you go!"

Marta pressed the sticker on a patch of lace just below Maggie's collar bone.

Maggie went back to the kitchen and tore open a bag of pre-washed lettuce bits. She poured it into a large yellow bowl. Some of the bits were brown. She picked them out.

She hoped Josh liked ranch dressing, because that was all they had. Next, she sliced up a loaf of French bread that was well on its way to becoming stale. Her serrated knife flattened the bread before cutting through the crust.

In the living room, Lucinda Williams's rich, throaty voice drifted from the iPod. Marta had recently developed a taste for country music. It baffled Maggie. All that pathos and pain didn't seem like Marta's style.

"We're not doing candles, are we?" Maggie asked.

When she got no answer, she leaned around the corner from the kitchen. Marta and Kyle were in a loose embrace, swaying to the music. Maggie wondered whose idea that had been.

"I don't care," Marta said, when she saw her. "Do we have any?"

"No."

"You're such a pinhead."

"I only meant that if you wanted candles, you'd have to go get them."

The buzzer sounded. Marta and Kyle pulled apart. Marta turned off the iPod. Maggie stood still, bread knife still in hand. The buzzer screamed again.

Kyle trotted over and hit the button by the intercom. A minute later, before Josh could even knock, Kyle pulled open the door and introduced himself with a hearty handshake.

Josh wore a pair of torn jeans, a button-down shirt, and a clip-on bow tie. He had product in his hair. He gave off the same spicy scent as before. He regarded Kyle warily.

Marta swooped in like a hungry owl after a rabbit. As she approached, she slowed her stride, as if realizing her performance bordered on brash.

"Nice outfit," he said handing her a bottle of white wine. It complemented Kyle's red. Marta didn't know which one was supposed to go with chicken. She put the bottle on an empty shelf in the bookcase.

Maggie emerged from the kitchen to greet him.

"Whoa," Josh said.

"It's a game," Kyle said.

Josh looked intrigued. Either that, or he was terrified. He studied Kyle again, then calmed, as if sensing his gayness and realizing he posed no competition.

"Yeah? What are the rules?" Josh asked.

"You have to figure out who's who by the time we finish dinner," Marta said.

"And what do I get if I win?"

"Nasty boy!" Kyle said. Maggie was flooded with dread. Kyle was going to make a pass at Josh before the evening was out. She could feel it.

They trooped into the living room. Marta asked the men to sit. Though she hadn't told Maggie what she intended to do next, Maggie knew enough to just wait and take her cue. She hoped whatever it was wouldn't go on so long the chicken got cold.

"Wine!" Marta said and clapped her hands.

"Wine!" Maggie echoed, and fetched Josh's bottle of white from the bookcase. Both women went into the kitchen. Marta was deft with the corkscrew. She brought the open bottle to her nose. She squinted and examined the label.

"That idiot brought a dessert wine!" she whispered furiously.

"Hang on. Maybe we have another red somewhere."

In the cabinet over the refrigerator was the bottle their stepfather had given them for Christmas, from an upstate New York winery. He was friends with the vintner.

"Not that one, it's too expensive," Marta said.

"Look, do you want this damn thing to go off, or don't you?"

Maggie grabbed two glasses in each hand, and Marta took both bottles of red wine. They set up on the coffee table. Josh was on the couch talking excitedly to Kyle, who'd just asked about Josh's new play, and what he saw happening in the theater in the next few years. Any conquest involved getting the object of your desire to talk about himself, Maggie realized. Was that why she was such a failure with men? Because she couldn't take the time to listen?

Maggie sat next to Josh. Marta sat on the floor by the coffee table, since Kyle had already claimed the fancy wingback chair that had belonged to their stepfather. They drank. Josh watched Maggie closely. She touched her right earlobe, something she did when she was nervous. She had removed her gold hoops on Marta's order. Jewelry was personal. It identified. Marta wasn't wearing the silver ring she always placed on the middle finger of her left hand.

Josh turned his attention to Marta, who sat with her legs crossed—something she didn't normally do, but which Maggie always did.

Very clever.

"So, you decided to be a case study," Josh said.

"Anything in the name of art," Marta said.

"I wouldn't want to be a twin," Kyle said.

"And have to share the spotlight?" Marta asked.

"What spotlight? No one ever paid any attention to us," Maggie said.

She explained that their big sister, Angie, got much more attention than they did. Also, their younger brother, Foster.

"I thought there were five of you," Kyle said, looking right at Maggie. He was well acquainted with the details of her family because she spoke of them often. Neither the wig, nor the switched perfume had fooled him one bit, she realized. Was Josh fooled, or just pretending to be? Had they ever actually fooled anyone, or had people just said so because at the time they'd been children?

"We have another brother, Timothy. He didn't get a lot of attention either," Marta said.

"Oh, right. I remember you saying that," Kyle said to her.

Everyone tasted their wine.

"Dally, when did you first want to become an actress?" Josh asked Maggie.

"When I was ten. There was a play at school. I was Rapunzel. I just *adored* it."

"So, you let down your hair?" Josh's fingers brushed the back of her itchy wig. She froze. Marta watched him. She held the wine in her mouth without swallowing for a moment.

"I thought you wanted to study them, twins-wise," Kyle said. "Shouldn't you be taking notes?"

Josh tapped his forehead.

"Mind like a steel trap?" Kyle asked.

Josh laughed.

"More like a steel sieve," Marta said.

Josh didn't laugh. He turned to her. "Now, Dilly, a question for you. Do you prefer to work in oils, pastels, or watercolors?"

"Pastels," Maggie said. Marta shot her a quick, punishing look.

"She always likes to answer for me," Marta said.

"I do not."

Maggie was flushed from the wine she'd had. Marta wasn't.

"All you have to do is figure out which one's the better drinker," Kyle said to Josh, indicating Maggie's high color.

Marta and Josh always drank a lot when they got together. Maggie was far more moderate, something Kyle often complained about when they were out on the town. He liked to party, and he didn't like to do it alone.

Josh stared at Maggie, which only deepened her blush. She met his gaze and forced herself to hold it.

"When I was kid, there were identical twins next door," Kyle said. "Boys. Very cute boys. They were like a popsicle, fused together. A smooth, orange popsicle." His voice grew misty at the memory. "Jimmy and Johnny Reardon."

"Like Dilly and Dally Dugan," Marta said.

"Only it's really Maggie and Marta Dugan," Maggie said.

"I like hers better," Josh said, nodding at Marta.

"Anyway, Jimmy and Johnny had twin beds, and later when they got older, they tried having separate rooms. They tapped on the wall in between well into the night, every night, in a code they invented all by themselves. They also invented a spoken language, crude, not very complicated, but again, which only they could understand. Did you girls ever do anything like that?"

"No," Maggie and Marta said in unison.

Maggie thought suddenly of the poor cooling chicken sitting forlornly under its tin foil hat. Then she thought of a cartoon character who lives in a basement and also wears a tin foil hat to keep aliens from reading his thoughts. But the chicken had no thoughts, right? Especially since it had no head.

"What the hell are you laughing at?" Marta asked her sharply. She'd doubled over, and tipped sideways, convulsing with hilarity. She waved her hand to say she couldn't possibly explain. She pulled herself together. Tears ran down her warm cheeks. Josh found this particularly alluring, and he leaned forward to touch his lips briefly to hers.

"Go ahead, help yourself," Marta said. She put down her glass firmly on the table, got up, and left the room.

"I'll go. I can always get her to calm down," Kyle said.

Maggie leaned back and closed her eyes. Maybe Josh would kiss her again. Maybe she should ask him to.

She opened her eyes to find him staring at her intently.

"Who am I?" she asked.

"Maggie."

"When did you decide that?"

"I realized I already knew."

"So much for the great ruse."

She removed her wig and scratched her scalp. Marta returned, walking fast and highly agitated. She stopped, surprised to see Josh and Maggie weren't making out.

"Oh," she said.

"Where's Kyle?" Maggie asked.

"Bathroom."

Marta took her wig off, too, and tossed it to the floor.

"I guess this was all pretty stupid," she said.

"Made for good material," Josh said.

"If you can figure out how to use it, you mean."

Josh reddened.

Kyle returned, and asked if they were going to eat.

"That depends on how you feel about lukewarm chicken," Maggie said.

"Buk, buk," Kyle said.

"Or we could all go out," Josh said.

"Only if you're paying," Marta said.

"You two go. We'll hang here," Maggie said.

Marta gave Josh a commanding look, and he got to his feet. He glanced regretfully at Maggie as he followed Marta into the foyer, where she grabbed her purse from the coat rack and yanked it angrily to her shoulder.

"Don't you want to change, first?" Maggie called after her.

The slam of the door was her reply.

chapter seven

Marta spent that night at Josh's, and texted Maggie in the morning that they'd be at a friend's place in the Hamptons for a few days.

This was the second time in as many weeks that Marta had bailed out on her. Why was she so jumpy, anyway? The dinner party had been *her* idea. She wanted to confuse Josh, and they did. So, why was she mad that he kissed her? Marta should be home, laughing at him, calling him names, ignoring his calls.

Instead, she was punishing Maggie. Well, if Marta thought she was just going to sit there and take it, she had another thing coming.

Maggie got her mother on the phone and said she needed to buy a used car in a hurry.

"Whatever for?"

"I'm moving out."

"Why? What happened?"

"I'll tell you later."

"Are you in some sort of trouble?"

"No, but if I go on living here, I might be."

Her mother accepted this with a studied silence. Then she said to call her back when she found a car and let her know how much to transfer into her account.

Maggie texted Kyle that she was going out of town. She also texted her older sister, and brothers. To Marta she said nothing. To Marta, she might never say another word.

"You'd regret that," Leah said. She accepted Maggie's appearance upstate in Sullivan two days later with a neutral attitude, as if she were a rainstorm that would soon pass. Her attention focused when Maggie said she'd brought all her canvases in the back of the used minivan she'd bought.

"I'm not sure where I'll be living. It just made sense to bring them with me," she said.

"So, you're out of the city for good?"

"Yeah."

"You might regret that, too."

"Have you?"

"Not yet, but then, I've only been here about a week."

Leah rented an upstairs apartment in a house that had been converted to provide income for the old lady that lived below. The old lady's son had tried to get her into a nursing home, but she refused. He thought a tenant would provide another set of eyes on her condition, a chore Leah was less than happy to perform. She'd been asked to look in once a day and report anything out of the ordinary in exchange for a rent reduction of seventy-five dollars a month. The apartment had two bedrooms. If Maggie would take charge of the landlady, she was welcome to the second room rent free. Maggie would've rather paid rent than do that, but after buying the minivan, she didn't want to ask her mother for more money.

The room contained only a bed. They went over to Goodwill, so Maggie could get a dresser, a mirror, a rug, and a lamp. Leah helped her get everything into the minivan, then up the narrow stairs and into her room.

"Why are you being so nice to me?" Maggie asked.

"Maybe it's all part of an elaborate plot to mess you up."

"Could be."

"You have serious trust issues, girl."

"Probably."

Leah arranged for Maggie to stow her artwork in the neighbor's garage. Frank Donley was an easy sixty, or sixty-five depending on the light. He walked as if battling a fierce wind. He said his son used to keep a couple of classic cars in there until he got divorced and had to sell them. As for his own truck, he didn't mind if it sat out, because he didn't use it all that often.

In that case, Maggie asked if she might use it as a work space, too. Frank thought for a moment while he scratched his head.

"Sure. Help yourself," he said.

To open the garage doors, you had to pull really hard on the wooden handles. Maggie's first attempt earned her a few splinters. There were two filthy windows that took quite a while to scrub clean.

A wide plywood shelf was installed on three walls. Maggie arranged her canvases on one side. The side under the windows was where she would work. The third side held cardboard boxes and tools. The garage wasn't heated. Something would have to be done about that before winter came.

She'd been out of the city for three days. Kyle texted her, wanting to know when she was coming back. He missed her. Sean had finally dumped him, which was okay, because he'd just met someone else, or rather someone he'd known before, and "that situation" was about to be rekindled. Maggie figured it would last a couple of weeks, and he'd be back in touch when breaking up once again made him feel abandoned.

Marta, still in the Hamptons, began texting her every couple of hours asking why she wasn't responding. Finally, Maggie replied *I'm on the lam*. The memory of them holed up together watching old movies stirred something painful in her. She ignored it and focused on her work.

It was time to give up on bottles and doorways, and she thought it must have been good karma that made her leave the photo album of her work behind. She had an unused pad of sketch paper and a box of black pastels. She took both outside, behind the garage, and sat on the dry grass, grateful for the sun. Her blouse and skirt were light-weight cotton, and she realized she'd left most of her warmer clothes back in New York.

The first few smudges were soft, loose, and came gradually to form the outline of a woman in a hooded garment, walking through debris, broken furniture, an empty shopping cart, a coffee maker lying on its side. Bombed buildings rose chaotically in the background, the result of Maggie's rapid strokes. Smoke plumed thickly in the distance, and through it all the woman's expression was slack, vague, incomplete. Her displacement had stolen her identity, her individuality—her very humanity. Here was genuine tragedy, not the small sorrows of a girl with an alcoholic father and a bitter mother.

Her phone rang, and she reached for it without thinking.

"Finally! Jesus. Where the hell are you?" Marta's exasperation sounded genuine, not put on.

"I moved back upstate."

"You went home?"

"No."

"So, where are you?"

"Never mind."

"What the hell? Why didn't you tell me?"

"I think you know the answer to that." Maggie kept her eyes on the woman she'd created.

"This *can't* be because of Josh!"

Maggie said nothing.

"Is it because you're having trouble painting?"

Maggie hung up. She forced her attention back to her drawing. It was poorly arranged. The eye wasn't drawn to the woman, but to the mess all around her. But maybe that was the point. That someone forced out of her home becomes part of the larger destruction.

Too obvious. This woman needed to carry the woe *within* her.

Maggie turned to the next blank page and began again. This time the woman sat on the ground by a tree whose branches were bare. She held a baby to her breast. The baby looked like a large potato with a head. Maggie used her thumb to smudge the lines here and there, then applied the pastel some more until the baby looked like a baby. Imparting sorrow to the mother's face was daunting. Her turned-down mouth looked like a lame emoji. Her nose was a lopsided blob. So, again she smudged, blended, and eased the slippery pastel around the paper until she'd managed to obliterate the woman's features entirely. Her face was one big shadow.

That's it!

What better way to depict a loss of humanity than to be faceless?

Of course, it had been done before. *Everything* had been done before, but so what? This was a good idea, and she just had to run with it.

Leah found it clichéd. Maggie's spirits fell.

"Look, don't listen to me," Leah said. "Just go for it and see what happens." She was dressed to go out in a black silk pantsuit and high-heeled sandals. Maggie admired the blue stones in her earlobes. Leah always cut a figure, even when she was just wearing a paint-stained sweatshirt and jeans. She kept looking at her watch. Digger was on his way up from the city to take her to dinner and spend the night on account of the five-hour drive, but in a motel, not with her. He was late.

"He probably hit traffic," Maggie said.

"He should have called."

"Maybe his phone ran out of juice."

"He could charge it in the car."

"Maybe he doesn't have a charger."

Leah nodded. She flopped down in the nearest kitchen chair and poured herself a glass of wine.

"He was borrowing someone's car. Maybe it broke down," she said.

"Maybe he got abducted by aliens."

"Maybe he drowned in a can of paint."

"But not black paint."

Leah threw her head back and howled. The high notes she hit were amazing. Then she stood up, left her untouched glass on the table, and looked at Maggie.

"Fuck him, anyway. Let's go out," she said.

Maggie's minivan smelled of the previous owner's cigarettes. Leah asked if she'd gotten a discount because of it. Maggie hadn't negotiated the price at all. Leah was astounded. Then, after a moment, she said she figured when you were rich, you probably didn't worry about stuff like that.

"I'm not rich," Maggie said.

"Someone is."

"My stepfather."

Maggie took her time to parallel park the van in a tight spot in front of a dry cleaner's. The car behind her honked. She hated driving. She always had. The driver in back sped around them angrily. Leah was already out and on the sidewalk, peering at the parking meter and consulting her watch. Neither of them had any change. The spot was free after six o'clock, still forty minutes away. They decided to risk a ticket. They were both gripped by a spirit of adventure.

The bar Leah aimed for was two blocks up. Just as when they'd been at the Met, she walked ahead, not looking back. Maggie quickened her pace to keep up. Her cowboy boots were slightly too big. They were crimson and badly scuffed. Marta would say something nasty about them, but Marta wasn't there. Maggie had picked them up at Goodwill the day before. It occurred to her that the last few weeks of her life had been punctuated by footwear that didn't fit.

All commercial establishments in the State of New York had been smoke free for some time, but the air inside Ricky's was thick. Maggie thought of Kyle and the tony gay bars where he liked to hang out mooching drinks from good-looking men. He wouldn't like the décor—wooden booths and scratched linoleum, but he'd appreciate the patrons, the majority of whom were male, and not bad-looking at first glance. At least they weren't all old and fat, which so many around town seemed to be. Leah's body changed the minute she walked through the door. She wasn't rigid and moving fast, but fluid, looking around leisurely for a place to sit. She turned every head in the room and knew it. Maggie drew her share of glances, too. She'd changed into a pink sundress with spaghetti straps.

Leah chose a table in the middle of the room. Maggie would have preferred a booth in back, near the swinging door that led to the kitchen. She felt exposed and uncomfortable. She needed a nice glass of cold white wine, which is exactly what she told the sour-looking waitress who took a while to show up.

"Chardonnay, if you have it," Maggie said. "If not, a good Fumé Blanc. Or champagne, if you sell it by the glass."

The waitress looked down at her. Maggie studied the folds in her neck.

"And for you?" the waitress asked Leah.

"Makers Mark, straight up."

Maggie was glad people had stopped staring at them. She just wanted to sit, drink her wine, which was generically white and on the fruity side, think about her new project, and ignore the fact that Marta was still calling and texting her.

When she mentioned it, Leah said, "You can't just cut her off like that. She's your sister. She'll never leave you alone."

Leah finished her drink. She was flushed, bright-eyed and swaying in her chair to Fleetwood Mac, and Stevie Nicks' rich voice: *I'll follow you down 'til the sound of my voice will haunt you. . .*

"Silver Spring" was one of Marta's favorite songs.

Maggie took out her cell phone and turned it off. She choked down her wine and asked the waitress for another round.

"What happened between you two, anyhow?" Leah asked.

"I put the moves on the guy she's been seeing. Only she wasn't seeing him at the time."

"Man."

"Then she invited him to dinner, dressed us alike, even down to the same wig, to see if he could tell us apart. When he thought I was her, he kissed me, and she freaked out."

"I still don't get why you're mad at her."

Because I don't want to be a sidekick anymore. The one who always goes along.

"Incoming," Leah said about the tall blond guy making for their table with a frothy mug of beer in his meaty hand.

"Marta Dugan! I thought that was you! I told my buddy Ken—you remember Ken, right? —and he said I should come over and say hi."

Maggie stared at him.

"Hi," she said.

He looked first at her, then at Leah, then back to her.

"George Pratt. Don't you remember me?"

"Oh, sure. George. Good old George! How the hell are you?"

He sat down. Some of the beer foam landed on the table. He wiped it off with his shirtsleeve. His wide easy face reminded her of a ham.

"Good. I'm good," he said. "Been back for about two months now."

"Back from where?"

"Iraq."

Leah shook her head. "That must have been a wild scene."

George nodded without looking at her.

"I didn't see the worst of it, that's for sure." He drank his beer, staring at the table. Then he said, "So, what are you doing in Sullivan?"

"Getting out of the city."

"I heard you moved there."

Leah watched Maggie, wondering how long she would keep it up.

"You still acting?" he asked.

"Of course."

At that, Leah laughed. George turned her way.

"Didn't catch your name," he said.

"Lisa."

"My sister's name is Lisa."

"I didn't know you had a sister," Maggie said.

"Come on! She's the one that first brought you to the house!"

When had Marta met this girl? She'd never said a thing.

"I know. I was only kidding," Maggie said.

"I've seen guys who really lose their memory after getting blown up by an IED."

His voice had a hard edge now. Maggie didn't like it, and wished he'd leave.

George shook his head and stared into his beer.

Another guy appeared and put his hand on George's shoulder. "Hey, man, you wandered off in the middle of the game."

In the back was a pool table, surrounded by three other hulky meatheads.

"Right, sorry about that," George said. "I just wanted to come over and say hi. Whose turn is it?"

"Yours, man. For about the last ten minutes."

George stood up and walked off without saying anything more. His friend caught Leah's eye and shrugged. He must be used to looking after old George.

The waitress put down two fresh drinks. "Those guys over there bought your round," she said, tossing her head in the direction of the pool table.

"Mighty nice of them," Maggie said.

"You going to be ordering any food?" the waitress asked.

"I don't know. Are we?" Maggie asked Leah.

"Sure. What's good here?"

"Anything fried," the waitress said.

Maggie went over the menu. "Everything's fried."

"I like fried chicken," Leah said.

Maggie asked for two orders of fried chicken.

The food came. They ate, and went on drinking for another two hours, until Leah told Maggie she damn well better be sober enough to drive. Maggie hadn't had as much to drink as Leah, but she'd still had a lot more than she was used to.

"I can handle it," she said as they wobbled down the sidewalk. "I'm my father's daughter."

Though it wasn't even nine o'clock, the streets were empty. She drove precisely, and only went over the curb once when she turned the final corner onto their lane.

Digger sat on the front steps, leaning up against one of the columns. His face was in shadow, but the set of his shoulders said he had not enjoyed his time there.

Leah looked at him and said, "Forget it."

"Where the hell were you?" he asked.

"Where the hell were *you?*"

"I called you about nine times."

"I left my phone here."

Maggie went inside alone. They came in a little later, and, judging from the creak of Leah's bed, forgot their differences at least long enough to accommodate the matter at hand.

chapter eight

Josh needed Marta close to remind him of Maggie, to help him get the words down, to be his muse. The failed dinner party haunted him. He replayed it again and again, always with the absence of Kyle and Marta. He was consumed with the idea that Maggie's soul was completely different from her sister's, that their sameness was only on the outside.

Marta wanted him to look at her the way he had looked at Maggie. She wanted to be awash in his longing. In the huge home of his friend in the Hamptons, however, the only longing Josh expressed was for another drink, and his laptop, where he continued to hammer out his screen play. Marta swam laps in the Olympic-size pool, reliving the dinner party, too, only in her amended version, it was she whom Josh had so gently kissed. Maggie had some inner light that drew people to her. She always had. There was no change Marta could make in her own attitude, behavior, or appearance that would grant her that same gift.

She felt that's what Josh had to get on the page—how one's spirit and soul were unique. Rather than explore the nature of sameness, he needed to probe the truth of difference in two genetically identical human beings.

As Marta rested, spent from her third swim of the day, Josh approached. He rolled up the legs of his khaki slacks, sat beside her, and dangled his bare feet in the water. He made a kicking motion that reminded Marta of going to summer day camp when she was only about six or seven. She hadn't liked swimming then and tended to linger on the edge of the pool, immersing her feet and shins to see if that would satisfy the counselors who were determined to teach her how to float.

She shared her thoughts about the direction his play could take.

"You read my mind," he said.

"Yeah?"

"Because you're totally perceptive. Also, a bit brilliant."

He leaned in and kissed her slowly at first, then with more intensity. He broke off before she was ready. Her breathing had quickened. It was hard to slow. To help, she looked at the bobbing surface of the pool.

Now. It will all happen now.

She met Josh's eyes. What she found there was a blend of curiosity and disappointment.

"I'm not her," she said, "and I'm not less."

He put his arm around her shoulder, but not as a lover would. He was trying to be kind. It didn't suit him. It didn't suit her, either. She wasn't used to kindness.

"You're wonderful just the way you are," he said. He seemed to mean it.

Two days later, they had sex, after sitting up late discussing the play. He read some of it to her. It was flowing now. The twins went back and forth talking through the pane of glass, the warmth from their palms like an aura tracing their delicate fingers as they finished each other's sentences, just as Josh planned they would. Yet, every now and then the twins surprised one another with an unexpected remark. Marta wondered if the audience wouldn't get bored watching two motionless figures sitting on a floor, with a backdrop of . . . what exactly?

"Haven't decided yet," Josh said. "How about something from your childhood?"

"A messy room. Stacks of newspapers everywhere. Empty bottles on a table."

"The shadow of an overflowing laundry basket?"

Marta thought for a moment. "Well, fine, but the audience will want to know whose clothes are in it, how long they've been there, and if the girls are responsible for washing them."

"It's good to keep them guessing. Holds their interest," Josh said.

"Yeah, but have to answer those questions by the end."

"I will, I will, don't worry about it."

In the morning Josh watched her as she perched on the stool, her elbows on the huge granite kitchen counter. She was fresh from the shower. The tendrils of her hair glistened. She stared angrily at her phone.

"What's up?" he asked.

"Maggie's being a butt."

"What do you mean?"

"She moved out and won't tell me where she is."

"Seriously?"

"Yup."

Josh sat down. He was getting tunnel vision.

"You have to find her," he said.

"She's not lost, she's just doing her thing. Whatever it is."

"Your mother must know where she is."

"Probably."

"You can ask her."

She turned her wary blue eyes on him and bore a tunnel into the bottom of his brain.

"Why the hell would I?" she asked.

Josh said nothing.

"Find her yourself," she said. "You're obsessed with her."

"No, I'm not."

Marta put her phone in the back pocket of her denim shorts. She slid off the stool, rinsed out her coffee cup, and put it carelessly in the dish drainer. She pulled her long wet hair into a knot.

"You're a lousy actor, Josh. I know you were thinking of her last night," Marta said.

Josh's blushed. When she tried to walk past him, he stopped her and embraced her roughly. She didn't soften. He kissed her. She kissed him back, then pulled away. She was sure Maggie would have remained in his arms.

"I bet she calls you in a day or two," Josh said. Marta continued on her way and went upstairs.

At the end of the week, he came with her back to the city to soften the blow of the empty apartment. Marta wasn't bothered by it. In a way, she was relieved. Maybe Maggie had seen something she should have, that they were getting on each other's nerves even before the ruse. But soon the space felt like it needed something more, and she asked Josh if he'd stay a couple of days.

"Sure, why not?"

"One thing. I like being alone after sex. So, can you sleep in Maggie's room?"

"Yeah, I'm fine with that. If she comes back, I'll split."

"She won't come back."

"How can you be so sure?"

"Because she's my twin sister."

He asked if she had any wine. His bottle from the dinner party was still in the kitchen, but he didn't want that. He took what remained of the red Kyle had brought.

"Did you guys have a fight?" he asked.

"No."

"So, why—"

"Look, I really don't know."

"I thought you knew everything about her."

"Clearly not."

He turned thoughtful.

"I should find a way to use that for the play," he said.

Marta sipped her wine. Josh's remark made her consider again her passion for the theater. Being on stage had obsessed her since high school. She went to every audition for every ragged production, and finally landed something solid, Emily in *Our Town*; she even tried out for the school choir, but was told she had no ear for music and should probably stick to the spoken word; then, in the city, she showed up for one cattle call after another, for parts she didn't get, in plays that ran two, maybe three weeks. And the supporting roles she landed—playing a teenager named Nora whose best friend gets caught shoplifting, and then playing Bridgette, a maid in a fancy country house where the mistress, a brilliant, complicated, aging beauty, berates her because she's an easy target—earned her modest praise, nothing more.

Something turned inside her, exposing a hard, shiny surface.

"I'll play both parts," she said.

"Yeah? How?"

He'd need to write a series of soliloquies. She'd wear some kind of oversized garment, a cardigan sweater maybe, that she could slip off one shoulder to indicate that the other character was now speaking. Or maybe turn away just long enough to put on a pair of glasses, or the light could drop, and she'd just slip them on. Even better—she could simply pause, then present a very different behavior, like someone with multiple personalities, as in, what was that movie? The one about that woman in the fifties?

The Three Faces of Eve, Josh said.

But did identical twins ever have vastly different personalities? Marta conceded that no, they probably didn't. They'd have to stick to Plan A, or a revised Plan A. As long as she was the only one on stage.

He knew she was right. She understood drama, Maggie didn't. He twirled his glass, making the wine dance. The stage set changed in his mind. They didn't need a laundry basket, only a trimmed down version of this very room. A blue velvet couch, and a Persian rug, or a Persian rug knockoff, and there on the floor would be Marta sitting cross-legged. He needed to fix the image in his mind while he hammered out the rest of the play, revising the dialogue he'd begun in the Hamptons, which he now saw was childish, centering on toys and snacks, and contests about who would fall asleep first. He must write about them as women, not necessarily the women they were now, but those they would surely become when this stupid fight was long forgotten.

"I think that sounds awesome," he said.

"Make it so gradually the audience has trouble telling them apart. Just when they think they're clear on who's talking, they realize it's actually the other one."

Her smirk dared him to ask where she'd gotten that idea.

Later that same day he returned with clean clothes in a backpack. She apologized for the state of Maggie's room. Maggie didn't dust very often. The carpet needed to be vacuumed. Sometimes they talked about having a cleaning crew come in once a month, but neither thought the expense was worth it. She asked him if he wanted her to change the sheets. He'd brought a sleeping bag, so no need. She was going to go lie down for a little while. She'd gotten another bottle of wine while he'd been gone and polished off most of it on her own. When she got up, they could go out for dinner. She hoped the rain would stop.

Josh loved the rain. He bet Maggie did, too. The sound of it brought back his childhood home in Montclair, on a street lush with maples and oaks. They ruled the seasons, really, and of all the ways he loved those trees—the sudden green buds when snow still lay on the ground; their autumn fiery brilliance; even their bare, twisted branches, reaching skyward like yearning, hungry spirits—the best was the reassuring *tick, tick, ticktick,* of raindrops on their wide, flat leaves.

He put his backpack on the floor. The furniture was simpler than he thought it would be, given how generous their stepfather was. The double bed had a white wooden headboard. The dresser was in the same white wood, and the mirror above it had a photograph wedged between the glass and the frame. A little blonde girl in a cowboy hat sat on a rocking horse, grinning for all she was worth, showing a charming gap where her two front baby teeth had been. He had a similar picture of himself in a Superman costume. His mother had mailed him the picture a couple years ago when she was cleaning out a closet. Sure, he'd kept it, but he had no interest in putting it where he could be reminded every day of what he was like at that age.

He removed the picture and turned it over.

Marta, age 4, at the Dickinsons' annual BBQ.

So much for narcissism.

The drawers contained nothing, except for the bottom one where he found an empty box of tampons. The night stand contained only an unused condom. Who was the lucky guy who'd been told he didn't need it after all?

He lay down on her bed and pressed his face into the pillow. There must be a way to reach her. If he got ahold of Marta's phone, he could scroll through the text messages and find her number. It was definitely worth a try.

She'd left the phone on the table in the living room. She hadn't programmed a password, or used another security feature, and he was able to get right in to her text feed. The list was long, and nothing was identified as belonging to Maggie, except one number she'd nicknamed

"Duo." He called it. The phone rang and rang and went to voicemail. Maggie's recorded voice said, "I've gone to the moon on gossamer wings. I'll call you back once I return to earth." Of course, seeing Marta's number, she wouldn't pick up.

He entered the number in his own phone, and designated it as belonging to "Gossamer." He walked down the hall and stood for a moment outside Marta's closed bedroom door and listened. There was nothing. When he returned to the kitchen, he stood by the window, looking down at the street, and called her.

"Hello?"

"Hey, it's Josh."

She was silent for a moment.

"Hey, what's up?" she asked.

"Your sister's been looking for you."

"Is that how you got my number?"

"I got it from Kyle."

He wasn't sure how he was going to explain how he'd done that, since she no doubt assumed, correctly, that he didn't have Kyle's number either.

"And you're being a good Samaritan, trying to save her some legwork?" she asked.

"Something like that."

"If I wanted her to know where I am, I would have told her."

"Fair enough. But you can tell me. I'll keep quiet. Promise."

"She'll ask you where I am, and you'll have to say you don't know, which she won't believe. Or, you'll have to lie. Either way, it's a shitty position to get stuck in. I don't want to do that to you."

His heart quickened. Was her concern an expression of affection? Or was she just being overly considerate?

"Well, can you narrow it down a little for me?" he asked.

"Why?"

"I'm worried about you. Taking off like that. And I've been working on the play, and really need your input."

"I'm sure Marta can cover that."

He could hear her getting tired of the conversation.

"So, you're okay?" he asked.

She paused.

"I will be," she said.

"What needs to happen first?"

She took a longer pause this time.

"I have to go. Thanks for calling."

"You've got my number now. Call me sometime, okay?"

She hung up.

Down in the street, where he'd been looking during their conversation, someone was trying to park a mid-sixties Cadillac. The space he was trying for was big enough, but he kept coming in at too sharp an angle. He ran up over the curb more than once. A pedestrian yelled at him. Another driver honked. Finally, the car glided into the spot perfectly. For every good thing about New York there was an equally bad thing, like tight parking, noise, rude people. He'd lived there two years, and most days felt lucky to be there. Not today, though. Today he wanted to be wherever Maggie was.

Marta stirred in her room. Water ran in the bathroom sink. The toilet flushed. She appeared, one side of her face pink from being pressed into her pillow. She picked up her phone, apparently unaware that she hadn't left it on the kitchen table, but out in the living room, and stared at the screen. She punched in a number

"Who are you calling?" Josh asked.

"My sister."

"She won't answer."

"My *other* sister."

She brought the phone to her ear, then asked Josh if he could give her a little privacy for a few minutes. He went into Maggie's room, but didn't close the door. He needed to hear her end of the conversation.

The sister seemed to be doing most of the talking. Marta was quiet for a long stretch and then said, "Yeah, but what about me? I mean, this is so totally messed up!"

More silence, broken now and then by a sullen "uh-huh," and then, "Okay, whatever. Yeah, bye."

Josh crept into the hall, then more confidently into the living room where Marta sat on the couch, arms crossed, fuming.

"What's up?" he asked.

"She thinks it was time we took a break, Maggie and me."

She said the other sister, Angie, was a social worker, and big on giving advice, which in this case was to chill and let Maggie do whatever she was doing, wherever she was doing it.

"Does she know where she is?" Josh asked.

"No."

"Does she have any good guesses?"

"Jesus, Josh, give it a rest!"

He sat beside her. He put his arm around her. He felt responsible, he said. He was the one that caused the rift by going along with the ruse in the first place. He hated the idea of them pulling apart because of him.

"It's not because of you," Marta said. "It's because she couldn't take failing at painting."

"Her stuff doesn't look like a failure to me."

"Yeah, but it's not what you think that counts. It's what *she* thinks."

Josh admired the depth of this insight. He leaned in and kissed her.

"Not now. I have to pack," Marta said.

"Why? Where are you going?"

"Angie thinks I should swing by upstate tomorrow and see everyone. I'll probably spend the night."

"Oh."

"Come, if you want."

"And meet your family?"

"Why not?"

"Who will you say I am?"

"My friend from the city. What else would I say?"

"Okay, sure."

Marta stared at the Persian rug. It, too, needed vacuuming. Would Maggie keep her new place any cleaner?

I miss you.

That was the first time she'd admitted it, but rather than feel relieved, her frustration only deepened.

"Bring a sweater or two. October can be cold up there," Marta said.

He asked if she wanted to have sex. She said nothing, just got to her feet, took him by the hand, and walked him into her bedroom.

chapter nine

The wipers of the rented car lulled him. Yesterday's rain continued, only softer now. An air freshener in the shape of an evergreen tree swung idly from the rearview mirror. He hated how it smelled.

Marta had little to say. They had another two hours to go, and just then were ascending the gradual plateau of the Pocono Mountains. He'd checked his cell phone about thirty times since getting in the car. Brad, the guy whose house they'd borrowed in the Hamptons, called when he returned from the trip he'd been on at the time to say Josh's girlfriend had done a nice job with the kitchen. Josh had cleaned it, not Marta, but he'd kept that to himself. It was okay for Brad to think he had a girlfriend who was handy to have around. His mother had left two messages, the first about the neighbor's dog who dug up her carrots, the other about a second cousin in Florida she was hoping they might go see together over the holidays. His mother volunteered at a food bank several days a week. She had a slew of friends she'd known for years, yet she couldn't seem to fill her time well enough to keep her from bothering him almost every single day.

Thinking that made him feel bad. He should be more patient with her. She made it possible to live in the city and not have a job. His father had been a successful tax attorney, with family money of his own. He'd established a trust for Josh when Josh was about ten. It stipulated that he would not have control over the funds until he attained the age of 30. His father died suddenly when Josh was 11. Last year, when he turned 26, he tried to persuade his mother to let him have access to the principal. She refused. Whenever he needed money over and above his already generous allowance, she gave it to him. He never spent on anything lavish, like a car or an expensive trip. That might come later, when the money was entirely his.

Until then, he'd have to bring his dream to life on the cheap and draw talent from his circle of post-college friends. Everyone was an aspiring actor or dancer. They all had day jobs, usually in a restaurant, though one girl, Dierdre, tutored grade school children in math. Her parents felt that her skills were wasted in the arts. Her mother was an economist and insisted that a calling with a clear path forward was much better than gambling on the uncertainty of the theater.

He and Dierdre had had an affair last year. It started casually, as they all did, then came to that inevitable point where things either got more intense or just burned out. She wanted less of him, he wanted more of her, and that was the first time he'd been in that position with a woman. He'd wondered about it ever since. Was it that same old story, that he was drawn closer precisely because she pulled away? And did everything between a man and a woman come down to a struggle for power? When they broke up, Brad assumed it was once again Josh's choice, and Josh didn't set him straight. His silence earned him a lecture on needing to change, treat the ladies a little better, or face the prospect of never finding "the one."

Josh's phone buzzed in his pocket. He took it out and looked at the number. "Gossamer" lit up his screen. He declined the call, praying she would leave a voice message. The message icon displayed a moment later. He told Marta he should probably hit a restroom in the next few miles.

"Coffee on a road trip is always a bad idea," he said, aware that his voice was overly cheerful.

It took half an hour to find a gas station. Marta got out and ran her card through the automatic reader on the pump. Josh went into the men's room, which was filthy up to the ceiling light, and listened to Maggie's message.

"Hey, it's me. I talked to Kyle, he says he never gave you my number, so I'm figuring you swiped it off Marta's phone, or else she just gave it to you, which I totally doubt, because she's kinda jealous of whatever it is between us . . . chemistry?" Pause. "Well, I gotta go. My roommate wants me to drive her to the store." She hung up.

He used the toilet, and rejoined Marta.

"Taking a leak always make you this happy?" she asked. She ate potato chips from a small single-serving bag.

"I'm just in a good mood, that's all."

She patted his knee, leaving a smear of crumbs and salt on his denim jeans. "Well, good. Stay that way."

He shot off a quick text to Maggie.

On the road. Will catch up in a bit.

Marta's family home was huge, at the end of a long driveway separated from the road with a black iron gate. The circular driveway had two cars in it: an old collector's-item Mercedes and a late-model Land Rover. Stone columns stood on either side of the front door. Marta and Josh walked into a large foyer with black and white floor tiles. They left their backpacks by a potted rubber tree plant whose leaves were dusty.

Marta's mother was in the kitchen, sitting at the counter with another woman Marta introduced as their housekeeper, Alma. The mother was petite, dark-haired, with a sharp knowing look in her eyes. Alma was a good ten to fifteen years older, gray-haired, round, also with a keen gaze. Both women were each working their way through what looked like a glass of white wine. A half-empty bottle was on the far end of the counter.

The mother—Lavinia—shook Josh's hand. Her grip was impressive. Marta had said before that she'd sold manufactured homes. Josh bet she'd done pretty well, with a handshake like that. When she smiled, he could feel her charm.

"Good drive?" she asked Marta. Marta shrugged. She stared into the open refrigerator for something to snack on. There was a baked ham; several containers of peach yogurt; one of cottage cheese; a pound of butter; and a head of brown lettuce. She closed the door.

"Guess we're eating out," she said.

"Yes," Lavinia said.

"Who with?"

"Just you, me, Alma, your friend here, and, of course, Chip."

Marta didn't like the thought of being trapped in some high-end stuffy restaurant for several hours. She suggested ordering a pizza, instead.

"I'm in. But skip the pepperoni. It comes back on me," Alma said.

Lavinia invited them to sit down at the table nearby, since she and Alma were occupying the only counter stools.

"Where's everybody else?" Marta asked. She removed her platform sandals. They pinched, but she appreciated the three extra inches they gave her. Josh was only about five foot eight. The sandals let her look him in the eye, more or less.

"Chip's in his study. He'll be out in a bit. He's got Mel in there."

Lavinia said Mel was Chip's old friend. Alma said they were probably knocking it back.

"I mean Angie, Tim, and Foster," Marta said.

"Oh, they'll probably swing by at some point," Lavinia said.

None of the kids lived at home anymore. Sometimes Marta wondered how her mother liked living with just Chip and Alma in that echoey barn. She could never tell what her mother really felt about anything, unless she were angry. You always knew her mind then.

Lavinia asked if they'd like a glass of wine.

"Sure," Josh said.

"Do you prefer red or white?"

"Red, I guess."

Lavinia pointed to the small butler's pantry between the kitchen and formal dining room. There he found a wine rack stocked with both red and white wine. Judging from their elegantly drawn labels, this was quality stuff. He chose a red from California because it was a place he always wanted to go, and for a moment he saw himself in LA, with Maggie, directing his first indie film.

He returned with the bottle. Alma pointed to the corkscrew on the counter. Lavinia pointed to the cabinet to the right of the kitchen sink, where the wine glasses were stored. Pointing was a habit Marta had inherited, he thought, recalling how she pointed to his phone when it rang, and to a half-empty glass of water she might have left on the counter and didn't feel like getting herself.

He had trouble with the corkscrew, and Alma said she'd do it. He watched her sturdy hands grip and twist. He wanted to ask her all about Maggie, what she was like when she was younger. He couldn't, of course, with Marta and her mother right there. When Alma had poured out two glasses of red, and refreshed the white for both herself and Lavinia, she reclaimed her stool, leaned hard on her elbows, and asked, "So, what's the deal with Maggie taking off?"

Marta said nothing for a moment. Josh tensed.

"I think she got stuck. You know, in a rut with her painting. She had to leave the studio she was in, and she hasn't really gotten it together since," Marta said.

"What?" Lavinia said, "I just paid the rent on her space, or nook, or whatever it is. I guess I have to see about getting a refund. God, you girls can be so lazy about money. *Other* people's money, that is."

"She threw paint on someone's canvas. Wrecked it."

"Maggie did that?" Alma asked. There was a tone of admiration in her tone.

"Yeah."

"And they asked her to leave?" Lavinia asked.

"I don't know if they asked her to, but she did. Couldn't face them, I guess."

"You always think your sister's a wimp," Alma said. Josh got the feeling she'd been drinking for a while that afternoon. Her color was high.

"Well, isn't she?"

"Not this again," Lavinia said.

Two men entered the kitchen, one tall and on the portly side, the other much shorter, and also quite round, with a white handlebar mustache.

"Well, there you are!" boomed the taller man. Lavinia introduced him as Chip, her husband, and the other as his friend, Mel.

Josh shook hands with both of them. He stared hard at Mel.

"You look so familiar," he told him.

"Who, me?" Mel asked.

"Yes."

"And whom do I resemble?"

"Not Mr. Egghead," Marta said.

"Stop," Lavinia said.

"We used to call him that when we were little," Marta told Josh.

"Because, one, I love deviled eggs, and two, my head is as smooth as what the hen just laid in the coop," Mel said.

Josh said he'd had a great-uncle who looked just like Mel—same height, same blue eyes, even loved the same short-sleeved plaid shirts.

"What was his name?" Chip asked.

"Phil."

"Ah. Mel, Phil. Pretty darn close, wouldn't you say?"

"I bet you carry a handkerchief," Josh said.

Mel produced one from the back pocket of his khaki slacks.

"Gross," Marta said.

"It's freshly laundered. Here, see for yourself," Mel said.

Lavinia held up her hand.

"Don't you sweethearts have a game you can watch?" she asked.

"I don't know, do we?" Chip asked.

"Do you like baseball?" Josh asked Mel.

"Yes."

"I mean, like, are you totally into it?"

Mel thought for a moment and stroked one side of his mustache.

"Yes. I'd say I'm crazy about baseball," he said.

"So was my great-uncle."

No one spoke for a moment. Alma drained her glass.

"So, what's this I hear about Maggie leaving the city?" Chip asked.

"I told you all about that," Lavinia said.

"We're trying to figure out where she went," Josh said. "She won't tell Marta. Or, at least it seems she doesn't want Marta to know."

Marta looked pissed. Alma, amused. Lavinia, bored.

"Oh, well, she's living over in Sullivan," Chip said. He brought his hand to his mouth and stifled a burp.

"Oh, Chip!" Lavinia said.

"What?"

"She didn't want you to tell anyone."

"Marta's not anyone."

"Where's Sullivan?" Josh asked.

Mel used his thumb to gesture over his shoulder.

Alma said he was off, as usual, and pointed in the opposite direction. "Near Syracuse. I have a cousin there. Us kids used to call him 'Franky Wanky Doing The Hanky-Panky,' which is funny as hell on account of the fact that he'd been married three times. Damn fool keeps getting caught. Now, his second wife, Betty Lynn, she came at him with a baseball bat and—"

"Alma," Lavinia said.

"How far is Syracuse?" Josh asked.

"About fifty miles," Mel said.

Josh looked at Marta, but she was looking at her phone, then tapping the keys madly with both thumbs. Was she texting Maggie? What was she saying?

We know where you are. Chip blew it. Heading your way. I got Josh w/me. Repeat, I GOT JOSH.

But Marta was answering a text from Angie, who wanted to confirm that Marta was at the house, and that she'd be by after dinner. She had things to say.

Marta shared this with the group.

"That girl loves a soapbox," Alma said.

"She's a pain in the ass," Marta said.

"You need her. We all do," Mel said.

Marta stood up and said she'd show Josh where his room was. Josh went on staring at Mel until she said his name in a tight voice.

"Okay," he said.

They went up the curving staircase and down a long hall with thick carpeting and a series of prints on both walls, all of race horses. Marta said that Chip had once been the co-owner of a race horse, at least that's what she thought the story was, not that she ever really listened to him all that closely since he was so easy to tune out.

"He seems like an all right guy," Josh said.

"I thought Mel was your new idol."

"I'm sorry about that. It's just so *weird*. I mean, haven't you ever seen someone who looks exactly like someone you used to know?"

"No. But maybe I'm not as observant as you."

Josh ignored her. He wondered if he could skip out, rent a car himself, and take off for Sullivan. How would he find Maggie, though? He could just ask people in town if they knew her, but she hadn't been living there all that long. It could take weeks to catch up with her. Maybe if he just called and said he knew what town she was in she'd relent and invite him to visit.

The room he'd been given was tiny, with a single bed, and a tall narrow window. He threw his pack on the floor and asked Marta what she wanted to do until dinner. She was going to take a nap, but he was free to make himself at home. The television was in the finished basement, and he was welcome to watch whatever he wanted as long as Chip and Mel didn't mind.

She left him alone. He called Maggie's number. She didn't answer. He didn't leave a message, and then thought she'd find that odd, so he wrote a text message instead:

In Dunston with Marta. Chip says you're in Sullivan. Why don't I head up there and we can hang out? I'll leave Marta here. She wants to visit with your other sister. Let me know.

He was shocked when only a few seconds later, she replied with her address.

Marta had left the car keys on the kitchen table where they drank wine earlier. The kitchen was empty. He took the keys and went out the kitchen door, all the way around the side of the house, grateful that the sky had lifted. He soon passed by a large paneled den with tall windows. Chip sat behind a massive desk. Lavinia walked slowly back and forth in front of it, gesturing with her right hand. She turned just as Josh went by and stared at him curiously. She then continued her rhythmic transit, her right hand rising and falling to emphasize words he couldn't hear. Where was Mel, that spooky resurrection of his great-uncle? For a second, he was torn between wanting to return inside to look for him in the basement, to spend just a bit more time cataloging the similarities between the living and the dead.

But then he thought of Maggie.

chapter ten

Digger stayed two days, and then Leah told him to leave. He said he had to get going anyway, the co-op couldn't be rudderless for too much longer. Later, Leah told Maggie that this was always his way of saving face.

Maggie said, "He was brave to come and see you, then, knowing that you weren't really interested in him anymore."

"I'm plenty interested. In fact, I'm still totally on the hook, but I just can't have him around me all the time. I need my space."

Maggie understood. With four siblings, and Marta stuck to her like glue for her whole life, space was a luxury. Yet, having it could be lonely sometimes, too.

For the first time since leaving New York, she felt bad about not saying goodbye.

Maggie and Leah were cleaning the apartment, though they'd only lived there together for about a week. Leah didn't like dust, clutter, dirty dishes, tossed down magazines, chairs that weren't pushed in, unmade beds, including Maggie's even when her door was closed, or anything out of place. Maggie wrote her off as neurotic and let it go, because her own mother was the same way.

She thought about Josh calling her the day before. She didn't realize at first how glad she was to hear from him. When she called him after talking to Kyle, and he didn't answer, she was upset. Didn't he want to hear from her? Isn't that what he said? Then, when he texted to say they'd catch up in a bit, she didn't know what to think.

Leah said Mrs. Culver downstairs needed a quick visit. Leah had been the only one dropping down since Maggie moved in, because Maggie always said she'd go next time, and then begged off. Maggie hoped Leah wouldn't remind her about that, but the look in her eye said she was about to.

Maggie thought she should change out of her stained sweatshirt and black jeans into something a little nicer, but realized Mrs. Culver wouldn't care what she wore, and if she did, too bad. Old people made her uneasy, she decided, maybe because she'd never really been around them much. Although both sets of her grandparents had lived in Dunston for years after she was born, there was only one visit with each pair that she could recall. They were all dead now. Angie and her father, Potter, had gone to both of his parents' funerals, that much she did remember. Her mother's parents didn't cross the radar of her memory at all.

Mrs. Culver didn't answer Maggie's knock, so she rang the bell. When there was no response, she pressed her ear to the door to listen for any movement within. Slow, measured footfalls came towards her. The door opened all the way, revealing a small, tidy woman with a soft, wrinkled face and soft, blue eyes. Her white hair was cut short, with the same wisps Maggie's own stylist had bestowed up on her just a few weeks before. She wore an elaborately embroidered housecoat with a red velvet collar.

Maggie identified herself, and Mrs. Culver asked her to please come in, then led her back to the kitchen where she'd been having a cup of tea. Would Maggie care for one?

"Sure."

"I'm having the green today. Well, every day really since my doctor recommended it. Something to do with antioxidants, or cancer prevention, though at my age—and I'm not going to tell you what that is unless you're rude enough to ask, in which case I probably still won't say— these things are, for the most part, pointless. But I like the flavor quite a bit."

Maggie sat in a wooden chair. Its thick seat pad gave her extra height and made the table seem too small, like a poorly-chosen prop.

Mrs. Culver asked how she was finding Sullivan.

"Well, it's—"

"Not much, especially for a young person. But I think it's going to gentrify when that new high-tech place starts hiring. That's where the money is, isn't it? Computer coding?"

Maggie didn't know. She never paid attention to economic matters other than her own, but nodded wisely, as if she'd given the matter a great deal of thought.

"Are you getting along okay today?" Maggie asked.

"I get along okay most days. I don't know why my son worries about me so much."

Mrs. Culver poured tea into Maggie's cup. The handle was missing, she noticed, which would make drinking from it difficult.

Rain beat against the window over the sink, where a few moments ago there'd been pleasant autumn sunlight. Maggie hadn't noticed the darkening sky. Mrs. Culver turned her head in the direction of the sound, her cup halfway to her lips. Her hand trembled, and Maggie wondered if the storm had alarmed her.

Neither of them spoke for a few moments, and just sat, listening to the drops on the glass. Mrs. Culver lowered her cup and looked at Maggie. Her gaze was almost dreamy.

"You were such an angel when you were little," Mrs. Culver said.

Maggie hit a mental fast-forward to when she would report this to Leah, who would pass it on to the son.

"I was a pretty obnoxious kid, actually. Not as bad as Marta, though. Marta's my sister. My twin sister. My *identical* twin sister, actually."

Mrs. Culver focused. "She does looks exactly like you. I always found that remarkable." She paused. "To wear someone else's face is an extraordinary thing, don't you think?"

Maggie didn't answer.

"I wear my father's face," Mrs. Culver said.

"Okay."

"And in my family, that wasn't always a good thing. He was not well liked."

"Oh."

Mrs. Culver just sat staring into space after that until Maggie said she needed to be someplace.

"Tell your mother I said hello, and not to worry about the cake dish. It's hers to keep, if she likes," Mrs. Culver said.

When Maggie gave it all to Leah, Leah said the son, Jack, had mentioned that his mother was often confused about things.

"She needs to be in a home. I don't care how many pots of tea she can still brew," Maggie said.

"Easier said than done."

Josh texted saying he was in Dunston and wanted to drive up. When she texted back her address, she was filled with a pale yellow-green blend of dread and joy. Leah noticed her expression. Maggie filled her in.

"Well, proceed with caution," Leah said. "He's liable to cause something between you and your sister that might never get fixed."

Maggie calmed herself down by running the vacuum, although Leah had already done that; then doing a load of laundry, even though she only had a couple of T-shirts and pairs of underwear that were dirty; then making a shopping list because the refrigerator was pretty bare. Here, she stopped. She wasn't about to make dinner. She and Leah usually ordered from the Chinese place up the street. Josh could take her out. That's exactly what he could do.

She put on an ankle-length blue dress with charming cap sleeves. She wished then that she hadn't cut her hair. A dress like that needed the rolling tresses of a princess. She sashayed before the small mirror in her room, hungry then for the walk-in closet back in New York that had been her palace for almost two years.

About an hour after Josh texted to say he was on his way, she got a call from Marta.

"I'm in Dunston with Josh," she said. "He took off with the car."

"Yeah, he's coming to see me."

"Nice of him to let me know."

Maggie couldn't read her thoughts just then.

"Tell him to get back here no later than tomorrow. I'm trapped, awaiting the next Dugan Massacre," Marta said.

Maggie admired her for seeing that she and Josh might sleep together. Marta hoped Josh would keep his mouth shut about having slept with *her*.

"Tomahawks out and ready to strike?" Maggie asked.

"Soon. Angie wants a powwow."

"Why?"

"Because I told her you were blowing me off."

"I'm not blowing you off now."

"No, but you were damn frosty."

"Because you made me feel that Josh's kissing me was my fault when it wasn't. How was I supposed to know he'd do that? And how do you know he *didn't* think I was you, anyway?"

"I just got pissed off."

"Over something that was your idea in the first place."

They paused. Then Marta asked if she were ever coming back to the city. Honestly, Maggie didn't know. She was getting settled in the new place, she was working on a new project. She couldn't see uprooting herself again right away. She needed some time get herself together.

"Mom wanted to know why you left. I told her it was because of…"

"My painting. Thank you for not…"

"Saying anything about Josh. I know. But I couldn't…"

"Because he was there with you, right?"

They paused again, longer this time, as their thoughts followed the same path, until Maggie said, "I'll send him back unscathed."

"Don't put yourself out."

"That's what I'm saying."

At this they laughed.

"Maybe it'll be like getting out of camp," Marta said.

What, like when you faked an upset stomach, so you wouldn't have to go?

Sorta.

Maybe that's why you became an actress. You were quite convincing.

Mom saw through it, but didn't care, because it was cheaper just to send you.

That was their first separation, at age seven.

"Maybe I'll text you when camp's over," Maggie said.

"Be careful where you pitch your tent."

Then Marta had to go. Alma was ordering a pizza, and she needed to make sure she didn't get anything with mushrooms. Maggie agreed that mushrooms were nasty.

Maggie took her sketchpad into the living room and sat in the chair right in front of the window, so she could see Josh arrive. He would see her there, working away, serious in her intent. She would look at him with faint curiosity, as if he were coming to deliver the mail. Her demeanor would be cool, with a pleasant overlay, reminiscent of how her own mother handled dicey situations. Then he was there, parking and getting out of the car. He looked amazing in his high-tech running shoes and suede jacket.

He trotted up the walk and rang the bell. For a moment, she didn't move. She needed to keep it together. He rang it again, and she went down, her hand on the wall that separated the stairs from Mrs. Culver's living room, and let him in. He tensed when she shook his hand, a gesture she hadn't intended, but which just seemed to happen of its own accord.

"Hey," he said.

"The rain stopped."

"Yeah."

"You have any trouble finding me?"

He lifted his phone to say he'd used its GPS.

"You can't always trust that. It once sent my dad way outside of Binghamton when he wanted to be somewhere downtown. Of course, he was probably plastered at the time. He drank a lot. I probably told you that."

"Nope."

His eyes took her in from head to toe.

"Like it?" she asked.

"Sure."

He followed her upstairs, his tread echoing. He looked around the small living room, and she could tell he wasn't impressed.

"Where's the roommate?" he asked.

"In her barn, painting."

Josh took one end of the small couch, the only place to sit besides the tattered easy chair and a wide window seat Maggie and Leah wanted to get some brightly colored cushions for.

"So," he said.

She was still standing, looking down at him, completely at sea with the situation. "You met my family."

"Some of them."

"Who was there?"

"Uh, your mom, your step-dad, the housekeeper whose name I can't remember, and your step-dad's friend Mel."

"Oh, god, Mel."

"He looks *exactly* like my great-uncle."

"Yeah?"

"It was totally weird."

Maggie sat next to him. Their knees bumped.

"He probably just reminded you of him, that's all," she said.

Josh shook his head. His great-uncle had died only a few years before, and Josh recalled every part of his face. He was good with faces. She could ask Marta. He remembered who showed up at auditions. He could always place someone right away, even if he'd never been given their name. Maggie suggested that maybe Mel was a long-lost relative, way back in the family tree, though she privately thought that was nonsense.

"That might explain it. What do you know about him? Where he grew up, I mean?" he asked.

"I have no idea."

"Oh, well."

She offered him a beer, which he accepted. She didn't get one for herself. She asked how Marta was. She didn't say they'd spoken just a little while before.

"She's okay, I guess. We went out to the Hamptons for a week, so I could work on the play."

"How's it going?"

"Not too well, since you split."

"Sorry about that. I just . . . felt the time had come."

He drank from his beer, set the bottle on the floor then took her hand.

"I don't know how to say this," he said.

"Then don't."

He looked at her until she had to turn her gaze on something else, but that was only for a second. He kissed her.

She dropped his hand.

"What's wrong?" he asked.

"I'm not really ready for this."

"You were the other day."

Maggie conceded the point. She said she'd been trying to figure out what made her do it, and she realized that she must have some crazy wish to *be* her sister, if that made any sense. She might have discovered this before if she'd moved out sooner. She and Marta had spent very little time apart, which made this separation a valuable thing. She needed to know who she was, aside from Marta Dugan's twin sister. She tried to imagine that Marta had never been born, that it was just Maggie and her three other siblings; or that Marta had died at birth, and Maggie survived, but it was hard to think like that, because it seemed so cruel, willing someone out of existence. She realized, too, that this was what drove her work right now—she showed him the sketchpad, and the several versions she'd drawn of the faceless woman.

He was impressed, or pretended to be, and when Maggie registered her suspicions, she knew the evening was doomed. She couldn't sleep with a man she didn't trust. She then wondered whom she had ever trusted, male or female, in a binding, unquestioning way, the kind of bond she assumed should exist between a man and woman and had never observed, certainly not in her own fractious household. Her father remarried a woman who remodeled houses with her own hands and was, the children all agreed, actually very like their mother in terms of her capability and practical bent. They seemed happy. She couldn't tell. Her mother and stepfather seemed happy, or rather *he* seemed happy. She seemed generally disinterested. But they must have a deep, solid trust between them since it would be impossible to live together without it.

Until recently, the only person she had trusted was Marta, and not because Marta always treated her well, or was considerate of her feelings, but because she knew what she was thinking. Perhaps that—and only that—was the true basis of trust, knowing another's mind. And since it took time to learn the habits and inclinations of someone else, especially a love interest, maybe all you had to go on for a while was faith, and physical attraction.

She studied Josh while he studied her drawings. When he saw her doing so, he blushed. She lost ground then.

"It's a cool idea, facelessness," he said. He mentioned his great-uncle and Mel again, and said the circumstance reminded him of something he'd once read by an author named Milan Kundera.

"Have you ever heard of him?" he asked her.

She shook her head.

He was Czech, or Hungarian, or something like that, but he'd written this novel and all he could really remember about it, other than how strange and avant-garde it seemed, was his idea that all of mankind wore the same face. At the time he wondered if the author meant that the human face had basically the same structure across all individuals and populations; or maybe this was the impression an alien race might form, viewing us all from afar.

Maggie didn't know what to say.

"So, you're obviously on to something here, I think," he said. He put the sketchpad down on the coffee table, next to a small green ceramic vase that held a pair of silk roses Maggie had found at Goodwill.

"Thanks."

"But you were working a lot with color before, right?"

"Yeah, but now I'm digging just the black and white concept."

"It's hard."

"What is?"

"Being an artist. Any kind of artist."

"Like a playwright."

He smiled at her and pressed her palm to his lips. She counted slowly to ten, then pulled away.

chapter eleven

The light from the enormous crystal chandelier in the formal dining room fell cruelly on Angie's chin and the smear of pizza sauce she didn't know was there. Alma pointed it out. Angie swiped at it with her napkin. She'd come straight from work. Her tan pantsuit made her look older than 31. As a teenager she'd gone goth down to the black fingernails, nose ring, and black skull tattoo on her shoulder. No one meeting her now would believe she'd ever radiated anything but competence coupled with a slightly short temper.

It was that temper which she now tried to hold in check. She didn't think the problem was that Maggie and Marta necessarily needed some time apart, though taking time now probably wouldn't hurt, because they could have a chance to think for themselves and decide what they wanted to do next.

When she said this, Marta didn't understand. They were on their respective paths. What else was there to do but continue to pursue their dreams?

"Work. As in get a job."

Everyone around the table paused.

"We don't need jobs," Marta said.

"Because Mom and Chip support you."

"Isn't that our business?" Lavinia asked.

"I'm not saying it's not. I'm just saying maybe you work for a while, earn some money, see how the other ninety-five percent do it. Get some real-world experience."

Chip reminded her that the arrangement had been that the girls would be supported until they were able to support themselves. If one—or both—decided to take a break from her chosen pursuit, then the support would be withdrawn.

"We never intended to let them just sit around doing nothing," Chip said. He carved the slice of pizza on his plate with an elegant sterling silver knife and fork. The dishes they ate on were bone china, with a delicate pattern of blue lace around the rim.

"I know, I know, but it's been going on for years now, and I just don't think it's healthy," Angie said.

Alma cleared away the plates and asked if anyone wanted dessert. Chip and Angie did. Marta watched her weight carefully. So did Lavinia. Angie had always been a little pudgy. Every now and then she got sick of it, went on a crash diet, lost fifteen pounds, then gained them all back again within a month.

Marta reflected on this, watching her enjoy Alma's chocolate layer cake.

"You're jealous," Marta told her.

"Of what?"

"Having to work for a living when we don't."

"Girls," Lavinia said.

"I don't have to work for a living any more than you do. I want to work. I *love* my job," Angie said, fiercely. She mostly loved her job, that was true. She worked in a retirement home. The family members of the residents could be real stinkers, either making unrealistic demands, or ignoring the welfare of their parents altogether, all things she'd complained of many times before.

She had another bite of cake and pushed away her plate.

"Tell me this. How many roles have you gotten in the two years you've been in New York?" she asked.

"Two."

"And how much money did you make?"

"I don't know, some."

"Some."

"I'm not a bookkeeper."

"Or much of an actress, from the sound of it."

"Angie," Lavinia said.

Angie had always been able to drive a nail right into Marta's heart. She had that power over all her siblings, because she was the eldest and most hardworking of them all. She'd gotten her college degree from a local state school, while their brother Timothy attended Dunston University, which was Ivy League. Timothy worked in retail, which Marta found lame after such an expensive education. Their youngest brother Foster had also gone to Dunston, then didn't do much for a couple of years except knock around Europe and work on a fishing boat up in Maine, until he skewered his hand on a hook and had to have surgery. He still had numbness, which made working difficult. He found a job in a vet's office, taking care of the cats and dogs who boarded overnight. He seemed to like it a lot, but again, hardly a position commensurate with what had been invested in him.

"I do the best I can," Marta said. Something in her tone made Angie relent. She suggested maybe Marta might go back to school. Both she and Maggie only had associate degrees.

"I've thought about it," Marta said. That was true, but she always came to the same conclusion, that learning from professionals was more valuable than learning from professors.

"When's your friend coming back?" Lavinia asked.

"Josh? I don't know. He went over to Sullivan to see Maggie."

"Why?"

"He sort of has a thing for her."

"Is it mutual?"

"I don't know. She hasn't talked to me about it."

"Isn't he *your* boyfriend?" Alma asked.

"No."

"How could he possibly prefer her to you, or the other way around?" Chip asked.

Lavinia sighed, and put her hand gently on his arm. She reminded him that although the girls were identical, that was in appearance only. They were separate people, with unique temperaments. He'd remarked on that himself, from time to time, didn't he remember? The gentle chide caused a brief wince in Chip's blotched, lined face. Here Alma joined in by saying that as children, it tended to be Marta who started arguments and Maggie who ended them. In her own mind Marta agreed. She was a more aggressive person, she'd known it her whole life, and she never had any explanation for it, but perhaps an explanation wasn't necessary. It's just how she was.

Chip nodded. "I'm sure you're right."

Alma stacked his dessert dish on top of Angie's and brought them to the kitchen.

"Is *that* why Maggie moved out? Because of this guy?" Angie asked.

"I think she was getting bored in the city," Marta said.

Chip's eyebrows lifted. He found it hard to believe that anyone would find the city boring, especially a talented young person. And what on earth was in Sullivan to keep Maggie interested? He'd been there often enough to know it was a pretty quiet little place. He'd sold some double-wides for a development up there, Lavinia probably remembered, unless that was before she came to work for him, he couldn't recall just then.

Lavinia waved him away.

"Sounds like you've got yourself in a classic love triangle," she told Marta.

"Not at all."

"But you're interested in him, too, aren't you?"

Marta disliked how her mother could get ahold of something and not let it go. She supposed that's why she grew up to be such a good liar—it was the only way she could ever protect herself.

"No. We just hang out," she said. "He's writing a play, in fact. A play about Maggie and me."

Everyone at the table, again including Alma, who'd just returned, looked at her skeptically.

"No, it's a very cool idea! It's all about how we read each other's thoughts and finish each other's sentences."

"That's it?" Angie asked.

Marta realized that Josh was going to have to get much more innovative if he expected to fill two hours of stage time.

"I say he should summon the future," Chip said.

Lavinia looked at him crossly.

"He should write you through time. Does this connection last as you age? Does it change? Do you begin to lose track of one another as old ladies? Wouldn't it be interesting to have the characters pull apart in middle age, and then slowly come back together, psychically speaking, of course." He paused, drank some wine, savoring it. "Auditions will be tricky, given that you need twins. Can't be that many twins in the world who can act."

"I'm playing both parts," Marta said.

"Really? How extraordinary!" Chip had another sip of wine. Lavinia poured herself and Alma more, too. She didn't offer any to Angie and Marta.

"Of course, you could just get people who look alike in some way and make them up to suggest a closer resemblance. That would be fascinating, wouldn't it? The task of persuading the audience that they're actually observing a pair of twins up there on the stage."

Chip wasn't usually so expansive, at least not on any sort of artistic topic. He generally confined himself to golf, the stock market, and the latest ill-conceived project at the Dunston Chamber of Commerce, where he'd served as president for many years before getting fed up with entrenched interests that resisted moving the town in a forward-thinking direction. His enthusiasm now reddened his cheeks even more than the wine.

"How long have Josh and Maggie known each other?" Angie asked.

"Oh, a while. He comes over a lot. She's usually there. Or was, until she moved out, that is."

"I understand she now has a rent-free situation," Lavinia said. She sounded proud of Maggie's resourcefulness.

"Really?" Marta asked.

"Apparently the house she lives in is occupied downstairs by an old lady, and the son—the owner—wants her looked in on every day. The roommate told her she'd let her have the second bedroom upstairs for free if she'd do that, so she wouldn't have to."

So many things you didn't tell me. And won't tell me tomorrow.

The sudden flush Marta experienced let her know that Josh had not only reached Sullivan, but Maggie, too, in a way she hoped he wouldn't. The situation was clear. Josh was between them now, and they were going to have to make the best of that fact.

"Why don't you produce his play?" Marta asked Chip.

"What would that run, do you think?" he asked.

"I don't really know."

"Risky business, the theater."

"It can be."

"I need to see some financials. I don't want to throw money away."

Marta said Josh would get him everything he needed to make an informed decision.

Chip looked thoughtful, as if an old memory was then possessing him. "Hard to be young and ambitious and poor," he said.

"Josh isn't poor, but he doesn't have any real money of his own, not yet anyway."

Marta told him about the trust fund. Chip's eyes gleamed. He said in that case they could strike a deal, and if the venture lost money past a certain point, then when Josh gained access to the principal set aside for him, he could pay him back.

"We'll call it an incentive not to waste resources," Chip said.

Marta said that in an off-Broadway play there weren't any major expenses except renting the theatre itself. The actors would have to accept payment out of profits and forgo salary.

"Who would be willing to do that?" Lavinia asked.

"Everyone," Marta said. "To get an acting gig, something you can add to your resumé, is a big deal."

Her phone buzzed. It was a text from Josh, saying he was staying over in Sullivan, and would be back first thing in the morning. He apologized for taking the car without asking her. He figured she needed some time alone with her family and didn't want to be in the way.

Angie observed Marta's darkening expression.

"I'm sorry if you think I was hard on you. I just wonder about the big gaps of time between acting jobs, and what else you could be doing to further your career," she said.

"In other words, you just want the best for me."

Angie crossed her arms defensively.

"Girls," Lavinia said.

Angie had once written poetry, Marta remembered. She had discovered this back in high school, when Angie was then in college, and she borrowed her computer from time to time. Angie left all her programs open, including her email. Marta never found anything too interesting there, except a slew of rejection letters from places she'd submitted poems to. The poems themselves couldn't be found. Maybe one day she simply gave up and stopped writing, stopped submitting, and came to regret that. Was that why she was being such a pain now?

Maggie would know. Maggie could read people. Marta couldn't, which probably made her portrayals hard. On stage, she was the same person as she was off. People once said the same thing of Katherine Hepburn, so she supposed it wasn't such a bad trait, but in truth she admired any actor who could truly become someone else. She was going to have to imbue her twin's character with enough differences, so the audience truly appreciated her gifts.

She glanced at Chip, who was listening to Lavinia talk about the upcoming holiday season and what kind of decorating she wanted to do. She ran him. She probably had from the moment they met when she first started working for him. She'd run their father, too, only in his case her efforts were negated by his love of whiskey.

Chip's offer to back Josh's play would let Marta run Josh just as easily, because Josh was highly ambitious. If she forced him to choose between her and Maggie, holding the play over his head, what would he do?

Another excellent question was whether or not she'd ever do such a thing, and that depended on how much like her mother she truly was. She'd never thought of herself as possessing any of her mother's character traits. Now, watching as Lavinia put her hand lightly on Chip's arm when he voiced the smallest objection, Marta knew that laying down the law was something she could do, too, and would probably enjoy.

chapter twelve

Rather than being thrilled, Josh seemed bored by Marta's news about her stepfather's offer. She asked him bluntly if he were giving up the play; giving up on the theater in general; if so, to consider where that would leave her.

"No; no; and you'd be just fine," he said.

They were nearing the George Washington Bridge. Marta had never been so glad to escape from Dunston. Waiting for Josh to return from Sullivan had put her in a rotten mood, so rotten that she shot off a couple of nastygrams to Maggie, accusing her of going back on her word, to which she'd made no reply.

What Josh hadn't said was that Maggie turned him down. Her refusal had made him miserable. So had sleeping on her narrow couch, and the sly teasing light in her roommate's eyes when she found him there in the morning. Leah gave him a cup of coffee and told him he could take a shower. He accepted the first, and declined the latter, which he now regretted, because the stress he was under made him sweat like hell.

"Yeah, well, you don't sound very enthusiastic," Marta said. "Maybe I should find someone else who has a hot play he wants to get produced. It wouldn't be hard. I know lots of people with dynamite scripts."

She glanced at him. He stared out the window. Traffic slowed as lanes converged at the bridge. An old man leaned forward in the driver seat of the car next to them, trying to see how long it would take to get across. When the line of cars didn't move for several minutes, Marta turned off the engine. A light rain fell. The windshield slowly became harder and harder to see through.

"I know you guys had sex," Marta said.

"No, we didn't."

"Bull."

"Ask her yourself."

"She'd just lie."

"Jesus, Marta!"

She knew then it was true. She'd never seen him so depressed, so absolutely sunk in himself. And this presented another problem. She had no leverage if Maggie continued to reject him. In his heartsick state, he might not be able to finish the play. Could she persuade Maggie to let him have her long enough to get it written and produced? But that was like asking her to be his mistress, prostitute, or . . . *concubine.*

She flipped down the sun visor and looked at her reflection in the small mirror. Did her eyes now hold a harder light? Was she really capable of seeing people merely as things in her way, or tools to use to her advantage?

What if I'm really a terrible person?

She returned the sun visor to its original position. Some drivers up ahead had gotten out of their cars, despite the rain, to see why nothing was moving. After a few more minutes of being trapped there, in their heavy silence, cars inched forward.

Soon they were crossing the river, feeling very high above it all. Josh's heart lifted. The possibility of actually getting his own play produced was, in fact, great news, though not quite enough to blank out the memory of Maggie's trembling chin when she told him she would, under no circumstances, get into bed with him. Oh, but she wanted to! She even said as much: "Do you think this is easy for me?"

It would have to do for now, her self-thwarted desire.

He told Marta he'd put together some numbers for her to pass on to Chip.

"Oh, no, not me. You deal with him directly. I'm no go-between."

"Okay."

It took a long time to return the rental car, and then for the cab they had trouble hailing to wend its way downtown. By the time they headed up the steps of her building, Marta was totally burned out.

The sound of gentle jazz flowed sweetly through the door of her apartment.

"Hello?" she called out as she turned the lock with her key.

Kyle and another young man lounged on the velvet couch, drinking white wine and enjoying a plate of cheese and crackers. They both stood up, glasses in hand. Kyle was dressed more conservatively than usual, in blue jeans and a short-sleeved plaid shirt. His friend wore a black jumpsuit with a purple silk scarf knotted loosely about his throat.

"What the hell?" Marta asked.

"Maggie said it was all right, that you'd gone out of town," Kyle said.

"How did you get in?"

"I have a key. Maggie gave it to me a few months ago."

The friend looked sharply at Josh, who didn't notice, because he was staring at his phone.

"This is Edgar," Kyle said.

"God, you look just like her," Edgar said. His voice was throaty and rough, as if he'd just had a cold.

Josh put his phone away and stared sullenly at the two men.

"Do you want us to get going? We don't want to be in the way," Kyle said.

"Stay if you want. What are you drinking?" Marta asked. Their company was suddenly a welcome distraction.

"A good Russian River Chardonnay. Edgar works in a wine store. Awesome employee discount."

In the kitchen Marta saw two more bottles of wine. And in the refrigerator was a carton of fried chicken, a plastic tub of pasta salad, and a small chocolate cake. These guys knew how to do it right! She asked Josh to help her ferry the food over to the dining room table. She was hungry. Wasn't he?

Kyle and Edgar didn't say anything about her helping herself to the food they'd bought. Instead, they joined her. Josh stayed in the kitchen, where he could be heard talking on his phone to someone who obviously wasn't Maggie. He laughed, and spoke in light, teasing tones.

When he appeared, Marta asked, "Who was that?"

"My mom."

"Did you tell her about the play?"

"I did before."

"No, about getting a backer."

"Not yet."

"Wait, you have a play *and* a backer?" Edgar asked. He bit delicately into a drumstick. Kyle watched him.

"Looks like it," Josh said. He sat. Marta put some pasta on a plate and handed it to him.

"Let me guess. Your stepfather," Kyle said.

"Why do you say that?" Marta asked.

"Because he pays for everything."

Marta nodded.

"Do you have a theater lined up?" Edgar asked.

"Not yet," Josh said.

"Well, good luck with that. My cousin's an actor. Well, sometimes. Most of the time he's nothing in particular, but he knows tons of theater people. His last boyfriend was some big agent. Anyway, he hangs with them a lot, and space is at an absolute premium, unless you're a friend of a friend, et cetera. He told me it's easier to find something out of town, up the Hudson maybe, or wherever it is you just were. College town, right? Don't they a have a little playhouse there?"

Josh met Marta's eye. She could see him considering it.

"They do. The Hangar," Marta said.

She explained that it used to be an airport, back in the days of biplanes and all that. She'd made her acting debut there in middle school, playing the mother in *Charlotte's Web*. What she didn't share was that this was just after her mother and Chip married. The woman she portrayed on stage was nothing like the one who dragged them all off to live in Chip's huge, cold house. Was that where she learned about dichotomy and psychic disconnects? Or had that come earlier, watching her parents navigate around each other silently, yet communicating oceans of rage and despair?

"Earth to Marta," Kyle said.

"Sorry."

She drank and relaxed. It wouldn't be so bad, appearing at the Hangar. People she used to know would want to see her perform.

Oh, she's come a long way, hasn't she? Living in New York has totally agreed with her!

Edgar had some stage experience himself, as a set designer. He didn't do any of the actual building, he made the mock-ups in miniature. Had anyone seen the off-off-Broadway production of *A Christmas Carol*? About three years ago? He did the backdrop for Scrooge's office, dark smoky wood, brick, a low beamed ceiling. He hadn't worked in theater since then, stuck selling wine to stockbrokers in the Financial District, but he wanted to go back. Costume design, that's what he really wanted. He had a good eye and was more than handy with a sewing machine.

"Did you run that up yourself?" Marta asked, meaning his jumpsuit.

"God, no. I found this at a flea market in New Jersey."

"I love going to flea markets," Josh said.

"Really?" Marta asked.

"I found a first edition of Virginia Woolf's *To the Lighthouse* once."

"Wow. You never told me that."

"You never asked."

Kyle laughed. "Good one."

He mentioned a man he'd heard of who bought a ring at a flea market that turned out to have been given to Josephine by Napoleon.

"Can you imagine something like that just falling in your lap?" Kyle asked.

"You can fall in my lap anytime," Edgar said.

"Get a room," Josh said.

"Can we borrow Maggie's old one?" Kyle asked.

"No! Josh is using it," Marta said.

This caused raised eyebrows from both Kyle and Edgar. They finished their glasses and asked if they could help in the kitchen. Marta said she'd deal with it later.

Edgar wanted to hit up a new bar where his roommate worked. The roommate, a woman, said if he ever made it by, she'd slip him the first round under the table.

"Won't it be hard to drink down there?" Kyle said. His color was high.

"Oh, shut up," Edgar said, but Marta thought it was pretty funny. Did Josh want to go?

"Why not?" Josh asked. He just needed a few minutes to take a shower.

They headed out a little later. The day had turned cold. Marta's jacket was thin, and she took Josh's arm for warmth. Edgar and Kyle walked ahead, a bit unsteady on their feet but more or less maintaining. They talked animatedly about the place they were going. The crowd tended to be artsy.

Marta and Josh fell further behind, as they assumed an easy, unhurried pace despite the chill. Knowing that he was still exclusively hers thrilled her more than she cared to admit. But, did having sex with a man make him yours? And, if sex didn't equate with belonging, what did? What made two people truly intimate?

Secrets.

"You know, I once kidnapped someone," she said. Josh looked at her skeptically.

"It's true. When I was in high school."

"Why?"

"Maggie and I were trying to settle an argument about our cats. She had one in her room, I had the other one in mine, and they howled all night, wanting to be together. We figured they'd have to sleep in just one room, and we couldn't decide whose it would be. So we dared each other to do something risky, as a kind of contest. Afterward, we would decide who'd taken a bigger risk, and that person got to keep the cats."

"Why didn't you just trade off? Her room one night, your room the next."

"Oh. We never thought of that." Marta felt silly all of a sudden, talking about it.

"Who did you kidnap?" he asked.

"This girl we'd met the summer before, someone's daughter, they came to a picnic at the lake, friends of friends. She had Downs, and one day I was on the bus and she got on a couple of stops later. I followed her to the restaurant where her mother worked. She went there every day after school and hung out in the back for hours watching TV. I chilled there for a little while, and when I realized no one was going to come see how she was doing, I swiped her."

"Jesus."

"I just took her home with me. It wasn't a big deal. She didn't seem to mind. I think she kind of liked it, actually."

"Didn't her mother freak out?"

"Her number was in the kid's backpack. My mother called her up and said I found her riding the bus, and thought she looked a little lost, and so on."

Josh rubbed her arm. Clearly, he enjoyed the story.

In truth, Maggie was the one who kidnapped the girl, not Marta. Marta hadn't been involved at all. In fact, she'd forgotten all about the dare, and thought Maggie was stupid for thinking it was any sort of binding agreement between them. The cats ended up staying with Maggie because Marta had lost interest in them.

Kyle and Edgar stood in the doorway of the bar, waving them on. Inside, the place was warm enough that the windows steamed over. There was nowhere to sit or put their coats. Edgar tried to get the barmaid's attention. He had to call her name over the noise of the crowd several times before he finally caught her eye. She didn't seem glad to see him, and Marta assumed that was because she was the only one on hand to mix and pour drinks. Servers in short maroon skirts shouted order after order, then scurried off into the crowd again. They all agreed to stick with wine, but Marta wanted to switch to red, so they ordered one bottle of Cabernet and another of Chardonnay, which the barmaid put at the end of the bar with four glasses and a corkscrew. When a party by the window stood up to leave, Marta rushed to claim the table. Kyle, Edgar, and Josh brought the glasses and wine. Josh also had a menu tucked under his arm because he was still hungry.

"She's only spotting us a bottle," Edgar said.

"Which one?" Kyle asked.

"Whatever's cheaper. The red, I think."

"And how much is the white?"

"Forty-five."

"Jesus! No wonder you stay broke!"

But Kyle's tone was teasing, and Marta suspected he was head over heels in love.

It turned out that Edgar was also from Montclair, and he and Josh dropped into a detailed exchange about which block they'd grown up on, which high school they'd attended, whether one of them knew so and so, and if either could ever see living there again. Edgar asked about the play Chip had agreed to back, and Josh talked about the psychology of twins, as far as he understood it. He'd done some looking online about how twins relate to one another, how they describe their connection, which was all news to Marta.

Edgar said he'd seen a film he found on Netflix called *Twinsters*. Identical twin girls are born in South Korea, separated at birth, adopted by different families in different countries, and have no knowledge of each other until the one living in London is shown a YouTube clip of a movie in which the other twin, an American, plays a role. She is astonished at the resemblance to herself, and several weeks later, the same friend sends her a Facebook link with the actress's name. Contact is made, and they learn they have the same birthday. They meet in London, do a DNA test, and find that they are, in fact, identical twins. Josh asked Edgar to write the name of the film down for him in case he forgot it, and Marta realized he was getting pretty buzzed off the wine. The only things at hand were a napkin and a pen borrowed from a harried server ferrying a tray of empty beer mugs.

She was crossing the line from relaxed to woozy herself, and thought she should probably slow down, but the wine was delicious. She poured herself another glass and leaned back in her chair. She could see the entire bar from where she sat. She looked from one face to the next through the crowd, recognizing no one, yet not feeling lonely at all.

What would it be like to think you were the only one, and then find out you weren't? What if she were to meet Maggie for the first time by chance? Would they become friends?

They'd have lived different lives, around different people, in places the other knew nothing about. Without shared memories everything would be fresh. They wouldn't take anything for granted, because their history would start then, as adults.

She removed the wool cap she'd put on at the last moment back at the apartment, and let her blond hair fall around her. She eased the snarls out with her fingers. She'd borrowed her mother's shampoo that morning, and a hint of lavender wafted past.

A man at the bar stared at her. She was used to that, because she drew the male gaze all the time, but his was fiercer, more determined. He was dark and good-looking in a sloppy sort of way, like a messier version of Josh.

Edgar saw where she was looking, and said, "Yummy." Kyle nudged his knee.

The man at the bar came towards them, holding a bottle of beer. Finally, Josh noticed that the conversation around him had stopped, and he too watched the man approach.

"I was wondering where you went," the man said to Marta in a clear Hispanic accent.

"I've been right here."

Someone back at the bar shouted, "Luis! Don't forget your coat," and the man at Marta's elbow called back that he'd be there in a minute.

When he looked at her again, he said, "You decided not to cut it, then."

"No. I like it long."

"Where did you go? Digger said you bolted like a shoplifter."

"What else did he say?"

"I haven't talked to him for a while."

The couple two tables over rose to leave, and Luis took one of their empty chairs and squeezed it into the space next to Marta. She told him who everyone was. He gave each a quick nod.

She asked him what he was working on these days, which produced a heavy sigh.

Did she remember that series he was playing with, the kids in the park? The figures became more and more abstract, so that they seemed to disappear into what was around them—the swings and slides.

"Sounds really cool," she said.

Except that he wasn't sure how people would like the idea of vanishing children. It might upset them.

"Art is supposed to upset," she said.

At this, Josh looked at her, then at Luis.

"So, you work in the same studio space?" he asked.

"Used to. Couldn't make the rent, so I had to pack up."

"O-M-G!" Kyle said, dissolving into snorting giggles. Edgar leaned in and told him to chill.

"What?" Luis asked. He put his arm around Marta, causing her to sit up straight.

"She's got a twin sister, you know," Kyle said when he'd recovered.

"Marta. I know. *Man*, do I know."

"What did she say about her?" Kyle asked.

Luis shook his head and smiled.

"Come on, tell me!"

"Ask *her*, if you really want to know," Luis said, tossing his head towards Marta.

"Fantastic!" Josh said. He patted his pants pocket for the small notebook he often carried there, then remembered he didn't have it with him.

"Remember that," he said, pointing at Marta.

"He's writing a play about us," Marta told Luis.

"Yeah? Cool."

Kyle surreptitiously texted Maggie that he was out drinking with her sister and Josh, and that things were getting very interesting.

Luis had another beer. He talked about wanting to find another space he could paint in that was less expensive, which would take a while. Then he looked at his watch. He had to be at work at noon the following day.

He bent towards Marta and whispered, "Wanna get out of here?"

Marta nodded. She told the others that she was taking off, and to have a good night.

chapter thirteen

The weather in Sullivan turned cold overnight. Maggie went to the mall and got several pairs of corduroy pants, five long-sleeved shirts, four turtleneck sweaters, six pairs of heavy socks, a pair of sturdy, thick-soled shoes, and a stylish insulated jacket.

Frank gave her a couple of electric heaters, so the garage would be bearable.

She bought a pair of blue indoor-outdoor rugs to cover the cracked concrete floor. She also found a swivel lamp, the kind you clamped to a shelf, whose focused light was nice to work by. She picked up an easel at the art supply store, and a box of colored pastels. The tall kitchen chair, with its supportive back, came from Goodwill, as did the padded cushion she tied to the seat. Its pattern of daisies would keep her spirits yellow and bright.

The faceless woman evolved. No longer a refugee, she appeared in many places: at the park, reading a book; in an office, staring at a computer screen; driving in traffic; drinking with friends in a bar. The other faces around her were all fairly uniform. Any variation was with the eyes and the length of the jaw. Mouths didn't interest her, which she found odd, upon reflection. Did she not trust voices? Did she believe words caused harm?

Marta's had cut. Maggie wasn't a liar. She hadn't slept with Josh and was sure Marta sensed that. But for Marta, truth was less important than feeling wronged. She always needed some justification in her own mind for the next time she went on the attack.

Why attack at all?

"She has a warrior's heart," their father liked to say. He admired it. Their mother had a warrior's heart, too. Angie also was tough and determined. Timothy, Foster, and Maggie were quieter spirits, but they forged ahead in their own way. They simply operated with less fanfare.

After about an hour of sketching, Frank came to say he was going to go through his boxes and keep only what was worth keeping. Maggie understood that he was lonely and liked her company even though she didn't say much. She could work with him there. She was used to other people being near when she was trying to concentrate. Over the preceding days she'd learned that he'd lost his wife only the year before; that his son was estranged from him over some unspecified, long-standing feud; that before he retired he'd worked for the electric company as a meter reader, and boy, that could be cold work in the dead of winter. They could read them remotely now; did she know that? Great idea, except it put people out of work. Robots and computers were taking over everything these days.

Frank removed a photo album from the second box he came to and put it next to his tool box. He went through the pages slowly, sighing softly now and then, until he came to one page in particular that caused him to shake his head. Maggie noticed all of this from the corner of her eye, only because she'd suddenly become restless, as she often did when working. In New York, she would take herself around the neighborhood. She'd pick up a latté somewhere and clear her head. There, in Sullivan, her outings were brief, just a brisk walk into town and back. The whole thing was only about a mile. The idea of that circuit now wasn't appealing. Sullivan could be awfully quiet.

Frank saw that she'd lifted her head and was gazing away from her sketch. He brought over the album and put it right in her lap.

"Take a look at this," he said.

Old style photographs, with white scalloped edges glued to black paper, had been obliterated by a red marker.

"My boy did that. Now, these folks here, they're all dead, and were when he found them. And he wasn't a little kid at the time, mind you, but in his twenties, with some big grudge against his forebears."

"Why?"

Frank shrugged.

Shirley, his late wife, reckoned it might have been some deep alienation, a failure to connect. He had been a difficult child to raise. Lots of tantrums, bad moods, not being able to sleep when he got older.

"These were her people—two, three generations back," he said. "I never saw them before he raised his hand. We weren't the kind of couple that spent time with old pictures, so I have no idea what they looked like."

He glanced at her drawing.

"And here you are, choosing not to know," he said.

"True."

He reclaimed the album and went back to his sorting. She returned to her pad to find her interest waning even further.

She packed her things and went up to her apartment. She looked at her phone, which she now made a point of not bringing with her to the garage. A text from Josh read: *Sorry I pressured you. Won't happen again.*

Was he saying he was no longer interested in her?

She turned off her phone.

Mrs. Culver was being seen to at the moment by her son. His pickup truck was in the driveway. Footsteps below were audible, as if someone were pacing. The sound made her restless to the point of nervousness.

She got in the minivan and headed out to Leah's barn. The sky was chrome, and the air had that sharp, silvery smell that meant snow was on the way. Snowfall in Manhattan was magical, because the city could still keep its color. There, in a small town, with open country just beyond, snow would blend everything into white, black, and gray tones.

What must it be like to live where the world was full of color? Isn't that why Georgia O'Keefe loved New Mexico so much? And what about Frida Kahlo, with those luscious Mexican plants and flowers to inspire her? Maggie's native land had its own, to be sure, especially in the fall season that was now passing, but she hungered for more. What she craved was . . . *vibrancy*.

The lane that led through the farm was overgrown, narrow, and deeply rutted. She slowed to spare the van's suspension. She hadn't been so annoyed by the rough ride the first time she came there, perhaps because she was excited by the change of scene and the thought of a life without Marta. They'd been separated exactly two weeks. The thread connecting them had stretched with maddening ease over both time and distance, and she didn't feel autonomous at all.

Leah wasn't alone. A man took pictures of her while she painted. They both turned Maggie's way when she opened the new wooden door that had recently been installed. The black stove in the corner warmed the space beautifully. It was cozy, clean, and fabulous. Maggie felt a blue tinge of dismay as she compared it to Frank's garage.

Leah introduced the man as Carl, someone she'd met in town. Carl was probably in his forties, with a paunch and thinning hair, yet his eyes were keen as he stared at Maggie.

"I'm sorry. I see everyone I meet as a possible subject," he said. It took Maggie a moment to realize he meant subjects to photograph.

"He's got a small gallery. We passed it the other night. The Silver Frame," Leah said. Her pale green sweatshirt was spattered with dots and drips of pink and orange, a bright remnant of the colors of her old life. Maggie found the effect stirring.

"Are you going to display Leah? Your pictures of her, I mean?" Maggie asked.

"That's the idea."

Leah looked at Maggie, registering her presence more completely than a moment ago. She asked if she'd already knocked off for the day.

"Yeah. Frank came in and started going through boxes, and sort of drove me nuts."

Maggie told Carl that Frank was their neighbor, and that she worked in his garage.

"I used to use my dad's basement as a darkroom. He wasn't crazy about the idea. But then, he didn't like much of anything. Point is, artists are always refugees, looking for a home," Carl said.

Leah stood back from her canvas, which bore soft muted colors in shades of green and gray.

"Not only must we be brilliant, we must be well-housed," she said.

"This place is great!" Carl said.

"Needs a bathroom. My aunt gives me the stink eye whenever I ask to use her precious commode."

"Remember the bathroom in the old studio? How the sink was coming loose from the wall?" Maggie asked. There was a touch of fondness in her voice. She missed the happy times she'd had there.

Leah's expression said her associations with that former bathroom were of a different order, and Maggie felt like a fool for reminding her about the miscarriage. How long ago had it been? A month? A month and a half?

"That's her place, across the field?" Carl ask, peering through the spotless window by Leah's easel.

"Yup."

"Gonna be a long walk in the snow."

"I'll get snowshoes."

"Seriously, when the weather gets bad, you can use my porch. It's got a heater. I'm never home, anyway. And my son just left for college, so no one would bother you," Carl said.

"What I need more than your porch is a part-time job."

Leah had worked in a shoe store over the spring. She quit when the manager was rude to her, though she never specified what had been said. Then she took tickets at the Museum of Modern Art, a gig she loved because she could wander the galleries when her shift ended. Maggie admired Leah for making her life work without a lot of money but was glad she didn't have to do the same thing herself.

Carl went on snapping pictures. He moved on from Leah to the barn itself, then took a few of Maggie, but quickly lost interest when she couldn't follow his instructions about which way to tilt her head or smile with her eyes but not her lips. She asked to see what he had, anyway, thinking maybe she could pay for him to print off one or two.

He stood next to her, scrolling through the shots. She liked one he'd taken when she was looking at Leah's canvas. Though she was in profile, her interest in what she saw was clear. She looked focused, engaged, and intent.

"Do you shoot everything, or just people?" Maggie asked.

"Faces mostly."

When he started out, he took family portraits, and learned just how hard some people could be to work with. People had expectations he couldn't always meet. Sometimes they didn't like how they truly looked. This was especially true of women, though he hated to say it. He hoped Leah and Maggie understood. It was the world they lived in. Women were always judged so harshly on their appearance, it was no wonder they internalized it.

"And men?" Maggie asked.

"They're judged by how much money they make. So, for a struggling artist like myself, I was deemed a failure the moment I chose this path."

Leah snorted. "That's not exclusive to male artists. We're all failures, in the eyes of the world."

Maggie considered. She agreed there was too much emphasis on money. Her thoughts turned to her mother, who criticized her father for years for his failure in that regard. Then she married a man who had loads but found him just as irritating. But at least she'd stopped complaining about not having enough.

"My ex-wife had terrible self-esteem," Carl said. He held his camera but wasn't using it then. Maggie thought he must feel empty without it in his hands, as if it were a necessary part of him.

"Yeah?" Leah asked. She was studying her work, which was full of blocky forms, all tilted, as if about to lose their balance and fall. It represented her and Digger, Maggie realized. That's why the color palette had shifted so dramatically.

"She was lovely, but never believed it, even though I told her so all the time. Other men always expressed an interest in her, and she doubted them just as much. Then one day she went off with one. And you know what? She said it was because I never gave her enough attention."

There was no grief in Carl's voice, just a calm understanding of the facts. His eyes gave away the deeper truth of how painful it still was.

"I thought you said it was because of those sisters you were photographing at the time," Leah said.

"That's what she told me, but it was just an excuse."

"What sisters?" Maggie asked.

Carl's phone trilled from inside the backpack a few feet away. He went to answer it.

Maggie helped herself to the rocking chair Leah had gotten from her aunt a few days before. The aunt, a sour-looking woman who clearly disapproved of Leah's avocation, had brought it over in the back of her pickup truck, which bore the label Emerson's Dairy in faded letters.

Leah stood back from her canvas and regarded it for a moment. She seemed uninspired, almost bored, all of a sudden. She put down her brush and the small tube of paint she'd been holding. She never mixed her colors on a palette. All mixing took place on the surface of the canvas itself. Maggie wished her own eye were that good. She supposed it was a matter of training. When she returned to the use of colors—which she now felt was imminent—she would do as Leah did and turn the canvas into a palette.

Carl returned, looking cross.

"That was my ex. Guess she doesn't think the cost-sharing arrangement for Cory is fair. I reminded her it was her idea that he apply to a private college. We talked about the expense. Her second husband isn't wild about the tuition. Of course, she could get a job, but no, that's beneath her." He paused and took a couple more candid shots of Leah. "Well, I'll talk to the bank. See about a second mortgage on the house."

"How much is his school?" Maggie asked.

"Jesus, girl. Aren't you a little nosy?" Leah said.

"I'm just curious."

"All told, with room and board, books, living expenses, a little north of fifty-five thousand," Carl said.

Maggie had no idea if that were a little or a lot.

"What's he going to major in?" she asked.

"Hard to say. He's pretty into music. Maybe that."

"No money in music. And I know what I'm talking about. Digger was in a band for a while," Leah said.

"That's cool," Maggie said.

"Yeah, he painted and played at the same time. I mean, at the same time in his life, not like some funky act, up on stage, or anything."

"That would be awesome, though, if he did," Maggie said.

Leah frowned. Her mind had slipped off somewhere else. She wiped her brushes with a rag, then bundled them up to bring back to the apartment, where she'd wash them with dish soap, which worked as well as turpentine, but wasn't toxic. Then she draped a heavy cloth over the canvas she'd been working on, picked up the easel, and turned the whole thing around. Maggie had learned that this meant she wouldn't work on it again for a little while. She found it interesting that draping it wasn't enough. Leah needed that extra step to put it from her mind.

Carl packed up his camera and put on his jacket. He told Leah he'd have some proofs for her to go over soon. Leah nodded. Then he turned to Maggie and looked at her closely.

"This probably sounds awfully sudden, but would you like to have dinner with me tonight?" he asked.

"Really?

"I'm a good cook."

"Yeah? What's your specialty?"

"What do you like?"

"Spaghetti."

"With meatballs?"

"Of course with meatballs," Maggie said. "Use pork and veal along with the beef. Otherwise they dry out."

Carl looked amused.

"My mother's housekeeper told me that," Maggie said.

"Ah. Wise woman."

"She's kind of dense, actually. But she has a good heart."

Carl gave her the address, and suggested she come around seven.

Leah stood watching both of them.

"Don't feel like you need to dress up," Carl said.

"I always dress up for spaghetti."

He grinned. He was actually sort of handsome. She liked the lines around his eyes.

When he'd gone, Leah asked Maggie if she thought it were a good idea going to his house.

"Are you mad he didn't ask you?" Maggie asked.

"Of course not. Besides, I already have a date."

"Digger's coming up again?"

"No, not Digger."

Maggie waited while Leah refused to meet her eye. When it was clear she'd learn nothing more, she stood up from the rocker, and turned on her phone. There was nothing from Marta.

She was both sorry and relieved.

chapter fourteen

Luis's place was tragic, like the set of *The Honeymooners*. She and Maggie would watch that show late at night in their shared bedroom on the tiny television set their mother bought hoping it would keep them quiet. It did, except for the occasional outburst of laughter or dismay. And where *The Honeymooners* was concerned, the shock was over the idea that someone would keep a bathtub in the kitchen and cover it with a board when it wasn't being used.

Luis had that same bathtub, in that same kitchen, with that same board. Marta thought he might channel Jackie Gleason any minute and bluster not knowing up from down or dollars from cents. Of course, the idea of being the slim, elegant, wise-cracking Audrey Meadows had its charm. She could see herself as the long-suffering wife.

On the board that closed the sad mouth of the tub, Luis had arranged his art supplies: small vials of paint, a tin of watercolors, a cup of brushes whose bristles were so dry it was clear they hadn't been used for a while.

There was also a small sketchpad full of finely drawn architectural features, towers, Renaissance domes, cupolas with weather vanes, even an elaborate bridge spanning a choppy sea. Everything was rendered in the same cobalt blue pencil, a color that definitely lent drama to each subject, despite its small size. Against the wall under the window were three canvases, the playground series he'd talked of earlier. Their tones were muddy, almost indistinct. She preferred the drawings by far.

He lived in Harlem, on a block that hadn't yet gentrified. He assumed they'd take the subway up from the

Village, but Marta insisted on paying for a cab. She disliked the subway and avoided it. She wanted to hire a car service on a regular basis, something she'd mentioned to Maggie, which, like so many of her sensible suggestions, was met with apathy.

The bed pulled down from the wall. The mattress was thin. The energy Luis displayed made the wobbly frame squeal. Marta didn't, though it was hard not to, he was that good.In the morning, as they lay in bed, he ran his fingers through her hair.

"I'm so glad you didn't cut it," he said.

"Me too."

He told her he'd been thinking about her for a long time. Had she known? Had he given himself away?

"No," she said.

He made coffee in a percolator, the kind her parents used to have years before. She offered to buy him a drip coffee maker and bring him up to speed.

"You don't have to do that," he said. He was wearing an old button-down shirt and black jeans. He hadn't shaved for a few days. The effect bordered on devastating. Maybe he was what she needed to get over Josh.

Josh!

She hadn't thought about him once since leaving the bar last night.

They drank their coffee in his dingy kitchen. A cockroach scuttled across the countertop. Marta had lived with cockroaches as a child. She had a poignant memory of her mother on the telephone with the landlord, yelling at him to get an exterminator or she'd call the Health Department and say he was endangering her children. It took a few days, but the extermination took place, which required the house to be vacant and all the food removed or kept safely in the refrigerator.

"You should move," Marta said.

"Can't afford it."

She thought about Maggie's old room, now temporarily occupied by Josh.

"My sister is thinking of getting her own place. I might let you have her room. Think about it."

"Hey, I don't want to take things too fast here," he said, putting his arms around her so quickly she gasped.

"Sure, I get it."

"Don't get mad."

"I'm not mad. But I do have to go."

"Okay. I'll call you."

Marta stood still, about a foot from his door that had seven different locks.

"Your number's still the same, right?" he asked.

"When did I give it to you? I don't remember."

"When you joined the studio. Digger said we should all be able to reach each other if we needed something."

"Right. Well, no. I got a new phone, and forgot to have them port the old number over. I'll text you in a bit. Then you'll have it," she said.

"Why not just give it to me now?"

"Because I'm late."

He opened the locks swiftly, top to bottom, and kissed her on the cheek as she sped through the door.

She rushed along the trash strewn sidewalk, head down against the rain.

You're an idiot, an absolute idiot!

No more than eight minutes had passed when her phone rang. It was Maggie, wanting to know what the hell happened with Luis. Yes, he'd just called her, and man, was he surprised that her number hadn't actually changed. He didn't appreciate being bullshitted like that. He always assumed she was a fair, honest person.

"What did you say then?" Marta asked. She ducked into the doorway of a small grocery store, whose patrons looked at her crossly as they came and went.

"I told him I was scared. That it all happened so fast, that I just needed time to think."

"Good. That's a good answer."

"He said he'd have to think about the offer of the spare room, given that I obviously wasn't sure."

"Shit."

"Look, Luis and I were never super close, but he's a good guy, so don't mess with him, okay?"

"Okay."

They paused. A car honked, and the driver of the car ahead of it leapt out and began yelling. Marta shut her eyes. Maybe the city was getting to her, too.

"If he calls me again, I'm going to tell him the truth," Maggie said.

"Okay."

"I might just call him and get it over with, come to think of it."

"Whatever you think is best."

"What's wrong with you? You sound brain-dead."

"I don't know, maybe I'm a little hungover."

"Yeah, Kyle said you had quite the time of it."

"I should have figured he was texting you when I saw him with his phone. What did he say, anyway?"

"Just said you were all hanging out."

"Nothing about me and Luis?"

"Only that you left together. Obviously, I figured the rest out when Luis called and reamed me a new one."

"Look, I'm sorry. Really," Marta said.

They paused again. The drivers in the street continued their verbal rampage. The line of cars behind them grew, and more honks sounded.

"Well, I suppose it's only fair, given what almost happened with Josh. Emphasis on the word 'almost.' You had *no* right to accuse me of sleeping with him," Maggie said.

Marta's stomach dropped.

"I know. I'm sorry," she said.

"You really *are* in the shits, aren't you?"

Marta said she had to go.

The door to Josh's room was closed when she returned. She moved as quietly as she could. The remains of yesterday afternoon's party were still there. Josh could have cleaned up. She realized she had no idea whether he was tidy or a slob. When she stayed with him after Maggie's ruse she'd been so self-absorbed she hadn't noticed.

His jacket, dropped on the floor in the living room, clued her in. She picked it up. His cell phone wasn't there. Of course, he'd taken it into the bedroom with him. Had he and Maggie been in touch? No doubt they had, because he was in love with her. Why did she keep forgetting that?

She showered, put on a silk blouse and a pair of designer jeans, and because it was so chilly outside, slipped into a new leather jacket that was padded and warm. She wore stylish boots with a thick pair of socks. Lately, socks had become something of an obsession. A little store over on Spring sold racks and racks of them. She'd brought home ten new pairs just the other day. The ones she chose this morning had shamrocks. They made her think of her father, and his collection of shamrock ties. She hadn't talked to him for a while.

She caught him on a job site, and the connection was bad. What came through loud and clear was the concern in his voice about unexpectedly hearing from her. No, he didn't know that Maggie had moved out. He was sure it wouldn't be for long. Whatever it was would pass, and they'd be easily reunited. As he said this against a background of other voices and mechanical noise, Marta realized that he, like everyone in the family, herself included, had always seen her and Maggie as essentially inseparable, an equation already solved, a fact that could not be disputed. Until now.

He could come to the city later that week if she liked. Would Friday work? How about lunch in Little Italy, what was the name of that place she liked so much? Or how about dinner? Then he could stay over and not sweat the drive back. He'd only bring Mary Beth if Marta agreed. Mary Beth was his wife. Marta didn't care for her much. She pretended to be kind and gracious but was in fact pushy and hard. Marta said she thought Mary Beth didn't like the city much. Potter said that was true. She'd be happier at home.

They agreed to touch base in a couple of days. As she returned her phone to the pocket of her jacket—she'd made the call outside the coffee shop she liked to frequent—she realized this day just wasn't getting off the ground. She went inside and ordered a latté with non-fat milk. While she waited, she scrolled through her text messages until she found Rob's number. Last summer they auditioned together for a bit part in a play, a character whose gender didn't matter because it was just someone to round out the crowd. Rob got the part, which Marta didn't understand. Then she decided it was because he was tall and could be visible from the last row. They got drunk afterward to celebrate his modest success, and Marta railed against the director, saying he should have requested only actors over a certain height.

She met Rob soon after coming to New York. He grew up in Illinois in a family that didn't consider acting a career. His father was a mechanic and may have had artistic ambitions of his own at one time, judging from the strange sculptures Rob unearthed in their basement, which his mother said his father made years ago. The mother was a cook in an elementary school cafeteria. Rob said she always smelled like French fries. How she viewed his life path wasn't clear, but Marta sensed while she may not necessarily have supported it, she didn't object to his choice, either. Rob's only sibling, an older sister, had moved to Georgia years before, was married with five children. Rob adored his nieces and nephews, and saw them every chance he got, which was seldom, given how tight money always tended to be.

She called, but he didn't pick up. His voicemail greeting said he was working at the Westside Theatre on Ninth if anyone wanted him during business hours. Marta finished her coffee and hailed a cab.

She and Josh had gone to the Westside to see a play a few months before. It was the story of a Depression era family. Josh called it a poor knockoff of *The Grapes of Wrath*, but Marta found the characterization eerily familiar. The father was a drunk; the mother made of steel; the eldest daughter cracked the whip; the younger siblings hid out, trying to define themselves against the stronger female personalities under their leaky roof.

There was no one in the ticket office, so Marta went directly into the auditorium where a number of people filled the first few rows. Rob sat by himself. An audition was taking place. A woman on stage spoke in a heavy Southern accent that was clearly not her own, extolling the beauty of the cotton fields outside her window and what they meant to her family, the state of Alabama, and the whole world. From those few lines alone Marta knew the script was overwritten, and heavily clichéd.

When she finished her whining soliloquy, Rob thanked her for her time, and told the others waiting that auditions were over for the day. A quiet protest came up from the group of five or six, and Rob told them to return tomorrow morning promptly at nine if they still wished to be considered. He spoke firmly, but not harshly, and Marta admired his professional tone.

She approached quietly, then touched Rob lightly on the arm. He turned his head and smile the moment he saw who it was.

He stood up and embraced her. He smelled of cigarette smoke, and Marta recalled that he'd started vaping when they last saw each other. Obviously, he'd reverted to the real thing.

"What brings you here?" he asked.

"Wondering what you're up to."

He swept his arm grandly towards the stage. "Trying to find a lead for my roommate's play. He'd have been here, but he's home with some nasty throat infection."

"Bruce wrote a play?"

"Delta Damsel."

"Awesome!"

"It's sucks, but he got a backer, and here I am."

"The Delta's in Mississippi, not Alabama."

"I know. Let's just call it artistic license."

While Rob chatted with one of the women on her way out, Marta looked up at the stage where the only prop was a music stand the last actress had stood in front of to deliver her words of adulation. Marta knew this was merely an anchor point, something to help the actress focus.

"Who'd back a dog like this?" she asked when they were alone.

"Some old lady he dug up. Might be a relative."

He was glad she came by, it had been too long. What was she up to? Was she still working with that guy, what's-his-name?

"Josh. Yeah. And he's writing a play, too."

"Wow. About what?"

"Identical twins."

"Sounds like you made quite an impression."

"Actually, it was my sister who impressed him."

She told him the story, only her version had Maggie and Josh caught in the act when she innocently returned from a pleasant afternoon of shopping.

"Oh, man, that's rough," Rob said.

Marta shrugged. She'd adopted her brave stance, where she stood straight, with crossed arms. With her jaw squared, she clenched her teeth so hard that her eyes grew moist. The effect was not lost on Rob, who watched her with growing alarm.

"Hey, it's okay," he said.

She nodded, and let free one quick, gasping sob. He came closer and embraced her in a warm friendly hug. She allowed her back to bend just a bit, to give a sense of softening into him. He stepped back and looked at her with a merry gleam in his eye.

"You are such a faker!" he said.

"You believed me, for a minute, anyway."

"I did."

"Well, then. Guess I can still act after all."

He stepped even further back and looked at her intently.

"Were you ever in any doubt about that?" he asked.

"Always."

He reminded her that her performance in . . . what was that play? Where she was a maid? It had been nothing short of spectacular. All that silent suffering, the small gestures that gave the audience her rage, like how she used the feather duster aggressively, almost as a weapon; or how she stood, being dressed down by her boss, Lady what's-her-name, with her head bowed and hands clenched; and how her eyes, when she lifted them just once, to look into the dark theater when her reprimand ended, had been like laser beams.

"Didn't lead to much, though," she said.

"Come on. You know what it's like. You just have to keep trying."

And what about him? Was he still going out for auditions?

At this he paused.

No, he wasn't. He liked being off-stage more than on. Maybe it was meant to be that way, he wasn't sure, but the money was better, and money mattered, right?

"Right."

Marta went up on the stage. It had been some time since she stood on one. She wanted to see if it felt the same. It did, maybe even a little better now that the space was entirely hers. Rob watched her from below as she sashayed across the wood, arms out, as if being led in a glamorous romantic waltz by an invisible partner. She grew warm, removed her jacket, and tossed it into the first row.

"Wait," Rob said. He scrambled up to join her and went into one of the wings. He returned with a costume, a long dress patterned with daisies. He handed it to her to put on. It was too big in the waist and shoulders.

"Where's that inane script?" she asked.

"Just improvise."

"The scene?"

"Miss Caroline just found out that her overseer ran off with the money she gave him to pay her taxes, and now the sheriff is on his way foreclose on the property."

"Jesus, that's lame."

Rob nodded.

Marta shook her hair, so it fell chaotically, clasped her hands, and gathered herself. She thought about being poor, being told she'd have to wait for a new pair of shoes, learning they were moving out sooner than planned because they were behind on the rent, though this had only ever happened to the family once. Summoning the scene, she changed from a lady used to salons, poetry, and moonlight, into one who had learned to work with her hands to save what was hers.

"The blood of my father and grandfather have turned this rich land red." She lowered her head as if to pray, then raised it. She pulled further into herself, focusing on a sunbaked landscape. "I am born of this soil, and its strength runs in my veins. I have turned it with my own hands, stamped its dust from my feet. No man will take it from me, nor me from it without first claiming the last breath from my lips, and the last beat of my heart." She put her hand lightly on her chest, as if to feel the rhythm within. She bent her head once more, lifted it, then raised her arms over her head, pulled her hands into tight fists, and demanded that the heavens hear her.

Rob clapped and shouted, "Brava!"

Marta bowed. She slipped out of the dress, rolled it into a ball, and dropped it on the floor. She scooted off the stage. Her few moments there had made her cheeks hot and her fingers tingle.

When her eyes met Rob's, an idea took shape. She said a bad part played well could catch someone's attention. If the script could be overhauled—if the author would consent to some intelligent revisions, and yet keep his original intent alive—there might be something to work with.

"And you'd play Miss Caroline," Rob said.

"Damn straight."

"Let me see what I can do."

But where would that leave Josh, to whom she had more or less committed her talents for the foreseeable future?

For the moment, she didn't care.

chapter fifteen

<u>*Act II, Scene II*</u>

Dally sits alone in the living room of her new apartment. She is on the couch, hands folded in her lap, with a peaceful, resigned expression on her face.

DALLY

Do you remember our thirtieth birthday party? It wasn't that long ago, was it, yet it seems so. Maybe it doesn't feel that way to you. I don't know. I used to know. I used to know everything you felt, everything you thought. Now, I don't even know where you are.

Here Josh paused. He wondered if he should rearrange the acts so that instead of moving forward in time, they go backwards, growing younger, then thought that was too reminiscent of *The Curious Case of Benjamin Button*. It then occurred to him that there were really no new stories, per se, only how they're told.

I feel you, though. I always feel you. You're working in a job you don't like because the theater didn't pan out. Mom says you finally came to your senses.

(The stage goes dark. Dally slides the sweater off her shoulder and unclips her hair. She stands. The light returns. With her hands, she scans invisible items at the check-out stand of an invisible grocery store. Her movements are so regular, so precise, that the impression is robotic.)

DILLY

Yeah, I'm thinking about it, too, that big 3-0. They say what you're doing when you turn thirty is basically your life. I beg to differ, though I'm obviously in need of a better plan.

(Dilly leans forward to catch what her customer is saying. She nods, then pantomimes repacking an entire bag of items slowly, glancing at the customer every now and then to make sure her efforts are met with approval.)

Josh saved the file and closed his laptop. Marta was still out. He heard her come in that morning but stayed quiet in Maggie's room until she went out again. He didn't want the summary of her night with what's-his-name from the bar, assuming she'd say anything at all.

After she blew him off, he'd hung out a while with Edgar and Kyle. He didn't care that they were gay. He didn't have a lot of male friends, other than Brad, and found the company of other men refreshing.

Kyle kept pulling out his phone to text Maggie some more and Edgar told him each time to put it away. Finally, Kyle said he'd behave himself. Josh wanted to know how long he and Maggie had known one another, and how they'd first met.

In a *gallery*, of course, Kyle said with an exaggerated toss of his head. He'd been between jobs—at which point Edgar reminded him that he was always between jobs—and there was this stunning little creature standing before a new work by Meredith Klein—did Josh know her? Anyhow, she looked so sad, gazing at that gorgeous painting, hungry almost, as if she wanted to pull it off the wall and eat in up, inch by inch.

"So, I just had to talk to her," Kyle said.

"But—" Josh began.

"Not to pick her up. I don't swing both ways. Though, for her I just might."

At this, Edgar rolled his eyes.

"What? Soul like that doesn't come along every day," Kyle said. "I couldn't ignore her, just because she's a woman."

She *did* have soul, Josh thought. A whole lot of it.

He put his head down on his crossed arms for a moment. Edgar touched him lightly on the shoulder.

"You still with us?" he asked.

Josh lifted his head and sat up straight. He nodded.

"I think someone's in love," Kyle said.

"Leave him alone, and finish your drink," Edgar said.

It was true, Josh said, he was. As unlikely as it seemed and based on the briefest intimacy. Kyle explained to Edgar what he was talking about, and Josh felt suddenly exposed, because he didn't know Maggie had shared the event with anyone else.

"Wait, what, you thought Maggie was Marta?" Edgar asked.

"Yeah."

"And now you dig *her*, not Marta."

"I like Marta, too."

"Ooh, I feel a three-way coming on!" Kyle said.

"I'm not into that," Josh said, hoping to hell he'd managed to conceal the lie.

Edgar finished his wine and pushed away the empty glass. He waved for the server and asked for their bill.

"Oh, I'll get it," Josh said.

"You sure?" Edgar asked.

"Yeah."

While they waited, they fell silent. The bar was winding down, though a large group had just come in, and jostled cheerfully past them.

Josh asked Kyle how often he heard from Maggie since she'd left the city.

"Oh, probably every day, just to check in," he said.

After the bill had been paid, they left the bar. Josh went one way, Kyle and Edgar another.

Josh stared at his screen. He wondered if he should incorporate Luis' mistaking Marta for Maggie into the play, then thought not. The story had to be about the two women, not anyone around them.

He went into the living room. Though Marta's place was much larger than his, he missed his funky little apartment. He wasn't going to be able to work here. And there was something else he wasn't going to be able to do, maybe because it made everything just a little too easy.

He brought out his laptop and sat on the couch.

Dear Mr. Starkhurst,

Marta has told me of your incredibly generous offer to back my new play. I can't tell you how honored I am by your faith in my abilities both as a director and as a playwright. However, I feel I must decline. I am fortunate enough to have a large trust fund of my own on which I can draw at my own discretion. I would, though, like to offer you two complimentary tickets to the opening night. Details to follow in due course.

Yours etc.

Then he called his mother, told her the deal had fallen through with Marta's step-dad, and that time had come for him to have access to his own money. He was gentle, but firm. At first, his mother resisted as always, but then, to his surprise, she relented. She would call the lawyer. Papers would no doubt have to be signed. She'd let him know. And would he please think about that trip to Florida?

He said he would. When he hung up, he gathered the few things he'd brought with him, texted Marta that he needed to work in his own space and was heading home but would be in touch again soon.

chapter sixteen

The sisters Carl had photographed over and over hung on one wall of his house, a pleasant Victorian on a quiet winding street. It evoked a sense of longing the moment Maggie pulled up in front. As a child, she dreamed of living in a place just like it, so different from the small, shabby homes her parents struggled to pay rent on; and much more intimate and charming than the mansion her mother installed them in the moment she married Chip.

The furniture was modern, with sleek lines. The sofa had chrome legs. The coffee table's top was glass. What must have once been a carved mantelpiece was now a piece of reclaimed barn board that he'd distressed further with a blow torch. He'd kept the bullseye window frames, and some of the carved brass doorknobs must have been original to the home, too. She supposed blending new with old was a sign of sophistication.

The sisters decorated the wall between the living room and the dining room. Karen and Kay Mansard. Irish twins, Carl called them, and then explained this meant they'd been born less than a year apart. Maggie already knew that. Her younger brother, Foster, was only thirteen months younger than she and Marta, not quite Irish, but close enough.

They were clearly on the late side of middle age, in their fifties at least, so it wasn't likely that Carl had fallen in love with either of them, but who knew? Women fell in love with older men all the time. It was possible that he'd become infatuated. The series of both women seated on a couch where each picture was taken from a gradually shorter distance until their bodies filled the picture frame more than hinted at obsession.

In the living room, where he'd set out some crackers and cheese, and then poured her a glass of a very nice Bordeaux, he told her all about them. They lived in Connecticut and had come for the summer to stay with friends. The friends had a large house in the mountains. It was very pleasant there, and an ideal place for Kay, who'd lost her husband the winter before, to sit, gaze, sip tea, restore her soul. Karen came, too. Karen had never married. She lived with Kay and her husband on an estate belonging to the husband's family. There was an ambiguity in the husband's will about exactly how the estate was to be passed on. He and Kay had had no children, so the estate was presumably now hers, but he had added a codicil stating that Karen would be a part owner. What specific share would be hers was something the sisters would have to decide together. Kay was certain that this was his way of keeping Karen in her life. They didn't get along all that well, which made living under the same roof awkward at times. Their rancor stemmed from childhood, when Kay's parents put much of the responsibility for Karen on her. But maybe the parents knew something, because Karen never really got herself together. She tried a number of careers, including being an interior designer, and here he gestured to the room they were in, indicating that it was she who'd suggested the very furniture on which they sat. Nothing ever took, and she just stopped trying, settled in with Kay, and lived a life of relative leisure. Kay wrote children's books under a nom de plume, Charlotte la Blanche. Maybe Maggie had heard of her?

"No," Maggie said. Carl poured her a second glass and told her how nice she looked. She wore a pale pink, finely knit cashmere sweater and a pair of designer blue jeans with smart leather ankle boots, an outfit she'd brought up with her from the city. He wore jeans and a pressed button-down shirt with the sleeves rolled up to just below the elbow. He looked both capable and trustworthy, an impression enhanced by the physical distance he kept between them. They sat on opposite ends of his surprisingly comfortable red leather sofa.

Kay and Karen made it a project to visit a number of nearby towns. They came into his studio and wanted portraits taken. They weren't easy to work with. They were very particular about how they should be seated, or where their hands should go. Or rather, Kay was particular. Karen didn't seem to care. As Maggie could see, they looked quite a bit alike, yet there was never any mistaking them. What fascinated him was watching them interact. Kay always the boss, Karen always reluctant, a bit pouting, almost childish. He thought Karen was the prettier, didn't Maggie think so, too?

"I don't know. I'd have to go look at them again," she said.

"After dinner."

"Okay."

The food he served was delicious. The meatballs were moist, with little pockets of gooey mozzarella inside. He said he loved to cook but living alone often made it a chore. He passed her the salad bowl, saying salad should be considered a palate cleanser, not a first course. Then he asked about her plans.

"I just want to draw something decent," she said. "And then paint it. Then paint more and find someone who thinks my work is worth something." The salad dressing was a little heavy on the vinegar, and she took a sip of ice water.

"Do you think it's worth something?" he asked.

"Not really. Not yet, anyway."

"How long have you been painting?"

"All my life, really. I didn't get serious until a few years ago."

"You're young. You have lots of time."

"It doesn't feel that way."

"I know."

He asked how she knew Leah. She talked about the studio in New York, and what she'd done to one of Leah's canvases. At this he sat back and regarded her across the table.

"I know. It's awful. I just couldn't stand looking at it, seeing how good she is. It's probably the worst thing I've ever done to anyone. You can't image how bad I felt about it," she said.

"And now you're friends."

"Yes."

"She's a remarkable person, isn't she?"

"I'd say so."

Something about the tone of his voice made Maggie see that it was Leah he was after, that inviting her there this evening was a way to gather intelligence and improve his chances with her.

"She was friends with the studio manager," Carl said.

"Digger. They still see each other."

"Ah."

"He came up for a few days. Then she kicked him out."

"I see."

"She's too young for you."

The color rose in Carl's face. He dabbed his lips with his napkin and drank some more wine. So did Maggie. They finished the bottle, and he brought another from the kitchen.

"Some people have old souls," he said, opening the bottle, not meeting her eyes.

"True. Though I don't think it's her soul you're after. But it's none of my business. I'm sorry I said anything."

"Don't be. I like honest people."

Maggie thought back to her ruse and dropped down inside herself.

"Did I say something wrong?" Carl asked.

"No, not at all. I like honest people, too."

She offered to clear the table, and he said she was being silly. After he took their plates away, he offered more wine and asked if she wanted to hear the rest of the story about Karen and Kay.

"Sure."

Over the course of working with them, and this was for about a week, he got the feeling that Kay's dead husband had been in love with Karen. There were quiet remarks about how he looked out for her, worried when she didn't come down to breakfast, or found something to do in whatever room of the house she happened to be in. Kay didn't seem angry or jealous about this. No, not one bit. On the contrary, she seemed glad it had been the case. Now, maybe Carl had a dirty mind, and he hoped she wouldn't think so, but he started wondering if there had been some blatant sexual activity going on in the big house in Connecticut.

"You mean, like three-ways?" Maggie asked.

"I mean a ménage-a-trois."

"Isn't that the same thing?"

"Well, no. A three-way suggests a one-time occurrence. A ménage means something regular going on over time."

"You think they all slept together in the same bed?"

"Something like that."

"Bizarre."

"Yes."

Carl shared these thoughts with his wife, who said his obsession was creepy. He said he wasn't obsessed. He just found how some people chose to live fascinating. This led to a number of arguments where he was accused of wanting more than she could give him, which was ironic as hell, because it was she who said *he* was failing *her*, not giving her enough attention, wasn't interested enough in her. He came to realize she was simply projecting on to him her own thoughts, and the reckoning she had come to within herself about the state of their marriage.

"And where are Kay and Karen now?" Maggie asked.

"Probably back in Connecticut."

"Did they mind you keeping their pictures?"

"I think they forgot all about them. I contacted them several times to say the proofs were ready, but I never heard anything back."

"They didn't stiff you, did they?"

Carl smiled. "They'd paid up front. It was their suggestion, not mine."

"Maybe they just wanted to sit together and be looked at. *Interpreted*," Maggie said.

"Telling their story silently, with small gestures."

"Uh-huh."

"You're very perceptive."

"I ain't no dummy," she said.

"Nor much of a drinker, it seems."

That she was true, she said. In fact, she was pretty snockered.

He said she probably shouldn't drive herself home. He'd make up the couch for her since the spare room was full of his equipment.

"Okay, but no funny stuff," she said.

"Scout's honor."

He lent her a pair of pajamas that had belonged to his ex-wife. When she moved out, she didn't take much. In this case, Maggie saw why. The pajamas were hideous, decorated with small spaceships. But they were warm, even if they were way too big. This wife must have been about five foot ten, and outweighed Maggie by a good thirty pounds.

Carl got her settled, put the dishes in the dishwasher, went to his room and closed the door. Maggie took a last look at her phone. She scanned a bunch of recent texts from Kyle, all referring to being in a bar, the last of which said, *You will not believe what just happened!*

She was too tired for his drama. She'd catch up with him tomorrow.

chapter seventeen

Marta was mad that Josh bailed out on her. She wanted to make an entrance, tell him about Luis's sad little apartment, and then about her visit to the Westside. She wanted it made clear that even though she slept with him, brought him to Dunston, and urged Chip to back his play, she was a free agent who could come and go as she liked.

Yet she couldn't convince herself of this. Her heart was still his. Then there was the mess with Luis. That was a new low, for sure.

The day wore on, and her spirits sagged. She went through her phone, looking for someone to have drinks with. No one seemed appealing, no doubt because for the last few months the only person she spent much time with was Josh. And Maggie, but Maggie wasn't here. Maggie might not ever be here again.

She called her brother, Timothy. He said he swung by the house, but she'd already gotten back on the road.

"Couldn't take Angie's preaching," Marta said.

"Just ignore her. That's what I do."

"She thinks I should get a job."

"Yeah? What do you think?"

She said she didn't know, but she'd stumbled across a possible role that might do good things for her career. Could he see her as a fallen Southern belle?

"What about that guy's play? About the twins?" Timothy asked.

"You heard about that?"

"Sure. Chip's all excited. Mom thinks he's being an idiot."

"He can find another actress."

"How did he take that news?"

"Haven't told him yet."

She asked if he'd seen Maggie. He hadn't, but they'd talked. As far as he could tell, she wasn't crazy about living in Sullivan, but she was working hard and getting used to this new chapter in her life.

He asked what had caused the rift between them. She hesitated, then told him the truth. At this Timothy laughed and said he couldn't see Maggie doing that. And that was the whole problem, Marta realized, hearing him expand on how strange it was. Maggie had gone completely out of character, and Marta hated it.

"It's like I didn't even know her, and shit, I'm supposed to know her better than anyone, right?" she asked.

"You were always the boss of her. Maybe she was just trying to get back at you."

At this, Marta just let it out. The guy—Josh—thought he was in love with Maggie. Yeah, that's right, based on just one encounter. He went to see her when they came upstate. He even spent the night with her in Sullivan. Maggie swore they didn't do anything. Josh said so, too.

"So, first she wants to, then when she has the chance, she doesn't?" Timothy asked.

"Pretty much."

"Sounds like she just had second thoughts."

Marta couldn't imagine having second thoughts about Josh. She kept this to herself.

He asked if she'd kicked Maggie out. She said no, she'd left of her own accord.

"Maybe you guys just need a break, that's all," he said.

"Angie said the same thing."

"God, I hate agreeing with her."

He could come down to the city that weekend if she liked. She'd have to let him know. Their dad was coming in a couple of days, and she didn't want to have a family overload. Timothy was the one person who understood this. He loved their family, too, but only in small doses.

They said goodbye.

Talking to Timothy pulled her mood down another notch.

She put on her jacket and headed out to her favorite vintage clothing store. It was on Hudson, only a ten-minute walk. The bracing air brought a measure of clarity to her chaotic thoughts, and she reminded herself that she'd always been a logical, if sometimes ruthless person. To that end, there were several things she had to establish:

1) Should she accept that Josh's affection probably would never turn her way, and just go on using him for sex?

2) Would her decamping from his play make him withdraw from her completely?

3) What the hell was she going to do about the fact that her deceiving Luis was worse than Maggie deceiving Josh?

There they both were, lying and misleading men. They'd become *femmes fatales*, after having only a couple of boyfriends each, including rough one-night stands that probably shouldn't count. Then she considered that she had slept with both men in question, and Maggie had slept with neither, and a small nugget of pride settled in her heart. You didn't need intimacy to get a man in bed, but raw nerve, and in some cases, being willing to throw ethics out the window. Men did that all the time, didn't they?

The shop was called Rosie the Riveter. Marta didn't recognize the sales clerk, a tall, striking African woman wearing a dashiki and a colorful headdress. When she asked if she could help her find anything, her accent was pure Brooklyn. Marta was sorry she'd spoken so soon. She'd enjoyed the fantasy of being in the presence of an African queen.

It was a small, cozy space. The dressing room door was a curtain made of black velvet. The full-length mirror was old. Where dirt had collected on the back side of the glass there were splotches of opaque bronze. The first dress Marta tried fit her perfectly. It was plum colored rayon, with broad shoulders and a tight waist typical of the 1940s. If she had a hair ribbon, she'd look like Betty Grable. This kind of outfit required deep red lipstick, and long red nails. Seamed stockings, of course, though those were probably hard to find, and sturdy pumps.

"I'm off to sell war bonds," she said, as she swept aside the curtain and strode up to the sales clerk.

The woman looked down at her and grinned.

"You look perky."

"Uncle Sam needs perky to help smash the Nazis."

"You're a trip."

Marta curtsied. She went to another rack, and pulled out a low-cut green dress, which was too long. The hem fell to mid-calf, when it should have been just below the knee.

"You could have it shortened," the clerk said. "Wouldn't be too hard."

Marta thought of Edgar and his love of sewing.

A navy blue satin evening gown caught her eye next. She could see it worn with a large, sparkly broach, and an equally flashy clutch. The cap sleeves were charming. Were there any long gloves she could try on?

The clerk brought the only pair she had that reached above the elbow. The hands were too big, but Marta didn't mind. The effect in the mirror was just fine.

"All I need is a little Jimmy Dorsey, and I'm good to go," she said.

"You're really into the forties, aren't you?" the clerked asked.

"I used to watch a lot of old movies."

"Yeah? What are your some of your favorites?"

Marta thought of her late nights with Maggie. Saturdays were the best, especially in winter, when the falling snow deepened the quiet of their sleeping household. Maggie was into Claudette Colbert and Myrna Loy—*The Thin Man* series a great favorite. Marta preferred Jean Harlowe and Lauren Bacall for their tough wisecracks and unapologetic sexuality.

"*Red Dust, The Women, The Lady Eve,* though I'm always on the fence about Barbara Stanwyck," Marta said.

"I've heard of misspent youth, but this is beyond."

Marta's expression darkened. Then she walked regally across the short width of the store, smiling brightly. She turned and came back with the same measured gait.

"You could model," the clerk said.

"Not tall enough."

"Maybe. But you'll do."

"For what?"

The clerk—whose name was Monique—said this shop had been left to her, and she wanted to make the most of it. A friend of hers worked in a new boutique over on Spring Street, maybe she'd seen it, The Purple Hat—did she live around here?

"Yes."

Anyhow, the friend, Clarisse, said she'd display some of Monique's clothes in her window, which was way bigger than the one here, and if someone were interested, Clarisse would direct her to Rosie the Riveter.

"And in return?" Marta asked.

"In return nothing. She's my friend. She's helping me out."

Marta realized her attitude towards pretty much everything had gotten mercenary.

"What's your name?" Monique asked.

Marta told her.

"You carry yourself well. Are you a dancer?"

"Actress."

"Ah, perfect. If you're interested."

Marta would wear an outfit, stand in the window of the Purple Hat for, say, an hour, or until she got sick of it, then she'd change into a different outfit—they'd pick stuff that looked really great on her.

"Why don't you just use a mannequin?" Marta asked.

"Old clothes on a dummy look lame. Old clothes on a live person, who moves now and then, look new—better than new, really."

"You've really thought about this."

"Like I say, I inherited this place, and it's really all I got."

Marta closed the curtain and removed the dress. Back in her old clothes, she felt ordinary. She emerged with the evening dress on its padded hanger.

"How much do I get?" she asked.

"Twelve dollars an hour."

Beats what you're making now.

"I don't know. I might be getting a part soon," she said.

"I'm sure we can work something out."

Marta gave the dress to Monique, then folded up the long gloves slowly, meticulously.

"If you don't want to, that's cool," Monique said.

"No, I want to."

Monique said she wanted to find some of those old Norman Rockwell illustrations for the background. Okay, he was probably racist, at least judging from his pictures, but she'd never seen anything that better evoked the era.

They exchanged phone numbers. Monique wasn't sure yet when Marta would start, since that was something she needed to work out with Clarisse. She gave her the address of The Purple Hat, and suggested she go over and introduce herself.

"I'll text her now and let her know you're coming," Monique said.

Marta's eyes fell on her necklace, a choker of round, amber beads. Monique directed her to a matching ring for ninety-five dollars. Marta pulled out her credit card. Monique said she only accepted cash. Marta had just been to the ATM and produced five twenties. She thanked Monique and left.

Clouds had given way to a harsh, sterile sunlight that made her wish she had her Ray-Bans on her.

A man walking several dogs of all different sizes struggled his way up the sidewalk towards her. The dogs were exuberant, active, shifting back and forth, tangling their leashes. She assumed he worked with a service that did this for people, took their dogs out while they were at work. Either that, or they were all his, and he was an animal hoarder. He stopped to gaze through the glass of a storefront selling sleek headphones, displayed cheerfully in bright colors. Marta looked, too. How about a Lana Turner evening gown and a pair of headphones, blending old and new, luring buyers to see a vintage dress in a contemporary light? She'd have to mention that to Clarisse.

Clarisse's shop was a mess. The day before, a pipe had burst in the apartment above, and though the water was promptly shut off, a portion of the ceiling at the back of the store had been ruined, along with several boxes of merchandise, which she was in the process of assessing. Clarisse was a little old lady, "feisty," some might say. She wore a flowing tunic over a floor-length skirt. On each wrist were several wooden bracelets Marta suspected were African in origin.

Marta offered to help her sort through the boxed garments, and Clarisse waved her off, then pointed to a worn leather easy chair in the middle the floor. She sat. She wanted to know all about her. Marta stuck to her recent history.

"I admire anyone with an artistic calling," Clarisse said. She stood up straight, with a quick grimace of discomfort, which her hand, quickly placed on her lower back, confirmed.

"Why don't you sit down, and let me do that?" Marta asked. Again, she was waved off.

Marta continued. She'd been thinking about modeling in the window, and the sort of backdrop there might be. Monique had mentioned Norman Rockwell posters, and frankly, she didn't like that idea too well. What about items from the particular era she was modeling? Like an old radio, or some funky kitchen appliances? Or even an old vacuum cleaner? Anything that would promote a vintage atmosphere.

"In that case, I should go in there myself. I'm pretty vintage," Clarisse said, then coughed out a dry, throaty laugh.

"I've always wondered what life was like back then," Marta said.

"Pretty much the same as it is now. People don't really change one decade to the next. Some of them are good, some of them not so good."

"I mean not having the things we have now."

"We didn't know we didn't have them, so we thought we were doing pretty darn well."

Marta went on with her idea of a living tableau. How about adding a liquor cart, with Deco styling? She could wear an evening gown and hold a martini glass. She could see Clarisse warming to the idea.

"How do you know Monique?" Marta asked.

"She's my goddaughter. I raised her after her parents were killed. We were all anthropologists together, working on a dig in Kenya."

"Wow."

"They were run off the road by a wild truck driver."

"Jesus."

It was hard to think about, even now, Clarisse said. One day, there she is, mapping out where a two hundred-thousand-year-old skeleton was discovered, the next she's on a plane back to the States with a little girl who doesn't understand where her mommy and daddy went.

"I didn't have any of my own," Clarisse said. "Children, I mean." Her gaze wandered.

"Monique said she'd been left the vintage shop by someone," Marta said.

"Yes. By a man she used to take care of. She trained as a nurse."

"And you went into the clothing business, too?"

"I didn't see why not. Retirement can be a lonely, dull affair if you don't shake it up."

Clarisse looked Marta over, as if trying to decide if she were up to the task of modeling Monique's outfits.

"You're not very tall, but that's okay. People will be looking up at you," she said.

"Yeah, I guess so."

"What's today, Monday? Come back on Friday. I'll tell Monique it's all set."

"Okay."

They shook hands. Clarisse's palm was soft and smooth, and Marta tried to imagine it holding an ancient bone.

Back outside, in the rush of the city street, Marta felt that she'd been dealt good fortune not once, but twice. They might not make up for Maggie's leaving, and her stupidity with Luis, but it was a start.

chapter eighteen

Maggie would never become a seasoned drinker, not with how badly her head hurt as she drove home from Carl's. The phone calls with Luis and Marta made her temples throb even more. Despite all that, the evening itself left a pleasant memory. The scrumptious food; the odd story of Karen and Kay. She liked that she'd guessed Carl's attraction to Leah. Looking back, it was obvious from how intensely he took her picture.

Leah was in the kitchen, having an off day, she said. Because she couldn't face picking up a brush, she spread out a box of pastels and was making random slashes on a piece of paper, all in somber shades of brown, purple, and gray.

She watched Maggie pour herself a drink of water and said, "So?"

"So what? We didn't sleep together."

"You stayed over because . . ."

"Too much wine."

"That's what pasta is for—absorbing the booze."

Maggie sat. She studied Leah's page. The slashes seemed like a crowd of people, leaning, pushing together, yet at odds, not in harmony at all.

She told Leah about Luis and Marta.

"Wait, what? Holy shit! That takes some balls," Leah said. Her fingers were tinged, bruised-looking. Her chin was smudged, too.

"Not really. She said it was on the spur of the moment."

"Jesus. Good old Luis. So, wait, so he really *did* have a thing for you."

"What do you mean?"

"Digger thought so. I thought so."

"Huh."

Luis?

She had assumed until now that the whole thing had been at Marta's instigation.

Suddenly all of their casual interactions were cast in a new light. When he helped her move a large canvas up the stairs, did he want to stop and kiss her? Or when she stood, looking at his playground series, did he want to put his arms around her? He'd given nothing away. Or maybe she'd just been too self-absorbed to see.

Leah considered her slashes. Her brow furrowed. She flipped to a new, blank page. Maggie's eye fell on a blue pastel, the color of a robin's egg. She removed it from the box, and without a moment's hesitation pressed it gently to the paper, slid it upwards at an angle, adjusting the pressure of her hand so that the line became thicker and thicker the higher it went.

She and Leah both stared at it for a while, each deciding what should happen next. With some visible reluctance, Leah chose a green pastel, and dotted the blue line. Maggie felt a surge of joy, as if she'd realized that in that one moment, her whole life was about to change.

Leah didn't have such a momentous vision. She just flipped to yet another new sheet of paper, and resumed working in the same dark, dreary tones.

"Guess what? *Carl's* got a thing for *you*," Maggie said.

"Get out."

"Seriously."

"He said that?"

"Pretty much."

Leah shook her head, but the news pleased her, Maggie could tell. Maggie asked for a blank sheet of paper for herself, and if she could mess around with the pastels Leah wasn't using.

"Sure."

Her own supplies were right in her room, but she didn't want to get up and interrupt the flow.

First in yellow, then red, then bright blue, and finally in fiery orange the faceless woman's profile ascended from the bottom left-hand corner as if drifting into the sky. She was soon shadowed in soft lavender, smudged with deep pink. Leah looked at Maggie's page.

"You must have really been into coloring Easter eggs when you were a kid," she said.

"I never did that."

"Really? I thought everybody did."

"Nope."

Maggie returned the pastels to the box and washed her hands.

"Oh, hey, who did you have dinner with last night?" she asked.

Leah looked sly. "Remember that meathead in the bar who knew your sister? The guy he was with? I ran into him at the grocery store, and we got talking, and he asked me out."

"Really? Was it fun?"

"Pretty much."

"You like him?"

"Yeah, sorta."

"You going to see him again?"

"He's been texting me all morning."

"And now you're ghosting him."

"Just for a little while."

The guy, Darrel, worked at the hardware store, but his big passion was guns. He wanted to take her to the shooting range on Saturday.

"And are you into guns?" Maggie asked.

"Grew up with them."

"Sort of a funny thing to do on a date, don't you think?"

"A date's when two people hang out. Doesn't matter how you spend the time."

"So, you're basically off Digger?"

Leah shrugged.

Maggie took her drawing into her room and propped it up on the dresser. The progression of the faces, and the composition as a whole, was reminiscent of *Inner Child*. Luis had once said that it represented striving. At the time, she wasn't sure, but now she saw what he meant.

Luis!

She called him. It went straight to voicemail. She said she hadn't been honest before, because he caught her off guard. The truth was, he'd gone to bed with her sister. Marta was clearly having a tough time, because she would normally never do anything like that. It probably had to do with her moving out. She was living upstate now. Things in the city had gotten . . . well, she didn't really know how to describe it, but it was like opening a closet one day and having everything you've been tossing in there come crashing down on your head. If he knew what she meant. She probably wasn't making much sense. Anyhow, it was possible that her being gone—away from Marta—for the first time since they were kids, must have really upset her. He had to take her word. Marta just wasn't that kind of person.

Liar!

She hung up. She called Kyle. His voice was groggy.

"Do I make excuses for people?" she asked.

"What? Maybe, I don't know. Why?"

She told him everything. There was the sound of movement on his end. He was probably getting out of bed.

"You just wanted to protect her," he said. "You're that kind of person."

"I'm an idiot. She walks all over me."

"I think she walks all over everybody."

"Maybe."

"You sound down. I'll come up there and we'll have some fun."

"You don't have to do that."

"I know." He sounded relieved. Someone said his name.

"Well, I'll let you go," Maggie said.

"You sure? I got time to talk."

"Call me later. I'm gonna go hang out in my studio. Well, my garage-slash-studio."

"Cool! Be brilliant!"

They hung up.

Her phone rang. It was Luis.

"Is this for real?" he asked.

"Yeah."

He was having trouble getting his head around it. How could you pretend to be someone else, or let someone assume you were someone else? It was beyond unfair, it was sick. That was the only word for it. Sick.

She used her most soothing tone. Marta, no doubt, had too much to drink. Luis was a good-looking guy. She got swept up in the moment. She probably wanted to sleep with him from the moment she saw him. That made it easy to overlook the details.

"You mean, the truth."

"I guess."

"You *guess?*"

"Don't yell at me. *I* didn't do this. *She* did it."

"I know. And she's an asshole. So are you for defending her."

"Luis—"

He hung up.

Shit!

She punched in Marta's number, but stopped before making the call. What could she say now that would make any difference?

Loud music drifted up from Mrs. Culver's apartment. It was old, with a Doris Day flavor, saccharine sweet.

Maggie went down. As she came onto the porch, Mrs. Culver opened her door only a few inches at first, then when she saw Maggie, opened it all the way. A strong smell of cinnamon wafted out. Mrs. Culver was done up in a fifties-style dress, with a wide skirt and narrow waist. Her legs and feet were bare, and the bulging blue veins just under the red, scaly skin made Maggie lift her eyes and meet Mrs. Culver's, which were bright and merry.

"Won't you come in?" she asked. Maggie stood in the doorway. Mrs. Culver padded over to the turntable, lifted the needle, and swung the arm to the side. Then she turned off the power.

"Music is magical, don't you think?" she asked.

"Sure."

Maggie went inside. She hadn't visited since the son's truck was in the driveway, a couple of days before. Her laxity pained her for a moment, but seeing Mrs. Culver then, clearly in possession of herself, bare feet notwithstanding, reassured her.

"She's wonderful, isn't she?" Mrs. Culver asked.

"Who?"

"Rosemary Clooney."

The name rang a bell from an old musical she'd once watched.

"Yeah, sure, she's great," Maggie said.

Mrs. Culver gave a little smile. She sashayed to the right, then back again, and twirled to music only she seemed to hear.

"I'm sorry I haven't been by," Maggie said.

"Your little boy keeps you busy."

"Yes."

So much for being in possession of herself.

Maggie wondered if Mrs. Culver would invite her to sit. Mrs. Culver kept dancing to her silent tune.

"It smells good in here. Are you baking something?" Maggie asked.

"Those are scented candles from my son. He says they're good for my mood, my, what is it—*attitude*."

Mrs. Culver stood still, and a lost, vacant look came into her eyes.

"I like your dress," Maggie said.

Mrs. Culver pressed her palms to the skirt.

"I just got it," she said.

"It's very pretty."

Maggie looked past her into the kitchen, where dishes were piled in the sink. Washing them might relieve her guilt, and it would certainly help out Mrs. Culver when she came back from whatever memory lane she was on, assuming she would. One more look at her said she probably wouldn't.

"Why don't you come with me?" Maggie asked. Mrs. Culver didn't respond. Maggie took her hand and gently led her to the kitchen. She put her in one of the chairs at the breakfast table.

"You can talk to me while I tidy up," she said. There was an apron on a hook next to the refrigerator that was patterned with purple tulips. The shade was arresting, falling somewhere between lavender and mauve. Her faceless woman should wear this color, in a dress cut like Mrs. Culver's.

"I'll be right back," Maggie said. She hurried up to her apartment, where Leah was still at the table, glumly pushing her pastels around. Maggie got the sketchpad from her room, along with her own box of pastels. She returned to Mrs. Culver, who had put on the apron in Maggie's absence and was having trouble with the ties behind her back. Maggie helped her out of it and asked her to stand still for just a minute, so she could draw her picture.

Mrs. Culver lowered herself into the chair and leaned her face against her palm. She sighed heavily.

"Mrs. Culver?"

"Yes, Betty, I'm right here. No need to shout."

Maggie opened the box of pastels. Her hand hovered over the purple. She chose the green instead, hoping the complementary color would spur her imagination. She did a quick sketch of Mrs. Culver's face, lingering over her still prominent cheekbones, and the thick eyebrows which had remained black and made a strong contrast to her silver hair. It was hard to convey the empty gaze that came and went, but she managed to by aiming the eyes slightly down, as if what lay there, the stillness of the past, held her fast. The dress drew itself. As a girl, watching old movies with Marta, she often had a sketch pad in her lap to copy strapless evening gowns, wide-shouldered jackets, and capri pants worn by all those beautiful, glamorous stars. She never understood why Marta wanted to appear onstage instead of the silver screen. Movies were *it*.

Her rendition had Mrs. Culver's look-alike standing with her hands demurely folded, as if waiting to be invited onto the dance floor. Maybe she'd been waiting for years.

Across the bottom of the page Maggie wrote, *Remembering the Dance.*

She examined the face she'd just drawn, the lines that ran down from the outside corner of each eye. They were called "laugh lines," but Maggie could see them as tear tracks, too, that had worn down the soft flesh with salt and grief. Maybe the title should be *Longing for The Dance.*

She showed the drawing to Mrs. Culver, who stared at it uncomprehendingly, as if being presented with an ancient scroll written in a dead language. Then she put her finger on the image of the dress and a small, fleeting smile lifted her lips.

"What a looker," she said.

"You bet!"

Maggie washed the dishes, each one showing a rime of egg yolk. When she finished, she opened the refrigerator to find nothing inside except a stick of butter and a carton containing two eggs.

"Where do you keep your son's telephone number?" Maggie asked.

Mrs. Culver said nothing.

Maggie put away the apron, told Mrs. Culver she had to be going, picked up her things, and went upstairs.

Leah pulled the son's number off of her cell phone. Maggie's call went into voicemail. She was firm. His mother had no business living alone. Was he aware that she was subsisting on a diet of eggs? The time had come when he either had to arrange live-in care or move her into a nursing home where she could be seen to around the clock. She concluded by saying that her sister was a social worker on staff at a retirement community in Dunston, and that Maggie would be happy to get him her number if he needed some guidance making the decisions he must now make.

"God, I sound just like my mother," she told Leah.

"You lit a fire under him, for sure."

"We'll see."

Maggie showed her the drawing. Leah took her time looking. Looking, too, was an art.

"I like the green. It evokes envy, and greed," Leah said.

"For?"

"Her youth."

Maggie should have thought of that.

Fat flakes of snow drifted past the small kitchen window. The thought of an early winter made her feel both cozy and trapped.

chapter nineteen

Josh turned up on Wednesday, two days after abandoning Marta, and took her to dinner in a crowded, noisy bistro where conversation was a challenge. The tables were too close together, and the man behind them boomed on about basis points and bond yields. His date seemed to have nothing to say for herself.

Josh, on the other hand, had a lot to say. He said again that he appreciated the offer of Maggie's old room, but as he explained in his text, he needed his things around him when he worked. That he avoided meeting her eye meant there was something else he was struggling to get out.

Then he said he'd written to Chip that he wouldn't be able to accept his offer to back the play. Things had changed for him, financially. He was going to be able to access the principal in his trust account. He hoped both she and Chip understood that he preferred to remain completely independent where his creative work was concerned.

Marta looked at the bottom of her empty wine glass, where the dregs collected. On her middle finger she wore the ring she bought from Rosie the Riveter. It was too big for her hand, overwhelming it, and giving the impression that she was a child trying to look like an adult.

Then Josh was talking about taking some time off, out of the city.

"You just said you needed to be in your old apartment," Marta said. She was hungry. The server hadn't yet taken their order. She wanted the grilled cheese sandwich made with both goat cheese and cheddar, mostly because it came with a cup of homemade tomato soup.

"I know, I know, but down the road. For now, maybe a new scene would keep the vibe going," he said.

How could she not have seen before how unfocused he really was? They'd been hanging out together for almost six months. They'd spent hours talking about plays, sets, costumes, who was good in what role, who wasn't, the foibles of critics, the charm of undiscovered talent. Maybe she'd been so intent on getting what she wanted—a way onto the next stage and the one after that—that she just hadn't really taken him in. The fact that he was handsome and could further her career had suggested a depth and sturdiness he just didn't have.

"Any particular place in mind?" Marta asked.

"I don't know. West, somewhere."

At this, she grew alarmed. She had pictured him back in New Jersey, or maybe at the friend's place in the Hamptons, where he would be conveniently in her orbit when she wanted to sleep with him.

She put the palm of her over-ringed hand on her forehead.

"You okay?" he asked.

"Sure."

"If I do go, it won't be for long. Just until I finish the play."

The server finally appeared and sullenly wrote down their order. When she left, Marta apologized for running out on him with Luis the other night. She hoped that didn't have anything to do with his wanting to leave the city. He said no, he'd been thinking about it for a while, and besides, they weren't in a committed relationship, were they?

She hated herself for blushing. It happened when she got mad.

You always want to call the shots, don't you?

Maggie's voice made her even madder.

Marta went on about Luis, how he seemed so ordinary on the surface, but was in fact a deep, complicated person underneath it all.

"You got this from one night with the guy?" Josh asked. He held a half-eaten breadstick in his hand. Marta now registered that the server just dropped off a small jar of them. She helped herself.

"A woman knows these things."

He looked thoughtful for a moment, then ate the rest of the breadstick. He drained his glass of beer.

Did he regret getting physically involved with her?

Fine for you to regret it, but God forbid he should.

Shut up. I don't regret it.

"So, how *is* the play?" she asked.

"Interesting. Challenging. Keeps me up at night."

"Well, that's good, right?"

"Yup."

The couple behind them rose from the table. The man banged his chair against Marta's.

"Some people," Josh said when they'd gone.

"Yeah."

She told him about the job modeling vintage clothes. He said it sounded awesome. His phone, lying face down on the table, vibrated. He looked at the screen. She couldn't read his expression. He declined the call and put the phone in the pocket of his jacket, hanging from the back of his chair.

The food came. They ate. She did all the talking. She started to panic, and told herself she was being stupid, this outcome was for the best.

As they waited for the bill, he moved the stainless-steel salt and pepper shakers around on the table.

"Look, what I said before, about our not being in a committed relationship. I don't want you to think that I don't want to go on being friends," he said.

"Okay."

"It's just that this last turn was pretty weird."

"By turn, you mean sex. That you wanted. That you initiated."

"Yeah, yeah, I know."

He leaned toward her, although the noise level around them was still high.

"It just doesn't feel right, having sex with someone you're friends with," he said.

Are you kidding me right now?

She'd learned of his reputation not long after they met. The king of one-night stands. What the hell lay behind this sudden urge to reform himself?

Maggie.

"Yeah, you're right," she said. "I was going to say something, but I didn't know how."

"So, you're okay with it?"

"Of course."

He wasn't sure when he'd be leaving, not for a little while, at any rate, and they'd see each other a lot before then. She said that would be cool. Outside the restaurant they hugged briefly. He pulled away first.

The next day—Thursday—she called Rob. What was going on with the play? Did he think he could offer her the part?

He apologized for not having been in touch before. They'd found someone else, the backer's niece, who had a fair amount of stage experience. He'd been skeptical and waited to hear her read before putting in his two cents, and he had to admit, she was awfully damn good.

"I'm really sorry it didn't work out," he said. He sounded like he was walking down a sidewalk somewhere.

Then he said he'd heard of a new play opening up in a couple of weeks. The director was some guy from England, Spencer somebody, and he had a thing for blondes.

"What the hell is that supposed to mean?" Marta asked.

"For his female roles. He always chooses a blonde."

So now anyone with a bottle of hair dye was a contender? Rob understood her frustration. He really did. Maybe she'd like to help him with *Delta Damsel*, learn a bit about directing? You could never tell what it might one day lead to.

"The only thing I want to do, Rob, is act. On a stage. Before an audience." She was close to tears then.

"I know, I know. Look, I'm about to jump on the subway, so I'll call you later, okay?"

Marta hung up.

On Friday she went for her first modeling gig. The Purple Hat was closed. The door was locked. She peered through the glass. There was no one inside. She walked briskly, fueled by another rising tide of frustration, over to Rosie the Riveter where Monique greeted her with a doleful expression. She wore a pair of red plastic bifocals, and her hair was wrapped in a bright white turban.

"Hey," she said.

"What's going on? The Purple Hat's closed," Marta said.

"Clarisse broke her hip yesterday."

"Crap!"

"Yeah. She was up on a ladder over there, trying to scrape paint off the ceiling where the water leaked, and lost her balance."

"Oh, shit."

"I was going to call you, but I've been at the hospital with her most of the time."

"It's okay."

"We'll have to push back your start date, obviously."

Monique looked down at a pile of scarves on the counter and began folding them. She seemed tired enough to melt. The scarves weren't much, most of them nylon, one or two silk, not particularly vintage, just bright and cheerful accessories. Her phone trilled on the shelf behind her, and she turned to pick it up. Marta dug idly through the pile. An Hermés caught her eye. It was a fancy French label her mother liked to wear. They were timeless. This one here probably dated from the 1970s, given its pattern of bright overlapping pink and green circles. Monique's back was still turned. Marta shoved the scarf inside the sleeve of her sweater. She took the pad of blank sales receipts off the counter, tore off a sheet, and with an orange pen sitting by itself in a nearby coffee mug wrote, *Give Clarisse my best*, followed by a lopsided smiley face. She tapped Monique lightly on the elbow. Monique turned her way, Marta gave her the note, and gestured that she was leaving. Monique wiggled her fingers in parting and went back to her phone conversation.

She hadn't stolen anything in years and didn't realize how much she missed it. She and Maggie used to compete to see who came home with the most loot. Marta always won. Her hands were quicker; her awareness of where a sales clerk's attention was focused was much keener. Maggie limited herself to small items like a bottle of nail polish. Marta once produced a sage green cashmere sweater from underneath her shirt when she got home.

After she put several blocks between herself and the shop, she took out the scarf and looked at it triumphantly. The early winter daylight was bright enough to make her see that the colors were entirely wrong for her. She favored earth tones. Maggie was the one who went in for all those cheery, Day-Glo shades.

Yet as she waited for her father that night, she wrapped the scarf loosely around her neck. Looking at her reflection in the full-length mirror in her walk-in closet made her think she could become someone else, someone better.

When Potter arrived, he admired the scarf, her jacket, and her amber ring. He said she must have learned the art of snappy dressing from her mother. They took a cab down to Little Italy, where he'd made a dinner reservation for them. They sat at the back.

He brought her up to date. He was working as a liaison on home remodel projects where his wife was the general contractor. He didn't want to sound critical in any way, but she didn't always handle the clients well. She got impatient if they couldn't make up their minds about a particular countertop or cabinet finish. He supposed she had a point, since things had to get ordered on time. He'd learned just to let the homeowner figure it out for themselves, which they always did, sooner or later. Praising their final choice made for good relations as they moved ahead. When people felt at ease, confident in their particular design aesthetic, they were much better to work with. And they recommended you to their friends. Dunston was in the midst of a remodeling boom, though Marta probably didn't know that, living her glamorous big city life.

In the middle of the pasta course, he finally wound down. They'd finished a bottle of Chianti. The light in his eye said he needed a second one. She asked if he wanted to order another and said if they didn't finish it the server would just put it in a brown paper bag, and they'd take it back to her place. He thought that was a fine idea.

When the second bottle arrived, Potter inspected the label, and tasted the small amount poured into his glass. He approved.

After the server had gone, he asked what was new with her.

"Oh, lots, actually. Looks like I have a small part in a play. I'm dating a playwright. And I got a job modeling vintage clothes. Doesn't pay much. But, as Angie said, I should get a job. That's not why I did it, though. I don't want her thinking she was right about anything, but I figure it won't kill me, you know?"

"Well, congrats all around!"

Is lying well what makes you a good actress?

I think you're conflating the two. An actress doesn't lie. She tells a different truth.

They ordered dessert. Marta relaxed into her falsehoods, aided by the wine, and her father's company. He always had a calming effect on her. Maybe because he did so much fibbing of his own when she was growing up. Had she come by it so easily because of him? If asked, he'd say he didn't really lie so much as put a positive spin on things. He was a diehard optimist. Marta didn't lie to persuade herself that she in fact had what she desperately wanted. She lied because she liked the person she became: fearless, bold, daring the world to see through her.

And yet.

There was no part in a play; there was no boyfriend; there was probably no job, because who knew how long it would take Clarisse to get on her feet again?

"What's the matter, honey?" Potter asked.

"Nothing. Just tired, I guess."

"You want to make it an early night? That's okay with me. I've got a room in midtown. It'll take a little while to get there by cab. I can drop you off first."

The night was cold. The stolen scarf gave her neck no warmth. They went over to Broadway to hail a cab. The first three were full. The driver of the fourth looked like he resented having to slow down at all to let them in. With the bagged bottle on the seat between them, Potter talked about how much he loved the city, and wasn't that funny, being just a simple upstate boy at heart. He patted her hand once in a while. She didn't respond.

While they were at a red light, he asked, "So what happened with Maggie?"

"What did she say?"

"I haven't talked to her. I got the story from Angie."

"So, you know about her throwing paint on someone's canvas."

"Yeah. She must have had a bad day."

Marta said she was clearly frustrated with her work and needed a change of scene.

"But she's in touch, right?" Potter asked.

"Sometimes, not often."

"Well, sounds like she just needs a break. You two have been in each other's soup for a long time now."

"All our lives."

She needed a few minutes of cold air on her face, so she asked the driver to stop at the corner and let her walk the rest of the way. She pecked her father quickly on the cheek as she got out and promised to call soon.

chapter twenty

The dark heavy wood of the lawyer's office was pretentious. The room felt stuffy, as if it had been sealed and only recently opened. Dexter Garrett had been his father's crony, and because of that long relationship, he felt it necessary to say some things now, in a calm measured voice intended to put Josh and his mother at ease, but which made Josh want to stand up and shout.

With wealth came responsibility. It was not for squandering. His late father had taken great pains to provide a solid, comfortable future for the family. The intended timeline was so that Josh could achieve a level of maturity he might not yet possess.

Josh's mother assured Garrett that her son was capable of making sound decisions. They had discussed the matter fully. In fact, they hadn't. It seemed to Josh that she agreed because she was tired of thinking about it. As Josh and his mother signed the documents in front of them, Garrett urged Josh to get good advice before withdrawing any large sum. Josh said he would, knowing he'd consult no one.

Now that the matter had been concluded, Garrett asked if he could offer them anything. Perhaps a small glass of sherry? Josh's mother said she would like one. Josh declined. He said he had to get going. He was anxious to get back to writing. Josh's mother reminded him that she would be going to Florida next month, and that he hadn't yet said if he were coming, too. He bent and kissed her soft, powdered cheek, shook Garrett's hand, and walked calmly past the very attractive receptionist. Once in the elevator, he pounded the mirrored wall in a gesture of pure glee.

The mood evaporated when Maggie failed to answer her phone. She'd been out of touch for about three days at that point. It had been a week since his dinner with Marta, and though she'd texted him several times saying they should get together, he had been noncommittal. He missed the sex and thinking that made him feel even worse.

Brad was in the city looking at some plans for an expansion on his parents' home in the Hamptons, where Marta and Josh had stayed. The parents spent most of their time in Arizona, and Brad had assumed the role of property manager in their absence. Josh sent a text saying they should meet up for drinks, and Brad said he'd pick him up at his place in about an hour.

In his mailbox was a letter from Marta's stepfather. He wished him well finishing the play and getting it produced. He had no doubt that a keen, perceptive audience would warmly receive it.

Was he put out that Josh turned down his offer? But then, he hadn't offered, Marta had asked. Marta had only wanted to help him, but he couldn't afford that sort of entangled obligation. He knew her well enough to see that she would use it as a bargaining tool whenever she needed it. It was one thing when a woman played those kinds of games where your heart was concerned. That was natural. That was to be expected. But where his work was concerned, he had to maintain his independence.

And now he had it.

Brad was his usual cheerful self, a trait that sometimes drove Josh nuts when they went to NYU together. Brad was one of those people who had trouble being serious yet liked to be around serious people. The women he dated tended to be sour and bad tempered, or uptight and nervous. One of them, Bethany something, came on to Josh at one of Brad's Hamptons parties when she pulled him into a hallway and told him he was the most amazing man she'd ever met. She was drunk, but he slept with her anyway without a bit of guilt since Brad had mentioned earlier in the evening that he'd gotten tired of her. Despite Brad's well-meaning lecture on Josh's taking women for granted, he didn't treat them any better.

Brad's parents were adding on a wing for his sister and her two children. She'd never married, something it took the parents time to accept. The children were from two different men, neither of whom was present in her life. The parents wanted her to get out of the city and raise her children in a proper atmosphere. The sister, Luann, wasn't particularly interested in how the children got raised, and Brad's parents hoped—assumed—that in comfortable surroundings she'd come to her senses.

"Which is such bullshit, because that's where she grew up. And the place she wanted to leave. Why they think she's going to become Super Mom just because she's right back where she started is beyond me."

Brad was at Josh's small kitchen table, in the same chair Marta had used when she stirred her tea the first time she stayed over. The memory was swift and sharp, as if he'd been kicked.

"People change," Josh said.

"Not her. Never her."

Brad wasn't a bitter person, yet his tone was full of resentment. Josh wondered if he were jealous of the attention his parents now gave her. But he'd had plenty of attention along the way, hadn't he? Gotten the best of everything? Even in college the parents were seldom in the picture. Josh had only met them once. Maybe he felt ignored. It wasn't the kind of thing Josh felt comfortable asking about.

"So, where's what's-her-name? The one you brought out to the house?" Brad asked. He pulled out a vape pen and started puffing away.

"She's around. Too busy for me these days."

"You break up?"

"We were never really together."

Brad shook his head and exhaled a stream of vapor.

"Wait, that's not going to mess up your play, is it?" he asked. Josh was surprised he'd even remembered.

"No."

"Good for you. Never let anyone kill the creative drive."

Josh went and combed his hair. He'd found a gray one the other day and tore it out. He examined his scalp for others. His hair line was just beginning to recede, something that had happened to his father at a young age, too. His mother said it was a look of distinction. Josh didn't agree. He used his new body spray, then thought the scent was too woodsy.

"What the hell, man?" Brad said when he returned.

"No worse than how you smell."

"Nice!"

They walked out. Josh lived in Tribeca in a building that was to be gutted and converted to loft-style apartments. He'd gotten a letter from the owner saying he had six months to find a new home. The last month's rent would be waived to mitigate the inconvenience. To Josh, the news was good karma, since it came just days after he realized he needed a completely new environment.

He shared this with Brad at the bar he'd gone to with Kyle and Edgar.

"Shit, you're leaving? Seriously?" Brad asked. The martini he was sipping had turned his cheeks red.

"Chill out. You can come see me."

"I'll have to. You won't know anyone where you're going. Wherever that is."

"How do you know I won't?"

"Oh, God. Don't tell me. Dierdre moved somewhere and you're hooking up with her again."

"No way. She's scary."

They laughed and asked for another round.

At the time, Josh thought he was in love with Dierdre. He thought so for months afterwards and projected an overblown sense of misery and rejection. That quiet introspective attitude had drawn other women to him. Not Marta. She hadn't cared. She was all about the stage and acting, and he wondered just how much acting she'd done with him, romantically speaking.

Maggie had committed the ruse, but she was the more honest of the two.

Of course, he was only imputing what he hoped was true. He didn't know for sure.

Brad fell silent. Only alcohol had the power to lower his mood. It was said you became the person you truly were when you drank. Was Brad's chronic cheer a front for some deep sorrow?

Josh's phone buzzed. Maggie texted, *Sorry I've been out of touch. Working on stuff. Making plans.*

Plans? What plans?

His fingers tapped madly, *Yeah? Like what?*

Art stuff.

What art stuff?

The usual—how to do it better.

Ah, gotcha. Are you home right now? Want to talk?

Can't. Carl's here.

Carl? Who the hell is Carl?

"Hey, you know that guy over there?" Brad asked.

Josh turned to see Kyle waving cheerfully from a few tables away. He wore a green felt hat with a floppy brim. He was alone. Josh lifted his own hand in greeting, and Kyle made his way through the crowd holding a pink cocktail.

Brad and Kyle were introduced. Josh asked where Edgar was. Kyle said, "He was supposed to meet me here an hour ago. He's gotten flaky lately."

"That rhymes," Brad said.

"No, it doesn't," Josh said. Brad mouthed the two words silently several times.

Kyle sipped his drink. He seemed like he was trying to make it last.

"What do you hear from Maggie?" Josh asked him.

"Just that she's working hard."

"Who's Carl?"

"I have no idea."

"She never mentioned him?"

"Nope."

Josh settled back in his chair. Kyle chattered on about maybe going up to see her before the weather got too wintry.

Brad said he wanted something to eat. Josh shoved the laminated menu standing up between the salt and pepper shaker towards him. Brad stared at it dully.

"You boys got an early start," Kyle said.

"Not really," Josh said.

No one spoke. The ambient noise rose around them.

Kyle asked what was new. Josh said he was thinking of leaving the city, going somewhere warmer for a while. He was tired of New York winters.

"Really? Maggie said the same thing."

"She did?"

"Yup. Guess they had their first snow up there, and she didn't exactly love it. I told her to go sledding." Kyle giggled.

"Who's Maggie? Is that the one you came out with?" Brad asked. His eyes were woozy. He wiped his palm on his button-down vest.

"No, that was her twin sister," Josh said.

"Yeah? Twins are cool."

"Sometimes."

"Identical or fraternal?"

"Identical."

"Very rare phenomenon."

Kyle tapped something into his phone. "'The incidence of identical twins is approximately four per one thousand births.'"

"That's only four percent," Brad said.

"No. Per *thousand* births. So, point-four percent," Josh said.

Brad nodded.

The server wandered past. Brad held up his hand. She didn't see him.

"Did she say where?" Josh asked.

"Where what?" Kyle asked.

"Maggie. Where she might go."

"No. Just where she won't freeze her beautiful butt off."

"Huh?" Brad asked.

Kyle said she had an exceptional one. He asked if Josh agreed. Josh said it was gorgeous. Brad looked blank.

"I'm not straight if that's what's worrying you, honey," Kyle said and patted Brad's meaty red hand, sitting slackly on the tabletop.

How about somewhere to warm your heart, and everything else? Josh texted her.

She immediately replied with, *???*

Maybe Carl wasn't anyone important. Maybe he was a neighbor, or a little kid she'd agreed to babysit. Maybe this, maybe that.

Kyle's phone rang, and he went to take the call in a slightly quieter corner of the bar. He came back and said Edgar was finally on his way, but that they were going someplace else, a party at a friend's. Did Brad and Josh want to come, too?

Josh said maybe another time. Brad said it had been a long day. And he was still hungry. Josh said it was a long ride out to the Hamptons, so Brad could crash at his place, and they'd get something from the deli on his corner.

"That place always smells bad," Brad said.

Josh bought him an Italian hoagie and cut it in half back at his apartment. Brad ate quickly; Josh ate slowly.

Josh brought out a sheet, blanket, and a pillow, the same ones he'd given Marta when she stayed there right after Maggie's ruse. He put everything on the couch next to where Brad was sitting. Brad took his hand.

"We talked about that," Josh said.

"At least I know who I am."

"I know who I am."

"Maybe. But you don't know what you want."

"Yes, I do."

Brad dropped Josh's hand.

"To write a brilliant play," Brad said.

"Yes."

"And to fall madly in love with the right woman."

"Eventually."

Brad looked at him sharply. He seemed less drunk.

"It's the sister, isn't it?" he asked.

Josh took their two plates into the kitchen. He poured Brad a glass of water and carried it back out to him.

"Get some sleep."

"And the play about the twins is because of *her*, not the other one."

"What do you want me to say?"

"Nothing. Goodnight. I'll find my way out in the morning."

In the quiet of his room, Josh looked at his phone. In response to Maggie's line of question marks he texted, *I'll call you soon.*

chapter twenty-one

The faceless woman developed small, delicate features. She was often more like a child than an adult. Her upturned nose gave this effect. Sometimes her eyebrows were thin and arched. Other times they were straight and thick. Her cheekbones tended to be high and well-defined. Her lips were full and sensuous. She was blonde or brunette, once even a redhead. In one picture, she was bald but with a robust gleam in her eyes, suggesting the hair had been removed by choice, not illness.

Maggie considered where the energy to transform her subject came from. Part of it was because of her new, non-Marta life. Her work was also fueled by a longing for Josh. People said suffering was good for the soul. Did being in love count as suffering? *Was* she in love? Or was she just lonely? She tended to think the latter, because she was on her own so much. Leah was busy juggling two men, Carl and Darrel. And her painting was moving ahead furiously. She put in long hours at the barn. When she came home, she looked both joyous and spent.

As the afternoon wore on, the drawing changed. The woman now had a body that enclosed a partially formed figure, perhaps a fetus that failed to develop and which her body never rejected, or one she could have gotten rid of but chose to keep.

Even with both electric heaters, the cold of the garage became too much, and Maggie went across the driveway to the house. The air had the sharp, silvery smell that meant more snow was on the way. There were no lights on at Mrs. Culver's apartment. Maggie stopped in the day before to see if the son had bought food. He'd put in bread, milk, a head of lettuce, and some frozen meals.

Maggie knocked on the door. There was no answer. She called out. She heard nothing. She went upstairs and took the spare key from the magnetized hook on the refrigerator and came back down. She dreaded what she might find.

"Mrs. Culver?"

She went room to room. The place was empty. A coat hung on a hook in the hall, a woman's coat, not very new, and not particularly warm. Had there been another, heavier one that Mrs. Culver put on when she left? But the son said she never went out. Maybe he came and got her. Wouldn't he have said something to her or Leah if that were the case?

The son didn't answer his phone. Maggie left a message. He called her back a minute later.

"What do you mean, she's not in the house?" he asked. He sounded breathless, as if he'd just climbed several flights of stairs.

"The apartment was dark, so I took the key and went in. She's not there."

"Did you look in the bathroom?"

"Yes."

"Did you look under the bed?"

"What? No."

He paused. Then he said he was on his way.

Maggie went up to her apartment to wait. She stared out the picture window at the darkening sky. The carved pumpkins on the porch across the street were lit. Halloween was a week off. She was pulled back to her childhood, to cheap costumes held together with safety pins. Some years, she and Marta went as different characters. Some years, they went as the same one. Since they moved a lot, and lived in several different neighborhoods, their resemblance often drew startled comments from the people who opened their doors.

"How on earth does your mother tell you apart?"

"It must be so fun, having someone who looks just like you!"

"Do you ever feel like you're not a whole person, because you're twins?"

That last was asked by an old man with trembling hands and sharp eyes. He looked down at them over his bifocals and said the candy he had was left over from the year before, but they were welcome to it. Neither girl spoke, though they helped themselves to a good handful each of what turned out to be incredibly stale M&M's.

Kyle had texted her just the day before to see if she wanted to come to the city for Halloween. She could stay at his place if she wanted, because Edgar was making himself scarce now. His message also said that he didn't think they were going to be together that much longer, and that sucked because the sex was good.

She couldn't go back this soon. The urban pull might overwhelm her. She didn't want to be in Sullivan then, either, which left the obvious choice of going home to Dunston. Of the three options, that was the worst.

Leah returned from the barn in a bad mood. Darrel was being a butt. She'd let it slip that she was seeing Carl, too, and he got all pissy about it.

"What did you expect?" Maggie asked. She was still glued to the window, and Leah asked what was up. Maggie told her about Mrs. Culver.

"She just took off?"

"Looks like."

"Oh, man. You were right about her needing to be put in a home."

Leah flopped down disgruntledly on the couch. She asked Maggie if there were anything to drink around. Maggie brought her a beer. She got herself one, too.

"Anything up besides Mrs. Culver?" Leah asked after a long draw on the bottle.

Maggie said she'd been thinking about Halloween. Last year she and Marta went out as Tweedledee and Tweedledum. Their outfits were hot, and hard to move around in. But they had a blast. This year, she had no idea what to do or even if she wanted to dress up.

"We could have people over," Leah said.

"You mean Darrel and Carl."

"I bet I could round up a few others."

They heard Mrs. Culver's son in the apartment downstairs, calling out, "Mom? Mom?"

"I'll go," Maggie said.

Jack Culver was a large man with a wide, sorrowful face. Sawdust covered his heavy jacket. A pair of thick canvas gloves dangled from one pocket.

Maggie asked if there were someone he could call, a friend of his mother's, someone she might have decided to go visit.

"She lost touch with most of her friends after my father died," he said.

Maggie nodded. "Even so, did she keep an address book anywhere? A list of phone numbers?"

"Maybe in her dresser."

Maggie went into the bedroom. The dresser held underwear, stockings, and a few scarves. The jewelry on top was coated with dust. So was the nightstand, and the small ceramic lamp which stood on it. Clearly Jack had overlooked the necessity of getting the place cleaned on a regular basis, but that cost money and he obviously didn't have much. That's why there were no home care workers around. But surely Mrs. Culver must be on Medicare, which would provide something.

Maggie looked dolefully at Mrs. Culver's costume jewelry—a broach with green stones; a bracelet with black stones; a bracelet with plastic pearls. Organizing someone else's life was no easy task. Her own mother was a master at it.

Jack sat on the couch in the living room, looking at his cell phone. When he looked up, Maggie shook her head.

"Maybe you should call the police. She could be wandering around, and it's cold out there," she said.

He nodded.

"They said this might happen," he said.

"Who?"

"Her doctor. The nurse. The last time I took her in. She's got Alzheimer's."

"I figured. She really shouldn't be living alone."

"She did great for a while. Lately, though . . . well, you know." He sighed. "Thing is, Pop made me promise to keep her at home."

"How long has he been gone?"

"Five . . . no, six years."

Maggie joined him on the couch. He smelled of freshly cut wood.

"She went downhill after that. People didn't come around. They'd all been his friends, really," he said.

"What did he do?"

"Ran the feed store. Everyone loved him."

His mother was a loner, he said. She got that way after his brother died, but that was before he was born, so he'd had to take on faith what other people told him. The death of a child is so hard on people, they say. Especially on the mother, though he was pretty sure his father suffered his share, too. Only he probably didn't show it. He was that

182

way, you know, brave face on everything. Always smiling, being pleasant. You had to be that way when you worked with the public. That's probably why he, himself, worked in a lumber yard. No one to bother you, just filling the orders, helping people get their wood in the truck. He left the sales part to the guys inside. He wasn't what you'd call sociable. Debbie, his ex-wife, said he wasn't fit for society. What did being fit for society ever do for anyone? That's what he wanted to know.

"So, it's basically just you and your mother," Maggie said.

At this, Jack's eyes welled.

"Call the police," Maggie said.

A car pulled up in front of the house. Both Maggie and Jack looked to see who it was. A middle-aged man got out and went around to the passenger side. He opened her door and helped Mrs. Culver out of the seat. Jack went down the stairs to meet them.

The man said he found her outside the grocery store looking a little worse for wear. He lent her his jacket, a puffy blue parka that made her look like a little girl, Maggie thought, watching from the porch. The man recognized her because he remembered Jack Culver's father, and figured she'd gotten lost. She didn't know her address, but it was easy enough to look up. Smart phones were great things, he said, especially if you had a decent data plan. Anyway, here she was, home safe and sound, and probably wanting a good, hot meal.

The man reclaimed his coat. Jack Culver took his mother's arm and led her up the stairs. She had on the same dress Maggie had drawn her in the other day. On her feet she wore bedroom slippers. The right one had lost its bow. She didn't look cold, but her teeth chattered. Maggie went to the bedroom, opened the closet, and found a thick gray sweater.

Jack stared at the sweater for a moment before putting his mother in it. It had been his father's, he said, and it was just sort of a shock to realize that she'd kept it. He supposed he should check around for more of his clothes, because what earthly good would they be to anyone now?

"You can donate them if they're in decent shape," Maggie said.

At the sound of her voice, Mrs. Culver focused on her. "I went to get Oreos for Jerry, but they were out."

"Come on, Mom, let's get you a nice, hot cup of tea."

"I'll make it," Maggie said.

"No, that's alright."

Jack seemed to want to be rid of her now. That was okay. She'd done her duty.

He led his mother into the kitchen, then walked Maggie to the front door.

"Jerry was your father?" she asked.

"My brother."

"Oh."

"They say with Alzheimer's you can remember things that happened decades ago, but not something that happened in the last ten minutes."

"Must be hard."

"For sure."

Maggie left them alone and returned upstairs. Leah was taking a shower and singing her head off.

Maggie's phone showed a call from Marta, but no message. She called back. Marta didn't answer until the fifth ring. She didn't say what had kept her.

"How are things there?" Maggie asked.

"Fine. Boring. When are you coming back?"

"I don't know."

"Okay, forget I asked."

Maggie said she was working hard on a new project. Marta said she'd had dinner with their father, and that he seemed fine. Oh, she also got a job at Rosie the Riveter.

"Really? A job?" Maggie asked.

"Yup."

"How's Josh?"

"Being an asshole."

"What?"

"Long story. Suffice it to say, I don't see much of him these days."

Maggie asked if she had any plans for Halloween. Marta was getting into vintage in a big way and wanted to put together a forties-themed costume. If only she could find a dress like the one Rita Hayworth wore in *Gilda*. But, strapless in this weather? Maggie said it could be cool, no pun intended.

"So, listen, the reason I called, something super strange happened today. Well, maybe not so strange, given this is New York City, but when I came home there was this old lady just sitting on the front stairs, looking totally out of it and lost. She was wearing a sweatshirt and sweatpants and asked me where Morris had gone. I asked who Morris was, thinking maybe he was a dog or a cat. But Morris was her husband, it turned out."

"Yeah?"

"I called the police, and they said they were already looking for her. She'd wandered away from her apartment and her daughter was frantic."

"Hard to see you as a good Samaritan."

"I know, right? But I couldn't just leave her there. She looked so sad."

I'm glad you called.

I know. Me too.

"Anyhow, that's all," Marta said.

"Okay, later."

Leah emerged, dressed in jeans and a blue turtleneck she got at Goodwill. She asked if everything were cool downstairs, and Maggie said someone found Mrs. Culver and brought her home. She wanted to tell her about the phone call with Marta and knew it would sound completely nuts. Leah said they should order Chinese again, if that were okay. Maggie said sure, she was pretty hungry.

chapter twenty-two

Monique called to say that Clarisse's recuperation was going to take a while, and that she was going to manage both stores during the interim but spend most of her time over at The Purple Hat. She needed someone to be on hand at Rosie the Riveter for about fifteen hours a week. Was Marta interested? Marta said she didn't have any retail experience.

"It doesn't matter," Monique said. "You know all about vintage clothes and could probably charm the skin off a snake."

Marta didn't know what to make of that. She thought she'd been straightforward, pinching the scarf notwithstanding. But, Monique didn't know about that. Her comment must be based on some put-on air she detected when Marta was flouncing around, talking about selling war bonds. Well, okay, so what? She was an actress after all, wasn't she?

Monique said if she were interested, to be at the store at eleven the following morning.

After only an hour on the job, Marta was bored out of her mind. No wonder she'd never had any desire to work behind a counter before. Of course, she'd spent very little time behind this one. Instead, she prowled through the dress racks, which upon close inspection, proved not to be very interesting. There were too many items from the 1970s and afterwards. Granted, the World War Two era outfits that Marta loved were hard to come by. She supposed you had to show up at estate sales or retirement homes after someone died, and hope they'd kept their favorite things, stored them lovingly, and their heirs were now willing to let them go for a song. How often did that happen? Maybe Marta should expand her horizons, open herself to the era of Diane Von Furstenberg, disco, *Saturday Night Fever*. When Clarisse got back on her feet, the tableau in her window could jump forward a few decades.

Over the next two hours, only three people wandered in. One woman bought a Coach handbag from the eighties; the other two just touched everything, held up a couple of dresses in front of the three-way mirror at the back, and didn't take Marta's suggestion that they try them on.

Josh texted, asking if she wanted to go for drinks later. She hadn't heard from him for four days, so she held off replying.

Her mother called and left a message saying she'd heard that Potter had come down for dinner, and she hoped it went well. Her mother liked to gather intelligence on her ex-husband's activities, and Marta was pretty sure in this case, as usual, she wanted to get a sense of how much he was drinking.

Timothy texted just to check in. She hadn't heard anything from her younger brother, Foster, in over a month, but then he was the most reclusive of them all.

Around one thirty, she locked up the place and went down to the deli on the corner for a sandwich. She wore a jumpsuit she'd taken from the store, with a flashy scarf tied around her head. Her image in the mirror right before she left the store was so perfectly Cheryl Tiegs she wondered if she could be a fashion consultant to anyone putting on a play needing period costumes. The idea of getting an inside position with a director or theater struck her as genius, and she didn't know why she hadn't thought of it before.

On her way back up the sidewalk, moving fast because of the cold, she stopped short when she saw Luis peering through the glass door of the shop. She fell back to their night together, something she'd thought about quite a lot.

She slowed her pace a bit to give her time to think, though the few seconds she gained didn't yield any worthy insights.

"What brings you to this corner of the world?" she asked. He turned and looked at her shyly.

"I wanted to talk to you," he said.

"How did you know where I'd be?"

"Maggie."

"You lost me."

He'd called Maggie that morning and asked how he could find her. She said she just got a job here.

"Why didn't you get my number from her and just call me?" Marta asked.

"I wasn't too nice to her on the phone the other day, and thought I better cut it short."

Marta unlocked the door. They went in.

The only place to sit was in a tiny room Monique used for her office. Two metal chairs were placed close together in front of a folding card table covered with papers and pens. On top of a file cabinet was a dead cactus. The fluorescent light overhead buzzed quietly.

She offered Luis half of her roast beef sandwich. He'd just eaten. He took off his heavy denim jacket. His T-shirt was splattered with paint in a variety of colors.

"So, I've been thinking . . ." he said.

"Yeah, it was wrong, and I'm sorry. I'm a shit for not coming clean, but I had a lot to drink, and then in the morning I had no idea how to explain." A piece of lettuce fell on the front of her jumpsuit. She'd neglected to grab some napkins on her way out of the deli. She brushed the lettuce onto the linoleum floor.

"I'm not here because I think you're a shit. Though I was plenty pissed after Maggie called me, like I said."

His hands were splattered, too. Maggie's hands often looked that way. Marta used to wonder why she didn't just wash up at the studio. Probably for the same reason Luis hadn't today. They were both used to the feel of paint on their skin.

The truth was, he didn't get along well with women as a rule. To be honest, he was shy around them. On some level, they probably terrified him. At this, Marta's eyebrows shot up. She had trouble seeing women as terrifying. Annoying, yes. Inconvenient, no doubt.

"They always seem in such control," Luis said.

"I take it you don't have any sisters, or close female friends."

"Only brothers. And I was pretty close with Leah before she quit the studio."

"And Maggie?"

He crossed his arms.

"We got along okay," he said.

"You had a crush on her, obviously."

"Yeah."

He looked embarrassed then, almost as if he wished he could just get up and leave. Yet, he stayed.

He wanted to get to the point. Did Marta want to see him again, and take things at a normal pace?

She wrapped up what was left of her sandwich in the white paper it came in and put it on the table by her elbow.

"You might be disappointed when you find out I'm not just like Maggie."

"Oh, I know you're not. You're actually very different."

She asked how he could possibly tell. They'd barely spent any time together.

"Well, call it a hunch, then."

"If you say so."

Could he make her dinner some time that week?

"Come to my place," she said. "I'll throw something together."

They hugged. She liked how he felt up close. She didn't want to let go. He stepped back and asked what day would be good.

"Friday?" she asked.

"Okay."

"Seven?"

"Sure."

She walked him out.

She took out a tray of costume jewelry, rearranged the pieces by finish and stone color, and put it back in the case. She reached in and helped herself to a large, fake gold bangle, and slipped it on her wrist.

She looked at her phone. There were no new texts or messages. She thought there might be something from Maggie, wanting a follow-up on Luis, or alerting her that he was trying to find her. Marta could let her know that they were officially going out. Maggie would be happy for her, wouldn't she?

A young guy came in wanting to look at plaid skirts. He was in a very sixties mood today, he said.

"It's cold out, you'll want tights, or a good pair of leggings," Marta said.

"You're a dear."

Marta could only find one skirt in plaid. It was a size ten. The guy was skinny enough to carry it off. As he stood before the mirror, turning from one side to another, Marta's eye was drawn down to his white, hairy shins.

In the end, he didn't want the skirt and chose instead a yellow sweater with a picture of a palm tree on the back. He put it on and struck a silly pose before the mirror, with his hands on his hips and his butt stuck out. He removed the sweater and handed it to her.

"I bet you're an actor," Marta said as she put the sweater in a paper bag with handles and the store's name written in cheerful green script.

"Paralegal. But I wanted to act, once."

"No good parts?"

"Couldn't afford to wait and find out."

No other customers came in that afternoon, and Marta's acute boredom returned.

Just before four o'clock, Rob called. Had she been looking at *Playbill*? There was a part she might be perfect for. She hung up and used her phone to access the website.

As usual, most were only for people who could sing or dance. The one Rob must have meant caught her eye, a serious drama about a young man who is seriously injured in a car accident and lies in a coma, visited by his girlfriend. The girlfriend is a strong person, but the stress she faces causes her to unravel. The actress playing the girlfriend should be between 25 and 29. Marta's heart quickened. To audition, she needed to prepare a short contemporary monologue. Auditions would be held that Friday, two days away. She hadn't had to do this for a while, since the parts she'd gotten before had been aided by an advance copy of the script, and knowing what scene was to be read onstage.

On a small pad of paper, she wrote key words: *death, coma, loss, longing, grief, guilt,* and *rage.* She considered each in depth. She sat in the office and scratched out one long paragraph, set the timer on her phone, and read it aloud. The text took only two minutes to read. Three minutes would be better. It struck her what short attention spans directors had. Then again, if she had to listen to thirty people read in one day, she'd want them to keep it short, too.

She called Rob back. Did he have time to listen to what she'd put together? He said he probably could. She could swing by the theater later if it weren't too much trouble.

She put the clothes she'd worn to work in her oversized shoulder bag. She closed the shop a few minutes early. Monique had asked her to slip the key back through the mail slot. She strode off in the jumpsuit she'd had on all day, and which she now believed was an amulet of good luck. The sleeve of her jacket pressed uncomfortably against the bangle, but she didn't mind.

The first cab she hailed stopped. Traffic was light, and they hit all the green lights.

Rob was waiting for her in the empty lobby. Rehearsal was over for the day. He'd gone down to the coffee shop on the corner a few minutes before and gotten them each an Americano. He remembered that she took both cream and sugar and hoped that hadn't changed.

"I owe you one. Not just for the coffee, but also the heads up about the part," she said.

"Forget it. Least I can do, after *Delta Damsel* fell through."

"I probably wasn't right for it, anyway."

They went into the auditorium. They draped their jackets on the back of two seats in the front row. Rob admired the jumpsuit and told her she had a real *Charlie's Angels* thing going on.

"Worst show ever," Marta said.

"I loved Farah Fawcett."

"She died a couple of years ago."

"Yeah, all over the news."

Marta put her coffee cup on the floor. She went up on stage, where the music stand had been replaced by a simple wooden table with a silver candlestick holding a two-inch candle stub. Next to this was a small glass pot of ink and a feather quill. There was no writing paper on the desk. If you wanted to depict someone wanting to compose a letter and discovering that an essential item were missing, wouldn't you leave out ink instead? Then she remembered reading somewhere that paper was in very short supply in the South during the Civil War, so maybe this omission was both clever and accurate. Would the audience notice and appreciate that? Or was it too subtle? It depended entirely on the scene. The actor would have to note the absence of the paper, and exclaim over it sorrowfully, ruefully, even angrily. That missing paper could motivate an entire soliloquy about everything else that had disappeared, never to return.

"Ready when you are," Rob said. He sat directly below her, legs crossed. He looked completely in possession of himself. Clearly, he'd gained a lot of confidence working on *Delta Damsel.*

Marta cleared her head. She summoned a sterile hospital room where a comatose accident victim lay connected to tubes, a respirator that rhythmically hissed and whooshed. The light falling on the face was harsh and bright. She turned to give the audience her profile. She stretched out her hands to suggest that she'd put them on the end of the invisible bed.

"You never listen. I told you that was a dangerous stretch of road, especially when it's icy. You always took it too fast, even in winter. It's like it was a test. But of what? Your nerve? You have plenty of that already. The way you pushed back at every bully in school. Facing down your art teacher who said you didn't have enough talent to make it. You've always been much stronger than you think. What did you need with a wild patch of country road?"

She paused, brought her hands to her face to indicate being momentarily awash in overwhelming grief, then let them drop slackly at her sides.

"Were you angry about what I said at dinner? That he'd never love you the way he loved me? Is that why you were going sixty, to put the miles between us as fast as you could? Don't you know there will never be miles between us, not really? Not even now, because I know you can hear me somehow. You can always hear me."

She turned her back to the audience. The heaving of her shoulders meant she was sobbing silently. The shoulders stilled, and she straightened her miserable posture into one of fierce resolution. She faced the bed once more.

"To lose a sister is a terrible thing. To lose a twin sister, more terrible still. How can I live in this world without the one who shared my mother's womb? You're a crucial part of me. In fact, you *are* me, and I, you."

She hadn't written those words at all, yet once on stage, other words just came. It was established canon that one should probe one's own life experience in order to summon authentic emotion, but this was involuntary, the voice of her own subconscious, proving she was more upset about Maggie's departure than she realized.

Rob gently reminded her that the character in the bed was male, not female.

"It won't matter. They just want to get a sense of my acting," she said.

"Which was remarkable."

"Yeah?"

"Absolutely."

She clambered off the stage and went back to sipping her coffee. Rob looked at her closely. She didn't meet his eye. Her tears were spontaneous, not forced. She couldn't answer any questions just then and was grateful that Rob asked none.

chapter twenty-three

Josh wanted to tell her in person, but couldn't wait, so he called. He was on his own now, he said more than once. Maggie asked him to clarify. He wasn't seeing Marta "that way." Also, there'd been changes to his trust fund, and he was now completely in charge of it. The first statement was important. The second, far less. But it was the second that changed everything, he said. He'd decided: he was going to LA and wanted Maggie to come with him.

If it hadn't been snowing, she might have hesitated. She might also have hesitated on the grounds that her work was going well, and she didn't want to jinx anything by uprooting herself again. Yet, it was the fact of her work's relative success that won the argument. She figured if she could create beautifully in a freezing, dull place like Sullivan, what wouldn't be possible in the sun and sand of LA?

And if they didn't get off the ground romantically? He said it didn't matter, they could just be roommates.

"Do you think this is crazy?" he asked.

"Completely."

That, he said, was a recipe for success.

They'd fly out and find a place. He'd cover the rent. She didn't know what to do about her paintings. He said to pack them for shipping, and to leave money with Leah so she could send them on later. He'd call her again tomorrow when he had the tickets lined up. She said she'd reimburse him for hers. He paused and said that was fine. He kissed the phone and hung up.

For a moment she panicked about what she'd just agreed to do. Her hands shook. Leah was out, which was good, because Leah had a way of asking blunt questions that would make her jitter even more.

She wondered about the minivan. She should sell it. She could go down to the used car lot and take the best offer. She liked the idea of having a cash reserve.

She drank a glass of water and called home. When her mother picked up, Maggie came right to the point. Her voice was calm and light, and listening to herself, she realized how happy she truly was. Her mother said it was sudden, given that she only recently arrived in Sullivan. Were things not going well there? Maggie said everything was cool. Her mother wanted to know how she was likely to feel being that much farther away from her sister, and if she'd come back at Christmas. Maggie didn't know. She thought maybe Josh's mother would want him home or come there to see him (which Maggie didn't relish one bit). At that, her mother said the idea of getting some sun had definite appeal, and she was sure Chip would love some SoCal golf time. Maggie's slowness in answering caused her mother to say they'd just have to wait and see.

Her mother asked how she was going to handle the rent. Maggie said Josh had offered to take care of that.

"Is he very important to you?" her mother asked.

"Not as important as he could end up being."

"Good answer."

Her mother said she'd miss her. Maggie was taken aback. Her mother was not a sentimental person. She told Maggie if she needed to go over her monthly stipend a little to cover moving expenses to let her know, but it shouldn't be by too much. Sometimes Chip raised his eyebrows when he went over the bank statement. Maggie said to give her love to everyone, including Alma. She'd call when she had an address. In the interim, she could be found on her cell phone, as always.

She called Marta with the news. Marta asked if she'd lost her mind.

"You barely know the guy," she said. There was noise in the background, and Maggie thought she was probably in a bar.

"But you do."

"So?"

"So you think he's all right? Not some nutcase."

"Ha! I'd never he say he wasn't a nutcase, but you're right, he's basically harmless."

You're not jealous, are you?

Trying not to be, but in truth, it wasn't working out between us.

The silent dialogue faded for a moment, but Maggie sensed some joy from her and asked what was good these days.

"Might have a part. I'm auditioning on Friday."

"Cool."

"When are you leaving?"

"Not sure. Early next week."

That's coming up fast. You sure you know what you're doing?

How can I be? Just have to wait and see.

"How did Mom take it?" Marta asked.

"Fine. She wants to bring Chip out."

"Jesus. Hope she'll change her mind."

"You can come out, though."

Now we'll be even farther apart.

I know.

"I'll bring Luis."

"O-M-G!"

"Yup."

Marta said maybe they could have a relationship. It was probably worth a try, anyway. Maggie hesitated, then admitted to herself that she'd never had any feelings for

Luis, and if he could make Marta happy, that's all that mattered.

"I'll check in before I leave," Maggie said.

"Okay."

Her call to Kyle went right to voicemail. She left a cheerful message that began with, "Guess what?"

The twilight fell in purple shades. The snow stopped, and clouds sped, revealing early evening stars. She texted Angie, Timothy, and Foster about her plans. The text to her father got an immediate one back asking if everything were okay.

Yes, Dad. Totally cool!

Can you make it down to Dunston before you leave?

Doubtful.

I can come out on Saturday, take you to b-fast? Maybe bring Angie?

Sure.

The next three days were frustrating. Kyle called back, begging her to change her mind. He was lonely, his job was terrible, he didn't know what to do with himself, and Edgar was being a jerk. Then he got another call and had to go. She hoped he was talking to someone who could both indulge his drama and afford his taste in everything. Then she felt bad for being cynical. Kyle had been a good friend to her, and she'd miss him.

Next, selling the car wasn't as easy as she thought it would be. There wasn't much of a market for used minivans in Sullivan. People preferred either small sedans or SUVs. The man at the used car lot said this slowly, carefully, as if she were a child who couldn't grasp basic facts. He offered her two thousand dollars less than she paid for it. It was late on Friday afternoon, and by the time his mechanic finished going over everything, and the title was transferred, and the cashier's check was prepared, it was too late to get to the bank. She'd have to wait until they got to LA. Josh had gotten tickets for a flight that Sunday out of Syracuse. They would have to change planes in Pittsburgh. He was going to rent a car and come get her around noon. The flight left at five fifteen p.m. She should be ready for a long day.

On Saturday she sorted her paintings, so that when they arrived in LA they'd be in some kind of rational order. They were spread out all over the small living room. Leah was by turns supportive and cynical. She lurked moodily behind the closed door of her bedroom, then sat on the couch and did her nails.

"You'll be back. LA's full of dipshits," she said.

"So is New York. Sullivan probably is, too. I haven't been around long enough to say."

Leah looked over the top of her pale blue toenails. Her eyes held a touch of regret.

"Thank you for letting me stay here," Maggie said.

"No problem."

Mrs. Culver had been moved into Hillside, the local nursing home. Jack was at the house earlier that day, trying to organize her things and probably not doing a great job of it. He came up to their apartment and told Leah he might sell the house but had no immediate plans to. It wasn't a question of money, really. He finally paid off the loan that made the upstairs conversion possible. His gaze wandered, then returned with a keen light. He just realized that Leah was sleeping in the room he'd had as a boy. Wasn't that something? Leah responded with kind, gentle words, and looked beyond him to where Maggie stood in the kitchen, heating herself a can of soup. When he left, Leah collapsed in a fit of giggles Maggie found forced. Leah felt sorry for him and didn't want to say so.

When she caught Leah looking at her again, Maggie said, "I owe you big time."

"It was just a bedroom. Don't get carried away."

"That not what I mean."

"I figured."

"I still don't know why it was so easy for you to let it go."

Leah recapped her polish. She blew on her fingernails. "It wasn't easy. But you were so unhappy, I just couldn't get up in your face about it."

Unhappy?

"I was fine. I'm fine," Maggie said.

Leah stared her down.

"Running out on your sister; now running off with her boyfriend."

"He's not her boyfriend. He never was."

"If you say so." Leah shrugged, picked up her polish, and went back to her room.

The breakfast with Potter got pushed back to lunch, then to dinner, because he couldn't get away. Just after six he called to say he was out front with Angie.

In the car he said a client was flipping out because the wrong size cabinets had gone in her bathroom. Mary Beth was up in arms, no way in hell she miscalculated. She knew how to use a tape measure. The cabinet shop was at fault. No question about it.

Angie's day had been bad, too. The retirement home faced a lawsuit from a resident's family, alleging abuse and neglect. The woman had died a few months before. She'd been a difficult person, refusing to be bathed, have her sheets changed, or her clothes washed. Angie found it interesting that in one's dotage and decline, sometimes a fierce spirit moved in and fought tooth and nail over everything.

Maggie hoped for the French bistro on the corner, but Potter said he heard there was a good Mexican place out on the highway just a bit. Maggie had been there with Leah just the evening before. She didn't mention it.

As Angie dug into the guacamole, she gave some advice she really hoped Maggie would take to heart. Acting on impulse was okay if the risk of disaster were small. Say she went out and spent four hundred dollars on a new purse she ended up not really liking. What was the consequence? The four hundred dollars. Now, to some people, that might be a considerable figure, but given their mother's . . . *generosity*, the consequence was nonexistent.

Moving across the country with a man she barely knew was entirely different, as Maggie must be aware.

"Of course, she's aware. She's not stupid," Potter said, enjoying his margarita with gusto.

Angie nodded in a small gesture of deference. She was fiercely loyal to her father, probably because she'd always been his favorite.

"If it doesn't work out, I'll do something else," Maggie said.

"You live in a floating world."

"What's that supposed to mean?"

"You do things and never suffer the consequences."

"That's not true!"

"No? What about that painting you ruined? Your friend just let you off the hook. She let you move in with her, in fact, right? It's as if she condones your animal behavior."

"Animal behavior?"

"Girls. Take it easy. This is a friendly dinner, we're having," Potter said.

"Tell *her* that," Maggie said.

Angie admitted that Leah's motivations were none of her business. That said, Maggie managed to get around people without even trying.

"Maybe I'm a witch," Maggie said.

Potter held up his hand. Everyone ate in silence for a few minutes.

"You have more influence than you know, that's all I'm saying," Angie said.

"Are you suggesting that I unfairly influenced Josh into inviting me to go to California with him?"

Angie had clearly considered this.

"I'm just some manipulative twit, is that it?" Maggie asked.

"No."

Angie said this situation had high risks and might have a bad outcome. She just wanted her to understand that.

"Because you care for me so deeply," Maggie said. She'd barely touched her food.

Her biting tone made Potter once again hold up his hand. Then he asked for the check. Did Maggie want to box her meal and bring it home?

"No," she said.

She didn't speak a word on the way back to her place, nor when she got out of the car. Before she closed the door, Angie apologized for being so hard on her. Maggie kept her silence. It was by far the best response she could make.

chapter twenty-four

They were used to New York City rents, so the price for the tiny house in Venice didn't shock. The realtor wore a silver jumpsuit and high heels that immediately reminded Maggie of the outfits her mother was keen on around the time she decided to leave her father. Women in LA had long hair, and Maggie's bob felt out of place. They spent two nights at a hotel after arriving and slept in separate beds. She didn't know if that would change or not. She wasn't focused on that, but on the new bright, warm place she found herself in, and what being there would mean for her work.

The house had a screened-in back porch that looked over a tiny yard separated from the neighbors by a brick wall draped with fiery red bougainvillea. Maggie claimed it for her studio. Josh wanted the second bedroom for his office. Each bedroom had a double bed. If things didn't evolve between them—and it was fine, either way, he said—he'd just use that room to both sleep and work in. Maggie said that wasn't fair. He was picking up the rent, after all. A corner of the living room could be converted to an office. Depending on how much privacy he required when he was writing, of course. She wouldn't bother him. They settled on sharing the porch. In his end they put a table, bookcase, and chair. On her end, a new easel and some canvases; also pastels, watercolors, several tubes of oil paint, and a tarp to protect the floor, which was already badly worn but didn't need further damage. He said two people sharing a work space were almost as close as two people sharing a bed. She let him kiss her. While lovely, her mind was elsewhere, on the positive energy she sensed from Marta, an orange glow, a color Marta never wore but one that brought her fully to mind. Their most recent exchange had been on the day Maggie arrived.

Made it to LA.

Congrats!

Even though the house came furnished, Josh wanted to buy a new sofa. Maggie thought he was being extravagant. He looked hurt when she said this, so she quickly added that she'd love to go shopping with him. She hoped he wasn't the kind of person who needed constant soothing and shoring up.

He liked leather, she preferred fabric. The pale blue he wanted wasn't in stock and would take twelve weeks to arrive from Italy. He looked at her as if to ask if she'd still be living there then.

She said it was a lovely color. In truth, it was too green.

They slept together the second night, and Josh moved into the larger bedroom she already occupied.

She might be falling in love. Why didn't she know for sure?

Because you're scared.

Her last serious affair had ended very badly. Jordan Case was a fellow art student who could sculpt as well as he painted. His abstract figures were inexplicably lovely. He smoothed and shaped them until the clay felt like silk. His canvases were joyous, mad rings of color and line. As a person, he was neurotic. His hand always seemed to find the glands in his throat, and he palpated them incessantly. Once, Maggie found him in her bathroom examining his scalp, parting his hair row by row. She asked him if he'd ever had lice. The question was poorly received. He told her she was shallow and would never amount to anything as an artist. He said beautiful people were worthless, because they were only decorative. She hurled an ashtray at him—he also smoked two packs of cigarettes a day and coughed riotously first thing in the morning. He relented, apologized, said he couldn't live without her. It was Marta who told her to get rid of him.

"Who needs that toxic shit?" she'd asked.

The pain of his insults lasted a long time. Her self-esteem had never been good. She blamed her mother and Angie for that. Also, Marta, though she preferred not to dwell on that now, with the distance of the country between them. She liked to think she'd grown up a lot since Jordan, that she was steadier on her feet. Her work proved it, she thought.

The faceless woman wore her hair in a variety of sixties styles—a Mary Tyler Moore flip; a French Twist; lastly enhanced with a luscious fall. She wore mini dresses; boots that climbed past her knees; a pantsuit. Josh asked what the time capsule was all about. Maggie panicked when she realized the vintage look might not resonate with people.

She started over. The faceless woman was naked. Her breasts were mere curves, her pubic hair a pale smudge. Josh asked why her sexuality was being denied. Maggie asked him please to let her work, and refrain from commenting. He sat down at his end. The rapid tapping on his keyboard was punctuated by long stretches of silence during which Maggie wondered if he were watching her. She maintained her focus.

The undeveloped fetus reappeared in a number of sketches. Its expression was either peaceful or terrified. Either it didn't mind its state of perpetual malformation or it hated it. The faceless woman—who should be thought of as something else now, since her face was well-wrought and compelling—appeared unaware of its presence.

"Nina," Maggie said.

"Who?"

"The woman I'm painting."

"Why Nina?"

Maggie said it was just a name that came to mind, a kind of alter ego, someone she might have been in a past life.

"That's not an alter ego. That's who you're reincarnated from," Josh said.

"Oh, who cares? You know what I mean."

He didn't really, but he let it go.

In the afternoons, the porch became too warm, and they moved inside. The living room had a ceiling fan they were glad for. Both remarked how hot it was for late October and recalled the chill misery of New York.

Leah called to say Jack Culver had asked for Maggie's phone number because he thought she was a real sweetie, not to mention quite a cutie, and wondered if she would go out with him. He was disappointed to learn that Maggie had moved away. He said he supposed that the difference in their ages would have wrecked any chance he might have had with her. Leah offered him a cup of tea, but he said he had to get going.

That evening Maggie and Josh walked on the beach. Holding hands felt more intimate than having sex. Maggie wondered about the power of hands to communicate and thought her work's focus on faces might need to shift.

The roller skaters were out in force. The men were shirtless; the woman in shorts; everyone in sunglasses. Some soared by with a galloping dog on a leash. One man had a backpack with a wide-eyed tabby cat peeking out.

The souvenir stalls caught Maggie's eye. She led Josh over to one. She was after a T-shirt. She'd remember it always as the first article of clothing she bought in California.

She rejected one that said, "LA is for Lovers," and was drawn to another with a picture of the pier at Santa Monica. The perspective was off, and she put it back. There was a stack of tie-dyes, a style she normally didn't care for because the designs were always too random, but one had only two colors, red and purple. This made sense to her. Simple was often better. She bought it.

"You're a strange creature," Josh said. He kissed her neck. She put a few inches between them. She'd never been much for public displays of affection.

"But adorable?" she asked.

"Definitely adorable."

A volleyball game was in progress a short distance away. The players, both men and women, were tanned and fit. Maggie felt her pallor and wondered how long it would take her skin to bronze.

Josh said he'd been on the volleyball team in high school and was pretty good. He'd perfected his serve. Maybe one evening he'd wander down here and see if anyone would let him play. Maggie thought of having the house to herself and said it sounded like a great idea.

As they continued to meander down the beach, he was drawn further back into his high school years. That's when the love of theater really took hold, he said. He and his mother would go up to the city and see whatever was new. After a while, his mother told him to go alone. She was a suburbanite at heart. His friends weren't really interested, but his English teacher was, Mr. Monsen, a crusty old widower who admired some of Josh's early attempts on the page. Mr. Monsen went with him a couple of times but insisted on buying his own ticket. Afterwards, they drank coffee before taking the train back to Montclair. Once, Mr. Monsen put his hand on Josh's knee, and to be honest, Josh thought he handled it with, what's that word, *aplomb*.

It occurred to Maggie that these were all things Marta must already know about him. They stopped to watch the sun drop into the sea. Josh told her to look for the green flash at the exact moment of its disappearance. She looked at him instead. Something yielded in her, and she put her arms around him. He hadn't expected the embrace but returned it forcefully.

When she woke in the early morning, she recalled the energy of their lovemaking. She slipped silently out of bed, pulled on the tie-dye T-shirt and a pair of yoga pants, and went out to the porch where Nina gazed calmly, perhaps recalling her own recent pleasures.

chapter twenty-five

To steady her nerves, Marta sipped a cup of hot water. She had to keep the steam from her face because her makeup was fresh and flawless. Her clothes were just as carefully chosen. She wore a pair of distressed jeans, a blue suede jacket, and the scarf she'd stolen from Monique, whose eyes, these days, turned sad at the mention of Clarisse.

She arrived at the theater early. Her hands were icy, her pulse rapid and uneven. She wished she'd asked Rob to come with her. Or even Luis, but she'd see him later that evening for their dinner date.

It occurred to her then that if the audition went badly, she wouldn't feel like having him over. She ignored that and focused on how it would feel to stand at the foot of the bed containing someone you loved dearly who would probably never wake up, never speak your name, never again look you in the eye.

The hopeful trickled in one by one, then a group all at once. Some were clearly much older than the part called for. One woman had to be in her sixties, judging from the lines in her face and the pouches below her eyes. Marta recognized the director. She'd read for him the year before, when she auditioned for the role of a middle-aged woman who finds a new lease on life when her husband is crippled by a stroke. She'd given it all she had, just the right blend of fear and courage, but the director, Angus somebody, said she didn't have the proper degree of pathos. When Marta asked what degree that was, he said the kind that came with time.

If he remembered her now, he gave no sign. Each actor got on stage and spoke stirringly of loss, redemption, never losing faith, never giving up hope.

When it was her turn, she improvised once more. The person in the bed was a long-lost friend who had abandoned her. She'd been summoned there by a nurse at the hospital who had found a piece of paper with her name and number in her wallet after the accident.

She put steel in her voice and crossed her arms, as if holding together what remained of her broken spirit.

"I know you can hear me, just as I know you now expect my forgiveness. Well, you won't get it. You'll never get it, even after you've been dead twenty—thirty years. I'm going to live a long time in the world without you, a world vastly improved by your leaving it. I'll put up a shrine on the tree you ran into thanking it for standing firm against your stupid little sports car."

She moved away from the bed and began to pace slowly up and down the stage, clutching and unclutching her hands.

"I'm sorry, that's too harsh. But you must know how your leaving affected me! We were so close, and then you were gone. People don't just leave people for no reason. Okay, you said you felt stale, needed a new start. Fine. I get that. But no word? Your cell phone didn't answer, then the service was discontinued."

Here she stopped and stayed silent a long time. Someone in the audience coughed.

"Yet you kept me in your wallet all this time, so I suppose you assumed that we would see each other again one day. Here we are."

Her voice broke on the last words.

The director thanked her for her efforts. His bland expression said she'd impressed him. This was confirmed when out of the more than twenty actors who auditioned, he told three, including Marta, to return the following week. In the meantime, they were each given a script with a highlighted passage. Each would read it. No variation from the text would be allowed.

Her first thought was to tell Maggie. Somehow, she didn't want to. But why? She'd already told her about the audition. It only made sense to follow up.

Maggie had been her first audience, when they were about five or six. Sometimes she was enlisted to play a supporting role, always someone to aid the heroine in her quest for justice and freedom. The rest of the family was seldom included. The twins were happy to be alone in their own private world.

When Maggie first picked up a colored pencil, did Marta show enthusiasm? She remembered being curious, occasionally critical, once or twice openly hostile. Where had this evil temper come from?

That evening, Luis was polite about the awful food she served him—an overcooked, salty pork chop; brown lettuce with bottled dressing; a side of frozen macaroni and cheese that hadn't gone long enough in the microwave. Parts of his were still hard. He asked if he could look around her kitchen. He was pretty good at whipping up a decent meal with whatever was on hand. He found a fairly fresh clove of garlic and a box of spaghetti. Did she have any olive oil? She thought Maggie had bought some for the roasted chicken she'd made. He found it on the counter next to the toaster.

"It's a good brand," Luis said.

"Do you cook a lot?"

"I have to. Eating out is expensive."

The cutting board was made of green plastic. Marta's mother had bought it for her at a high-end grocery store as a housewarming gift. She found it an odd thing to give someone who was clumsy in the kitchen.

"Maybe she was encouraging you to learn," Luis said.

"I doubt it."

He chopped the garlic carefully. Marta watched his hands. She thought back to how she had paced the stage, wringing her own. She was proud of herself for making it to a second round. She told him about the audition and getting a callback.

"Definitely worth celebrating," he said.

"I'll celebrate when I get the part."

"Celebrate now. Getting a callback's good."

He asked if she had any red pepper flakes. She said to look in the cabinet to the right of the stove.

As he went on making dinner, she asked him about himself. His parents had moved to New York from Puerto Rico just after they were married. All they wanted was to get ahead. He had nothing against that, money made the world go around, but it wasn't for him. So, like everyone else in the world, he waited tables. Before that he worked in a grocery store, drove a forklift around a warehouse, even taught art part-time at a private school on the Upper East Side. His older brother, Carmen, worked on Wall Street. His younger brother, Mario, owned a hair salon. That was enough entrepreneurial talent for one family, right?

Marta described how she'd grown up. Her mother was the only one who made a regular income, and with five kids, money was always tight.

"So, what happened? I mean, this is a nice place you've got here," he said.

"She left my father and married her boss. He was well-off. Still is."

"And he picks up the bill?"

"She makes sure he does."

"No strings attached?"

"Not really."

"Convenient."

Marta said her mother felt guilty.

"About what?" Luis asked.

"Well, it's a little complicated."

"I'm listening."

When they were young, the other three kids got the bulk of her attention. Her mother assumed that being identical twins meant they were a solid unit, and protected each other, *found* protection in each other, to be specific.

"And did you?" Luis asked.

"I guess. But we needed our parents just as much as they did. Eventually, she figured that out."

"So, the money is payment for an earlier neglect."

Marta didn't know. In any case, she didn't want to talk about it anymore. He said that was cool, he understood.

She asked him when he decided to become an artist.

"Probably the first time I picked up a crayon."

She told him she remembered Maggie doing the same thing. Around the same time, she'd discovered how fun it was to act out a story for someone else. It was like . . . leaving yourself behind for a while and finding that you were a little bit different when you returned.

"Interesting," he said.

"Do you feel like that when you work?"

"Sometimes. It's hard, though, because I have to stay super focused on what I'm trying to do."

He served her a plate of spaghetti. It tasted fabulous.

"Well, if the art doesn't pan out, you can always become a chef," she said.

"You sound like my mother."

"I'm assuming that's not a compliment."

"Just a statement of fact."

He wasn't cross. His brown eyes were full of a teasing light, aided no doubt by the good bottle of wine she'd bought.

She said Maggie was moving to California. He shook his head.

"What?" she asked.

"She just moved upstate, didn't she? Now on to somewhere else."

"Restless, I guess."

"Obviously."

She poured them more wine.

She asked if he'd been there that day in the studio when Maggie flung the paint. He'd left by then but remembered her mood had been getting increasingly strange. Marta reckoned that would have been what, four, five weeks before? She hadn't noticed anything out of the ordinary.

"Then the girl whose painting she wrecked let her move in with her," Marta said.

Luis looked up from his plate.

"Your point?" he asked.

"People let her get away with things."

"Leah's no pushover."

"Well, I don't know her, obviously. I'm just going off a long personal history with my own sister."

Then she said she was sorry for being crabby. She must still be on edge from the audition. Luis put their dishes in the sink and said he knew a great way to relieve stress.

He stayed the night and left early in the morning. He wanted to swing by his place and work on one of his canvases for a bit. His shift at the restaurant started at two. Marta had to be at Rosie the Riveter by noon, so it was just as well. She reflected on the evening. It had been good. The company wonderful, the sex spectacular.

She called Rob, told him about the callback, and asked if he could help her prepare. He was in the middle of something and said he'd get back to her soon.

She went to dress. Standing in the closet, it hit her for the first time since Maggie moved out how many clothes she'd left behind. Marta would never do that, but she planned things a little better. Marta was strategic, not impulsive. Of course, her leaving the bar with Luis had been completely impulsive, but then she'd been drinking. Maggie was impulsive drunk or sober (though she was seldom drunk) and seemed to be getting worse: throwing the paint on her friend's canvas; pretending to be Marta and putting the moves on Josh; leaving abruptly for Sullivan; and now, LA.

She looked at the winter clothes, on hangers and folded neatly on the shelves. For all of Maggie's recklessness, she took good care of her things. Marta had always admired the pale blue cashmere sweater. She put it on. She took a smart pair of black leather pants she couldn't remember ever seeing Maggie wear, and sure enough, the price tag was still attached. She ripped the tag off and got into the pants. They were slightly too small. Had she put on weight? Or had Maggie bought them without trying them on, discovered they didn't fit quite right, and failed to return them? Marta picked up the price tag. The pants were from a boutique on Madison. She'd take them over there, say she lost the receipt, and try to exchange them for store credit.

Then it dawned on her—she could sell Maggie's clothes and pocket the cash. If Maggie ever came back, Marta would just tell her that's the price you pay for abandoning someone. But no, that was going too far, even for her.

The Madison boutique refused to give Marta store credit, even after one of her better performances of crying to the manager and timidly accepting the tissue the woman offered, so she took the pants with her back to the Village and Rosie the Riveter. She'd also brought along the script pages to read over and get the feel of. Monique texted her to ask that she re-arrange the clothes into something more inviting. The only way to do that, Marta thought, was to sort everything by color, in the sequence of a rainbow, which she couldn't remember until she looked it up on her phone.

Though the day was cold, the heat in the store was fierce, and Marta's borrowed sweater made her sweat. The store was shaped liked a squared off U. The color scheme began to the left of the doorway and continued all the way around to end on the opposite side. Red, orange, yellow, green, blue, all the purple shades, ending with black. The problem was that most of the clothes were in darker tones, so the proportions were off.

"Oh, to hell with it," Marta said. She'd let Monique decide if it looked stupid.

She stood behind the counter and pulled out the script. She'd gone over it briefly the day she got it from the director. Now, in the quiet of the store, she focused.

ELAINE

Please don't go. Don't leave me. Wake up, Peter! Come back! I'm waiting for you. And I'll go on waiting for you even if . . . even if you never come back.

PETER'S MOTHER

What are you doing? You're supposed to talk about positive things, happy things, things he wants to hear! You go on like that, he'll sleep forever.

(Peter's mother, on the verge of tears, is quietly escorted from the room by a nurse. Elaine moves away from the bed and goes to the window. She turns her face to the sun and enjoys the warmth of it on her face.)

ELAINE

It's such a lovely day, Peter darling. Won't you open your eyes and see? Isn't this the best kind of weather? Falling-in-love weather, that's what it is. You know why I say that, right? The day we fell in love, the sun was out, the clouds were slow and gentle, the air soft. The green of the grass in the park—you said you'd never seen such a color.

The door opened, and two teenage girls giggled their way in. They each carried several shopping bags. One girl was tall, the other much shorter. Both wore expensive boots, distressed jeans, and poofy winter jackets. They set their bags on the floor and began to go through the clothes on the racks methodically, one garment at a time. The shorter girl glanced at Marta every few seconds, while the taller one kept her back to her.

"Can I help you find anything?" Marta asked.

"Oh, we're just looking," the short one said, in a heavy Russian accent.

Marta got off the stool and came around from behind the counter. She still had the script in her hand.

"Try the boutique at the end of the block," she said.

The tall girl turned and looked down at her.

"I'm still looking," she said, not in a Russian accent.

"Out," Marta said.

The tall girl blushed. "Who do you think you are?"

"Someone who's got no use for people who want to rip me off."

The tall girl stood perfectly still. Then she took a brightly colored polyester blouse she'd managed to drop into one of the shopping bags on the floor and handed it Marta. Marta looked at it. The fabric was cool and soft. No wonder the girl wanted it. Marta gave it back to her. She told them again to leave and said they should probably never come back.

When they'd gone, she put thirty dollars from her wallet into Monique's cash register.

Her little brother Foster used to steal spare change from her dresser drawer all the time. It took her months to figure out he was the one responsible. One morning, she announced to everyone at breakfast that she'd finally accumulated enough cash for that new pair of shoes she wanted, and sure enough, not even an hour later Foster crept into her room, observed slyly by Marta through the slightly open bathroom door across the hall. She could have gone ballistic but didn't. Instead, she broke down crying. She was genuinely hurt, because she and Foster always got along pretty well. He cried, too. In the end, she let him have the money. He had nowhere else to get it from. He wanted to buy their father a birthday present. She supposed good intentions counted for something in the end.

Those girls certainly had no good intentions. Then why had she let them take the shirt? Because she could see both sides: the outrage of being taken advantage of, and the thrill of doing something wrong.

She realized that very dichotomy would motivate her performance next Tuesday. The script called for grief, not anger, but both had to be present. Her first round had been full of rage and resentment, and it had clearly resonated with the director. She could play grief, too. Grief sharpened by anger.

She returned to her stool and read her part aloud, emphasizing certain words to indicate deep distress.

"Please don't *go*. Don't *leave* me. Wake *up*, Peter! Come *back*! I'm *waiting* for you. And I'll go *on* waiting for you *even* if . . . *even* if you *never* come back."

She was pleased. She got Rob on the phone and said he just *had* to come hear her read tonight. She'd take him out for *drinks* after.

He agreed. He loved her rendition. They both drank too much afterwards, and she had to put him in a cab back to Chelsea.

As she got ready for bed, her father called to tell her about the farewell dinner he and Angie just had with Maggie. It hadn't gone well. Angie hadn't been very nice, and Maggie went away mad. Marta could hear the worry in his voice. She didn't want to talk about Maggie. She said she wasn't feeling well but would call him in the morning, knowing she wouldn't.

This night, tomorrow, and the days ahead belonged to her alone.

chapter twenty-six

While Maggie's work became effortless, Josh stalled. Without Marta, there was no balance, no counterweight to the reality he tried to recreate. His focus on Maggie was personal, romantic, and passionate, yet she was impossible to capture on the page.

He asked her about growing up with an identical twin. She said she had nothing to compare it to.

He didn't understand.

"Well, it's all I know. I have no idea what it's like *not* to have someone who looks just like you."

"What about your other siblings, though?"

"Not the same."

"What do you mean, not the same? You all lived in the same house."

"I only ever shared a room with Maggie. Angie had her own. The boys had theirs."

Josh walked the length of the porch back and forth. He was in shorts. Maggie hadn't seen before how muscular his legs were.

Perhaps he wasn't making himself clear. Did they ever think they were the same person? Or two halves of the same person?

"No."

Liar.

So, she always felt completely herself, never borrowed, or, what was he looking for, *occupied?*

"You make her sound like a demon taking possession of me," Maggie said.

He thought there might be something in that he could use for the play, but then realized, no, that wouldn't work at all. It would turn off the audience.

He sat in the chair next to hers, facing the easel where Nina stood with folded hands, and black ivy vines growing from her head. The undeveloped fetus was separate, floating nearby, also with ivy vines for hair, though hers were red. The effect was dramatic because Maggie was using oil paint, not pastels.

She picked up her brush and began to fill in the background with broad strokes of bluish-green. She didn't mind having Josh so close when she concentrated. It might be a good predictor of their success as a couple.

He put his hand on her shoulder and she stopped, brush midair. She saw Marta, walking on a street somewhere in the Village, holding a paper cup of coffee and talking on her phone.

Josh removed his hand, and she pressed her brush to the canvas.

"I've been thinking about the day we met," he said.

"And?" Her brushstrokes narrowed.

"Well, what made you do it? Pretend to be her?"

"I didn't pretend. I just let you assume."

"Which was easy, because though I knew Marta had a sister, I didn't know you were an identical twin."

Crucial piece of information to leave out, don't you think?
Sorry!

Maggie asked him what Marta *had* told him about her.

Just that she was an artist and having trouble getting focused.

"She said that? I was unfocused?"

"She said you were struggling."

Didn't think you even noticed.

Hey!

Josh then asked what Marta had told Maggie about him.

Just that he was rich, working on a play, and wanted to break into directing someday.

"You know there was nothing romantic between us," Josh said.

"I figured that out when you looked so shocked."

They laughed about it, remembering.

He took her hand. She put down the brush. They kissed for a while. She knew he wanted to take her to bed, but she wasn't in the mood.

They pulled apart.

"So, why did you come on to me, when you'd only known me a few minutes?" Josh asked.

"Give me a break. What do you want me to say? I thought you were hot. Still do."

She could tell he wasn't entirely convinced, that he suspected she'd been spurred by something going on between her and Marta, which was true. She'd gotten tired of Marta always doing what she wanted and never getting in trouble for anything. She said nothing of this to Josh.

She said his writer's block wouldn't go on forever, that he just had to be patient. He said she was right, he already had an idea for a different direction to take the play.

"What if you met someone who looked just like you, but you weren't related at all?" he asked.

"You mean, like a clone?"

"No, because a clone would have to have the same DNA. At least, I think it would."

Maggie didn't get it. How could someone look exactly like you but be a different organism entirely?

"I don't know, but it's a cool idea, isn't it?"

"Sure."

She blended red into the blue to darken the area just behind Nina's vined head.

Nina seemed to approve of the color choice. Her eyes had warmed.

Josh said he'd been thinking about that friend of Maggie's stepfather, the guy that looked just like his great-uncle. He still couldn't get over the resemblance. Oh, he knew it was probably just that he misremembered his great-uncle's actual face, because faces were, in fact, very hard to remember. Think about it—when you haven't seen someone for a while, it's an aspect you recall, a gesture, but the face itself is really hard to summon. Did she agree?

"You said you were good with faces."

"Did I? When?"

"When you came over to Sullivan that first time."

"No, I didn't."

She sighed.

"I'm sorry," he said. "I'll let you get some work done. Let's try that Asian place over on Abbot Kinney later."

"Sure."

"And after, maybe hit up some boutiques."

"You don't have to buy me anything."

"Who said I was going to? I need a couple new shirts."

She knew he was teasing. He said just that morning that he had his eye on something for her.

He returned to his laptop, which he'd moved inside, out of consideration for the depth of Maggie's concentration. He wrote some notes about his new idea, trying to see where they might lead. After only a few minutes, his phone buzzed, and Brad's number glowed on the screen.

Brad said Josh wouldn't believe what that idiot sister of his had done. She told the parents there was no way in hell she was moving out of the city. She was doing just fine on her own, thanks very much. The parents were freaking. They wanted Brad to go into town and convince her to come back to Long Island, tell her it was better for the children. The problem was, he wasn't sure that it was. Kids did fine in a city, didn't they? Hell, you go anywhere at all in Manhattan and you see kids everywhere. He didn't like being turned into an errand boy. He was already taking care of everything out at the house, dealing with the landscaping company that routinely failed to maintain the yard, not to mention repairing that broken sprinkler head that sprayed water all over him one morning when he got back from a run. Yeah, he was running again. He found it good for the mind, as well as the body. Oh, and guess who he'd run into in a bar in Washington Square?

"Who?"

"Dierdre."

"Holy crap."

She hadn't changed. She was working for an architect, answering the phone. The math tutoring gig must have gotten old. She hadn't landed any parts, at least she didn't say she had. Brad hadn't asked. Josh can't have forgotten how touchy she could be. In fact, that one time someone at a party asked what she'd be in next, she said, "Your face." Remember?

"Yup."

Josh heard the car start in the driveway. He asked Brad to hold on a second. Better yet, he'd call him back in a minute, okay?

"Sure."

Maggie had already backed out of the narrow driveway when he opened the kitchen door. He trotted down the gravel, wishing he'd stopped to put on his flip-flops. When he reached the road, it was empty. Back inside, he saw that she'd changed her clothes before leaving. The yoga pants and tank top she'd been working in were lying neatly across the unmade bed. She hadn't left a note or sent him a text.

He told himself to get a grip. He called her phone. He heard it ringing on the porch.

Damn it!

Was this new, leaving her phone behind? Or had she just been in a hurry to get to wherever it was?

He lifted her phone from the wobbly wooden table they found at a neighbor's yard sale (Maggie said the best paint stands were old things no one wanted anymore) and scrolled through the calls and texts. The most frequent number was Marta's. There had been no activity for almost a whole day. That had to mean she was basically content with him. Otherwise, wouldn't she have wanted to complain to someone?

She didn't complain, really. If something bothered her, she tended to fall silent, knit her brow, and look charmingly fierce. He wondered what she kept to herself, if anything were about him, and knew he couldn't ask, because she seldom asked him anything other than practical things like where they might look for a dry cleaner. She was polite about his work but didn't delve too deeply. Maybe she was just giving him space and trying not to crowd him.

When she hadn't returned an hour later, he panicked. He thought about calling the police, but, in his anxiety, realized he couldn't remember the make and model of the car they rented. Then he thought to call the car rental company but couldn't remember its name. He kept her phone with him, checking it often to see if anyone tried to get in touch with her, maybe someone she arranged to meet.

But who? She didn't know anyone in LA. They hadn't met anyone, either, except for the listing agent who showed them the house. And they'd been together the entire time, except for two evenings ago when he went to play volleyball on the beach. The group who let him join their game played a lot better than he did, but were encouraging, not competitive. He told Maggie later it must be that mellow California vibe everyone seemed to have. He'd been out of the house less than an hour, but in that time maybe someone had come by. He remembered that the agent said her brother wanted a chest of drawers in the garage the previous tenant had left behind.

Josh went to the garage. The chest was still there. Maybe the brother had come, looked at it again, and decided he didn't want it after all. Maggie would have been polite and offered him a drink. When Josh got home from the volleyball game, she was drying her hair. Why had she washed it? She normally showered in the morning, didn't she?

He couldn't remember. He was totally flipping out.

He hadn't felt this bad for a long time.

Forty-five minutes later, Maggie pulled into the driveway, by which time Josh had resigned himself to the basic truth that either she'd return, or she wouldn't.

He stood in the back doorway and watched her get out of the car and remove a brown paper bag from the back seat.

When she saw him standing there, she said, "I got lost!"

"Where?"

"Somewhere south of Venice. I got totally turned around trying to find that specialty food store we passed the other day, and I forgot my phone, so I couldn't even use Google Maps. I stopped at three gas stations to ask directions, and the guys at the first two only spoke Spanish, and the third guy had no idea what to tell me because I forgot the name of our street."

She was flushed and sweaty. He took the bag from her and looked inside.

"What's all this?" he asked.

"Good cheese, good wine, good bread. And those little olives you said you liked."

"What's the occasion?"

"I reached a good stopping point and wanted to clear my head. I know you said Asian, but we can do that any time."

He hugged her awkwardly because of the bag in his hand. She hugged him back.

"Why didn't you ask me to come along?" he asked.

"You were on the phone."

"Brad called."

"The guy you went to college with."

"Yup."

She nodded. She said she'd take a quick shower, and then they could head down to the beach.

He asked if he could shower with her.

She didn't see why not. In fact, she said it could be fun.

chapter twenty-seven

Both Rob and Luis were beginning to lose patience. Marta had texted both of them and begged them to come by her place. Luis got there first; Rob fifteen minutes later. She was miserable. Her callback happened a few hours before, and she'd been so upset afterward she walked all the way home in the snow.

On top of that, it was Halloween. She missed Maggie. She wanted to call her, tell her the bad news, but then talked herself out of it.

So, instead, she complained to Rob and Luis.

"Being an understudy is good," Rob said, "I don't know what you're so pissed off about." His coat hung on the back of his chair. The phone in his pocket buzzed every few minutes.

"I agree. It was down to three, and you made the top two," Luis said. He'd come from work and wore black slacks and a white button-down shirt. He also smelled faintly of garlic. He worked in an Italian restaurant on the West Side, not far from the theater where *Delta Damsel* would soon be in full swing. Rob and Luis had established these facts while Marta was in the kitchen, opening a bottle of wine she'd picked up.

"Top two, but not top one," Marta said.

"Next time," Rob said.

"Or this time, if what's-her-name gets sick," Luis said.

"Janine Rayburn," Marta said.

"No kidding! I wondered what she was doing these days," Rob said.

They drank. Rob said he had to get going soon. His sister was in town for a couple of days, taking a break from the bliss of married life and motherhood.

Marta knew they were right. It was probably the best script she'd ever read. Maybe she could pressure the director to let her perform one night—just one lousy night—and see if the audience didn't actually prefer her rendition? Rob's said that probably wasn't a good idea.

He kissed her on the cheek on his way out, something he'd never done before, and Marta realized how sorry he felt for her. She was grateful for that, though she didn't normally take the sympathy of other people well.

Luis asked if she wanted to find some cheap costumes and go out somewhere.

"No costumes. But let's get some air."

"Cool. Though I have to warn you, I don't have a lot of cash on me."

"This again? How many times do I have to tell you to stop worrying about money?"

The air was bracing, so they kept up a brisk pace. The snow tapered. People were everywhere. A weaving Statue of Liberty went by, her torch pinned sloppily to the cuff of one sleeve. A man in a top hat struggled to keep up with her. An atmosphere of joy was palpable.

Marta felt better. She was proud of herself for how passionately she read the part. The director praised her interpretation. The woman reading the role of the mother took her aside afterward and said being an understudy could very well lead to great things. Her name would be on the playbill, after all. It was a tangible achievement.

With her arm looped through Luis's they went all the way over to Chelsea where a block of galleries was brightly lit and inviting. They entered one. There were two people speaking quietly in a corner. Luis looked closely at a series of collages featuring women's faces cut out of magazines and overlaid with geometric shapes in black and white. There were four works, collectively entitled *Proportionality*. Marta watched him study each one in turn with—what, admiration? Envy? Perhaps both.

About a year before, she'd gone to a performance of *A Doll's House* with Jill, another aspiring actress with whom she'd had a passing friendship after they met at an audition. Jill turned out to be shallow and not terribly bright, two strikes against anyone who seriously seeks to portray the heart and soul of another human being. The friendship was based on Jill's admiration of the way Marta had read the part they were competing for. Jill had grown up in New Hampshire, lived in a small apartment with two roommates, and supported herself working in a bookstore. She envied Marta's freedom with money. Marta paid for their tickets to an evening performance. Jill was clearly bored by the play, but Marta was entranced. The smoldering fury of Nora in the face of her husband's manipulation and dominance was striking. Marta wanted to be on that stage, in that role, being wholly true to Ibsen but also making it wholly hers. Afterwards she talked about this to Jill, who didn't understand what she meant.

"Well, look at it this way. You see a pair of shoes in the window and you admire them because they're beautiful. You really want them, but you can't afford them, and so the idea of someone else wearing them makes you envious. Two emotions, same object. Just depends on your vantage point," Marta said over drinks.

"I'm not into shoes so much," Jill said. "Seems like most people are. You read about these women who have hundreds of pairs of shoes. I just don't get it."

Marta didn't return Jill's next call, or the texts after that, and prayed she wouldn't run into her at any more auditions, which she didn't.

Did Luis find the work compelling? Was he jealous of the collagist's skill?

He caught her looking at him. He said, "I love cruising around galleries. I get so many cool ideas of things to try."

Admiration as a way to expand one's ability or expression. She hadn't considered that before.

A gray-haired woman with a pair of reading glasses on a chain around her neck approached Marta and Luis. She smiled warmly.

"I was hoping I'd see you again," she said and held out her hand to Marta. Marta shook it.

After a moment, the woman said, "Giselle Markham. Don't you remember me?"

"Of course."

"I just wanted to say I'm sorry it didn't work out with your *Inner Child*, but if you've got something new, I'd be delighted to see it. I wanted to let you know sooner that I was still interested, but I misplaced your number. I was going to try to get by your studio, but time got the better of me."

Marta introduced Giselle to Luis.

"A fellow artist, I assume?" Giselle asked.

"Yes."

"Ah. Tell me a little about your work."

Luis described his pencil drawings, and the series he was doing about the playground.

"Both sound interesting. Might I see some of them?"

"If you don't mind a trip up to Harlem."

"Your studio is there?"

"No. That's where I live."

"I see."

She handed him a business card from the pocket of her green silk jacket and suggested that he give her a call and say when might be convenient.

"And you. What have you been working on?" she asked Marta.

"Oh, this and that. I'm afraid we really must go. We're meeting some people for drinks, and we're already late."

Outside they laughed as they sped back towards the Village. Then Luis said he should call Maggie and tell her what Giselle had said.

"She's in LA now. I told you that," Marta said.

"I know. She would still want to know, though."

"Maybe."

"I just thought of something."

Maybe Giselle knew someone out there who might want to look at Maggie's stuff, a collector or gallery owner. He'd call her tomorrow and ask.

Marta asked, "Isn't Giselle going to wonder why I didn't mention moving?"

"I'll just say you're excited about going and were distracted."

Marta slowed her pace. The sidewalk was crowded and noisy. It was hard to hear, and she spoke loudly.

"Why are you trying to help her?"

Luis stopped. His eyes were hard.

"She's an artist. She's trying to get ahead. Why wouldn't I let her know someone likes her work?"

"Never mind."

"No, I want to know."

"No reason. I just didn't understand, that's all."

"Jesus. Are you jealous of your own sister?"

"Of course not!"

They continued, at a slower pace. She took his arm.

He said sometimes Maggie would talk about her in the studio, not at length, or anything very detailed, just about day-to-day things, like wishing she'd do her share of the grocery shopping, stuff like that. He often sensed some tension or unease between them.

"She complained about me?" Marta asked.

"No. But I could tell she wasn't entirely happy living with you."

"No one is ever entirely happy with anything."

"Don't be defensive, I'm just trying to explain what I mean."

He was sorry he accused her of being jealous, though Maggie sometimes said that about her, too. He recalled her talking about Kyle, and how close she felt to him, how glad she was for their friendship, then said Marta had issues with him for that very reason.

"That's not true. I just thought he was sort of flaky," Marta said.

"But you were with him that night in the bar."

"Yeah. He invited me and Josh to go. Maggie had given him a key to the apartment at some point—which I didn't know about—and he was there with Edgar when we got back from Dunston. I figured why not?"

Luis nodded. Marta said they could call Maggie now if he liked. He said to wait until they got back to her place. Marta hadn't gotten any candy for the trick-or-treaters, and Luis asked if there were families in her building. She didn't know, really.

"You haven't met the neighbors?" he asked. He stepped into a crosswalk and got immediately honked at by a cab turning the corner.

"No."

"I know just about everyone in my building."

Good for you.

You and your bad attitude!

Are you there?

Where the hell else would I be?

She saw Maggie standing on a beach with a drink in her hand. She didn't see Josh with her.

When they reached Marta's apartment, she called Maggie, who didn't answer. Instead of leaving a voice message, she texted *Ran into that gallery owner you met, thought I was you, said she wants to see more of your stuff. Luis will ask her to recommend a gallery out there that might take you on. More later.*

Then she didn't send it, though she told Luis she did.

chapter twenty-eight

By the following week, it was clear that Josh was in trouble with his work. He couldn't concentrate. He started one script after another. He flipped through the spiral-bound notebooks where he fleshed out ideas and tossed them angrily to the floor. When Maggie asked him what was wrong, he said he didn't know, maybe he missed the organized chaos of New York. Maggie said that made no sense. After all, there she was, just as unfamiliar with California as he was, yet moving forward full steam ahead. She'd bought more blank canvases and expanded Nina's existence onto each, along with the undeveloped fetus which she suspected was actually a twin.

He hung out at the beach a lot. He tried to teach himself how to roller skate, fell, and badly bruised both knees. He hadn't thought to rent kneepads. Maggie set him up with ice and ibuprofen. He gave her money to go out and buy a flat screen television for the living room. It then fell to her to set up the cable service and deal with Josh's irritation that the installation date was several days out.

He surfed the internet on his phone, quickly exhausting the limits of his data plan. When the cable company finally got the television connected, he added on an internet package that made it possible for him to use his laptop to read news stories, or so he said. More than once Maggie saw YouTube videos playing across his screen, often of something an animal was doing involving water, plastic balls, and other props invisible human hands provided.

She suggested he give up plays for the moment and write something else, like a novel.

"You don't just sit down and write a novel," he said.

"Why not? People do it all the time."

"You don't know what you're talking about."

She took the car and hit up the high-end boutiques along Abbot Kinney. She showed him what she bought, hoping it would get his eyes off his inane videos for a few minutes. He liked the scarf, the sandals, and the dress, but the belt with its big silver buckle was ridiculous and he couldn't believe she'd been so stupid to buy it.

She told him to go to hell. He apologized. She didn't care. By turns he either begged or bullied and then suddenly burst into a riot of tearful sobs.

"Whoa, Josh, take it easy, okay?"

He cried the way her father always had, with his face in his hands.

Her anxiety mounted. His weeping continued. She brought him a glass of water. He broke off long enough to drink some of it, then sat back on the couch, spent and silent. He wouldn't look at her. He wasn't looking at anything, really. Her phone rang inside her purse. She ignored it.

"Josh, talk to me," she said and sat beside him. She became aware that he hadn't showered. It was almost five in the afternoon.

She asked him what the hell was wrong, and he said haltingly that he honestly didn't know. Had this happened before? Yes, a couple of times, when he was in college.

"What caused it then?" she asked.

He wasn't sure. Too much stress, obviously. A sudden and complete loss of confidence. He became prone to panic attacks and couldn't leave his apartment. To be honest, he had to drop out for a semester and go home until he could cope with school again.

"Did you go to a doctor?" she asked.

He'd gone to several, one of whom suggested he might be bipolar. The therapist he saw last spring back in New York didn't agree. She felt he had an anxiety disorder and prescribed Xanax.

"You were seeing a psychiatrist?" she asked.

"A psychologist."

"So, you stopped going?"

Yes, right around the time he started hanging out with Marta.

"Did you tell her about it?"

"We weren't that close."

Maggie—1. Marta—0.

He looked exhausted. She asked him if he wanted to go lie down for a while. He said he was fine but could use a drink. They had a little wine left over from her visit to the gourmet food store. She brought him a glass. He took it down in one go.

She assumed he didn't have any Xanax with him?

No, the prescription had lapsed. In any case, he didn't want to take it again. It made him sluggish, not on his game, which he had to be to write. Maggie didn't point out that the depressed state he was in without it made writing impossible altogether, and that it was simply a matter of choosing the lesser of two evils.

He asked her to drive him to the store, where he bought more wine, a box of Pop Tarts, a head of lettuce, and some chicken breasts stuffed with cheese and olives they could bake up later.

Later, she found it hard to paint. His crying haunted her. Marta crossed her mind. Her energy still had a bright, warm color. She could use that familiar face around her now. But then she'd have to mention Josh's emotional instability, which Marta would somehow find a way to make Maggie's fault.

Over the next few days, Josh worsened. He slept late, went to bed early, drank too much, ate little. Maggie confronted him and said he had to go to a doctor. He told her to leave him alone. She took his phone off the nightstand one morning before he got up and found Brad's number. She hesitated. It wasn't right. But then, neither was this awful state of affairs.

At first, Brad was polite and expressed modest concern. When Maggie persisted, giving more detail about the depth of his despair, Brad said he had hoped Josh was beyond all that now. College had been hard on him, which Maggie probably already knew. He'd been plagued by his father's death, though it had happened years before. Maybe it was his mother's dependence on him that caused him to unravel, though that didn't seem likely, did it? Maggie said if his mother were so dependent, why hadn't Josh heard from her since they came west? Brad conceded the point, and then said the truth might be a little more complicated than either of them realized.

"What do you mean?" she asked.

He suggested that the mother's frequent phone calls were because she was worried about Josh's mental state. The idea that she was dependent might have been Josh's own explanation of her behavior.

"She'd still be in touch, though, wouldn't she? If she's so worried?"

"Maybe she figures—hopes—he's alright now."

"Or she's just relieved there's some greater distance between them."

Brad thought that might be the case. But if Maggie were truly curious, and since she obviously had access to Josh's phone, she could go through the list of recent calls and see if there were any from a 609 area code. Brad said to please keep him in the loop. And if the situation got really dicey, she needed to protect herself.

"Are you saying he could be violent?" she asked.

"I'm saying he can lash out. He did it to me a couple of times."

"Okay, thanks."

Maggie silently returned the phone. Josh stirred a little. She went to the porch. The breeze was fresh through the screens. She forced herself to concentrate on Nina, and to let her channel her creator's mood, the result of which was a red light in Nina's previously merry eyes, and thorns now embedded in her hair vines.

Just before noon, Josh emerged from their room, showered, clean-shaven, and wearing a new short-sleeved shirt he'd bought before leaving New York. Its pale blue color looked good on him. He told her he was really sorry for his bad mood, but it seemed to be passing now. He even felt like doing some writing. And you know what? He thought he might follow her suggestion and write a novel.

His voice was uneven. She asked him if he wanted some breakfast. He wasn't hungry but might be in a bit. He was sorry again for his mood. He didn't want her thinking it was any sort of a permanent thing.

"I still think you should see someone. Just to make sure," she said.

He promised he would. In fact, he'd already sent his old doctor an email asking for a referral here, if she had one. Otherwise, he could just Google someone up who had an office nearby.

She smiled at him, and a look of terror passed briefly over his face. He approached and kissed her lightly on the cheek. He smelled of his peppermint toothpaste. She stood up from her easel and hugged him hard. It took him a moment to ease into it and hug her back. But when he did, they stood that way comfortably for a few moments.

A little later he said the creative juices were stalled again, and he was heading down to the beach. Maybe there was a game going on. Did she mind if he went? She could come, too, and just watch, or bring her sketchpad. Maybe all the sunshine was why he was having trouble concentrating. Of course, she seemed to be cruising along just fine. What was her secret?

"I don't know. I guess I'm happy here."

Again, his eyes filled with fear. Then it was gone, and he was more like himself.

When he left, Maggie called Marta. Her voicemail recording had changed. Where it used to say, "I'm performing my way into the hearts of millions," now it was just, "You know what to do, and I do, too." Maggie knew instantly this meant Marta had moved forward somehow, that something good had happened.

You should have told me.

The message she left said she'd like a call back when she had time.

Then she tried Kyle, who picked up at once and sounded like he'd been drinking. Even so, he was alert, and followed her narrative easily. He was characteristically sympathetic. He'd had partners who went off the rails, too, and the only thing to do was be as kind as possible until you just couldn't take it anymore. He cautioned about getting sucked into a problem that might not have a good solution, and not to feel too responsible for something she didn't cause. She'd taken a big chance by moving across the country with someone she didn't know very well. She must have had a gut feeling that this guy was worth it, and if she still thought so, everything would probably be okay.

"I hope so," she said.

"Oh, darling! You sound so . . . I don't know."

"Skeptical?"

"I was going to say sad."

She wasn't sad. He had to believe her. She just called to get a reality check. She asked how things were with Edgar.

At this Kyle laughed and said Edgar was an absolute pain in the ass but had truly captured his heart. In fact, they were thinking about moving in together. Maggie told him to keep her posted.

"You too," he said. They hung up.

Leah was less kind. She said Maggie should get herself out of there, pronto. You can't live with someone who's unstable, she ought to know. No, she wasn't talking about Digger, and they hadn't actually lived together in any case. She meant her own mother. She wasn't going into all those details now. She said the big question was, would Maggie stay on in LA even if she had to quit living with Josh?

"I think so."

"Damn, girl, I should come check that place out."

"You should."

"Can't afford it. Not yet, anyway."

She was working in the grocery store part-time. When Digger quit paying her rent on the Culver place, she might have to work more hours. She might not even be there by then, in any case, if the house sold. She wondered if she could convince Carl to let her have his spare room, but Darrel might freak out about that. Yes, she was still seeing both of them. Why not? You only live once. Oh, Carl finally got her the digital proofs of the pictures he took that day in the barn. There was one of Maggie that was actually pretty good. She could ask Carl to send it to her. She might be able to use it as an artist headshot on a gallery brochure someday. Wouldn't that be awesome?

"Very."

Just after they hung up, a car pulled into the neighbor's driveway. Maggie went into the kitchen for a better view. She hadn't seen anyone in that house since they moved in. A man went up the steps, rang the bell, looked in the mailbox, and then under the door mat. She called from her front door, "Can I help you?"

"I'm here to pick up a set of keys from the realtor," he said. "She didn't leave them with you, by any chance?"

"No."

He called someone on his cell phone. The person didn't answer, and he didn't leave a message.

"You're the new owner?" Maggie asked, walking to the edge of the yard.

"Yes."

"I'm your next-door neighbor."

"I figured."

He came down the three front steps and held out his hand. His name was Riley Swain.

"That's got a ring to it," she said.

"Good for an actor, which I'm not."

"So, you're a . . ."

"Tax attorney," he said.

"Oh."

He was in his mid-thirties, not bad looking, and seemed nice enough.

"And you?" he asked.

"And me, what?"

"Well, let's start with your name."

"Oh, sorry! Maggie Dugan. I'm an artist. I just moved here from New York."

"City or State?"

"Both."

She gave a brief history. He'd never been to New York, but always wanted to go. He was a Californian, born and bred. And there weren't that many of them, believe it or not.

Josh returned from the beach and stood in the yard, watching her. His shirt was damp under the arms, and his hair was tousled. Maggie told Riley she had to get going.

"I hope you get your keys," she said.

"Yeah, me too."

When she reached Josh, she asked how the game went. He didn't say anything until they went inside. He splashed water on his face at the kitchen sink, then asked who that guy was.

"New neighbor."

"Looks like a jerk."

"Why?"

"Who wears a suit out here?"

"A tax attorney."

He stared at her. Maggie filled him in.

"Sounds like you got to know each other pretty well," he said.

"Yeah, during the five minutes we stood there talking."

He crossed his arms. She said she needed to get one thing clear: she didn't do jealous.

"Fine."

He left the kitchen, went into the living room, and opened his laptop.

Maggie tried Marta again, who still didn't answer.

chapter twenty-nine

For a week after getting the understudy part, Marta debated about quitting her job at Rosie the Riveter. She decided to keep it for a while to see how it went. If she got pressed for time, she'd give it up. Then the director's assistant called to let her know that rehearsals were being pushed back a couple more weeks.

"Crap! Why?" Marta asked.

The director was still casting for another play. It happened all the time. The assistant's voice had a trace of smugness, as if to suggest that Marta should know this. Marta thanked her and hung up.

Damn it!

She hated it when other people changed things.

She wandered into the closet and went through Maggie's clothes again. She put on a black leather coat. The collar and pockets were red and stitched with pink thread. She looked amazing in it. Her phone rang from the living room. She ignored it. She removed the coat and held it lovingly. She brought it to her nose, but there was no trace of Maggie's floral scent at all.

When her phone rang again, she swore, then answered it.

"Where have you been? I tried you like a million times," Maggie said.

"I'm at home. Just didn't feel like picking up. What's wrong? You sound on edge."

"I'm fine."

Maggie talked about the house they'd rented, her work, the boutiques she'd found, one of which carried amazing Mexican silver jewelry, and of course the beach.

Then she bluntly said Josh had sort of fallen apart on her.

"What do you mean, 'sort of?'"

Maggie said he was pretty down, and had trouble writing. Marta asked when it started.

"Pretty recently."

"You've been out there how long now?"

"Nine days."

Marta already knew that. She'd kept track of the days.

Maggie asked what he was like when they were together.

"We weren't together."

"I mean when you were hanging out. You were pretty tight for a few months."

"I guess."

Marta said sometimes he got frustrated with trying to get an acting troupe together. People's schedules were always hard to juggle. Then there was the problem of a decent script, not to mention finding an actual stage. Money was another issue. His allowance was generous, but his mother wouldn't let him at the principal of his trust fund.

Maggie said, "It's all his now. They went to a lawyer, and signed papers."

Marta was quiet for a moment. She asked if he were writing at all. Maggie said he'd given up on the play and was going to try a novel, but that too had come to nothing.

"What a flake," Marta said.

Now Maggie was quiet.

I'm sorry if that's harsh.

I know it's how you feel.

Marta said sometimes he wrote in a journal when he was in a bad mood. If Maggie could find it, it might tell her what was really going on.

"I know what's going on. His depression came back," Maggie said.

"You mean, it's happened before?"

"Yes."

Maggie gave her the whole story. As she spoke, it occurred to her that she was betraying a confidence. But the truth was important, and her keeping quiet wasn't going to help him. Marta said again to look for the journal. If he were using the same one, it had a black cover and a red silk book mark attached to it. It would show what he was thinking about.

"And what do I do then?" Maggie asked.

"I don't know. We'll figure it out."

We?

When they hung up, Marta went out to her favorite coffee shop. She was friendly with one of the baristas, and sometimes they chatted for a few minutes, but the place was too busy for that. Marta sat on a stool looking into the gray November light. She tried to remember if Luis worked today or not. She didn't hear from him quite as often as she had only the week before. Maybe he'd started a new project. If so, why hadn't he told her about it? Maybe now that he knew she was interested in him romantically he didn't think he needed to stay in touch so much.

Cynic.

I know, I know.

She dialed her dad's number to follow up on the disastrous dinner on Maggie's last night, then hung up before he could answer. She didn't really want to know what had happened. She could guess. Angie had been mean, critical, and then apologized. Next, she tried Timothy, but he didn't answer. She texted Rob, asking what he was doing. He didn't respond. She finished her coffee and went down to Rosie the Riveter, even though she wasn't scheduled. She could hang out with Monique, maybe offer to do a few chores off the clock. Anything was better than sitting by herself in her apartment.

The lopsided color scheme Marta had put in place had been redone. It seemed like the clothes were sorted first by decade, then by type, then by color. It looked better.

Monique wasn't surprised to see her. She said she figured she might be by.

"Why?"

"Isn't there something you'd like to tell me?" Monique asked.

"Like what?"

Monique put her hand on the cash register. Marta told her about the girls she caught shoplifting. She realized she should have written up a receipt and put it in the office where the others were kept. Monique probably couldn't figure out where the extra money had come from.

In fact, Monique said, she'd been waiting for Marta to tell her about the silk scarf, the bracelet, and the jumpsuit.

"I don't know what you mean," Marta said.

"I saw you take the scarf." Monique pointed to a small mirror high on the wall behind the counter, angled to show the entire store.

"Why didn't you just fire me, or call the cops?" Marta was surprised by the defiance in her voice.

Monique had done her share of mischief when she was younger. She liked to think of herself as a forgiving person, an understanding person. That's why she kept quiet. But time had gone by now, and it was clear Marta wasn't going speak up, so she had to.

"Okay, I'm sorry about the scarf. I'm happy to pay you for it. But I don't know about the bracelet and the jumpsuit. Really."

Monique said she kept tight control of her inventory. She supposed it had to do with her training as a nurse. She knew how to both observe and keep exact records. And she had an excellent memory. She found the items gone and knew she hadn't sold them herself. She might have assumed Marta sold them and forgot to add the receipts to the stack, but the register was wrong. Being a cash only store made it very easy to see what your transactions were or should have been.

"How much do I owe you?" Marta asked. The defiant tone was gone.

"Four hundred and thirty-five dollars."

"I don't have that much on me."

"Come back when you do."

The door opened, and a woman came in holding a little boy by the hand. She let go of him, so she could look at the rack of vintage shoes. The child looked up at Marta with round blue eyes that reminded her of Maggie's.

And mine, too, I suppose.

The woman tried on a pair of sling backs. She asked the little boy what he thought of them. He put his finger in his mouth. She removed them, put on the boots she'd worn in, and asked Monique if she had a bag for the shoes.

"Yes, of course."

Monique handed it to her across the counter. After the woman gave Monique thirty-five dollars and left with the little boy who carried the bag for her, Monique asked Marta why'd she'd come down today, if she weren't going to come clean about the items she took.

"To tell you I'm quitting. I got a part in a play."

"Congratulations."

"Rehearsals don't start for a couple of weeks. I suppose if you really need me, I could work until we get underway, but I'm in the middle of a big family problem."

"Oh?"

"My sister left town, and no one knows where she is."

Monique shook her head, whether to acknowledge the tragedy, or make it clear she didn't believe her, Marta couldn't tell.

"Okay then, I accept your resignation. But see that I get paid, okay?" Monique said.

"Okay."

Marta couldn't think of anything more to say, so she left the store and started walking. She was five blocks away when she realized she hadn't asked how Clarisse was doing.

chapter thirty

After two days of rain the mild weather returned. Josh took himself back to the beach. Maggie had hoped that being stuck inside would make it easier for him to write something, but it didn't. He only wrote in the journal Marta mentioned, which he took back to the bedroom and stashed out of sight. They hadn't had sex for days. She didn't miss it as much as she missed the Josh she used to know. How could confidence, wit, and passion all evaporate so quickly? Nothing had changed in her. If anything, she had improved. It was as if her strength sapped him. But people didn't work that way, did they?

The journal was easy to find. He'd put it in the dresser drawer with his socks and underwear. She sat with it on the bed, thinking she'd have to straighten the cover when she stood up again. Josh had gotten very fussy about how the house was kept. So far, she'd complied with his requests because she thought it was a good sign that he still cared about something. She opened the journal to the red silk bookmark.

When we dropped acid in Bear Mountain State Park and came down the trail, for a moment I didn't know if I were awake, walking beside Brad, or asleep in bed, dreaming it all. I had lifted off from reality and was startled into the recognition of my solitude. The other night, in the pull of too much wine, reality was again usurped, because Maggie's body is the same as her sister's and responds to mine exactly the same way.

How could that be possible? They didn't have the same fingerprints (they'd established that at an early age). The freckles on their backs were different. Obviously, Josh hadn't noticed.

Their sameness overwhelms me, isolates me, reminds me that I'm alone, and far from everything I have ever known.

Maggie closed the journal, and put it carefully back in the drawer, on the right side, under his boxers.

She'd never known loneliness as he described it. Growing up with an identical twin and three other siblings, they were all present within her, to one degree or another. Even now, across the country, Marta could still be felt as strongly as ever.

What she read disturbed her. Loneliness was one thing; losing touch with reality was another.

When Josh returned from the beach, he seemed calm. He embraced her and told her she smelled nice.

Like Marta? she was tempted to ask.

She realized that question would always be there. There was no way to avoid it.

For the rest of the morning, Josh worked on his laptop. She studied Nina for a little while, then put a blank canvas on the easel. She worked in two colors, orange and blue, in free-handed circles, sometimes intersecting, sometimes not. Where the circles didn't intersect, the paint was paler, not so intense. The greatest vibrancy was where the circles crossed.

Josh said they should go out for lunch.

"Sure. Let me wash up and change."

"Put on something nice."

"Don't I always?"

She returned in an ankle-length white dress and sandals.

"You look like a Greek goddess."

"A short Greek goddess."

He'd changed, too, in the second bedroom. He wore a bright silk shirt patterned with flowers, and tailored shorts.

She thought they looked very LA. Someone meeting them now would never associate them with New York.

They decided to walk to the commercial district. He said he thought they should buy a car and return the rental. That sounded fine to her. He'd heard from his mother. She was asking about Thanksgiving. Did Maggie think she'd like a trip to Florida?

"To meet your mother?"

"To have Thanksgiving."

She didn't know. She'd think about it.

Over a bottle of delicious California chardonnay, Josh said he'd gone back to the play. He thought he could move forward with it now.

"I've been meaning to ask you," Maggie said, "now that we've been together for a bit, what differences do you see between me and Marta?"

Josh swirled the wine in his glass, which threw a dancing golden light onto the table cloth.

For one thing, Marta tended to be crabbier, and Maggie tended to talk less.

Maggie nodded. What about their similarities?

"Well, you both snore," he said.

"Lots of people do."

"And you sound just the same when you sneeze."

"You remember the sound of Marta's sneeze?"

"Yours made me remember it."

Maggie ate more of her salad. Josh watched the fork travel from the plate to her mouth so closely it bothered her.

"You both like bleu cheese dressing, and you both kick off your shoes the minute you come in, and then can't find them again," he said.

"I feel like I'm living in a petri dish."

"I'm sorry. I've always been hypervigilant."

He brought up the car again, saying he'd always wanted a BMW. What did she think?

She didn't have an opinion. It was his money, he should get what he wanted.

He slid a small box across the table toward her. The brown paper was adorned with a lovely purple bow. The name of a jewelry store they'd gone into their first week in town was printed on the edge in gold script.

She opened it. A pair of emerald earrings sat on a blue velvet cloth. She knew the wires the stones were mounted on were eighteen karat gold, because she'd asked the clerk to show them to her. She also knew each emerald was point-six of a carat in weight, and that the pair cost Josh close to five thousand dollars.

"Josh," she said.

"Put them on."

She removed the gold hoops she'd worn every day since she bought them for herself almost three years ago and inserted the emeralds. They were heavier than the hoops and tugged at her earlobes.

"Perfect," he said.

She removed the right one and started on the left when he asked what she was doing.

"They're awfully fancy for every day, Josh."

His expression caught her off guard. That was how he looked on the day of the weeping fit. Was he going to weep again, right there in the restaurant?

She put the earring back in.

So, this is how it's going to be.

He held her hand all the way home. The wine and the sunlight made her head hurt. She'd have to buy herself a hat. She told Josh she was going to take herself out shopping in a little bit.

"Really?" he asked.

"I have to get something to go with these earrings, don't I?"

"Sure."

"Stay here, get some work done."

She took the car and drove into Santa Monica. She wanted to get out of Venice for a while. She parked in a garage, then found a coffee shop with lots of outdoor seating. She got Marta on the phone the minute she sat down. She said couldn't live with Josh. She gave her reasons, ending with the look on his face at lunch when she started to remove the earrings.

"He bought you emerald earrings?" Marta asked.

"Really good ones, too."

"Wow."

Marta said his obsession was odd, given how casually he used to go out with one woman after another. Maggie must have struck some deep chord in him. She didn't say this meanly, or with envy. Maggie thought about mentioning what Josh had said in his journal about their being just the same in bed, but knew it wasn't the sort of thing she could ever say. As Marta talked about how to stage a strategic retreat that wouldn't totally flip him out, Maggie knew the real reason she had to go was she couldn't stand his not being able to tell them apart in the dark. It never would have been an issue if they both hadn't slept with him.

"From now on, let's never go to bed with the same guy," she said.

"Deal. Not that it's likely to come up again."

"And let's not fight anymore. About anything."

"Okay."

"Were you super mad that I left?"

"Hurt, more like it."

"I'm sorry."

"It's okay. I probably had it coming."

Marta said she knew she was a pain in the ass. She just wanted what she wanted, when she wanted it. But she could try to be less bossy. That was doable, right? Maggie shouldn't expect any radical change, though. She'd come into the world this way, after all. Isn't that what the family always said?

"I don't think they know us as well as we know each other," Maggie said.

"True."

Maggie said they always thought she was a wimp, that she didn't stand up for herself. Marta said that might be why she had made so many sudden moves lately.

"To prove I'm not?" Maggie asked.

"To prove you can make a decision and still have the right to change your mind."

The conversation lulled for a moment. Maggie looked at the people on the street, and thought how each soul contained some grief, some unresolved issue beyond their control.

Marta asked if she would stay in California. Maggie said she would, for at least a few more months. She'd have to get their mother to cover the rent when the proceeds from the sale of the minivan ran out.

"What minivan?"

"The one I bought to move to Sullivan. I sold it right before I left."

"Did you tell Mom?"

"No."

"Oops."

If the matter came up, Maggie would say she was letting Leah use it for the time being. By then she'd have figured out how to explain that she'd gotten rid of it months before.

"You've been thinking about this a lot," Marta said.

"No, just making it up as I go."

"You can always sell the earrings if you get hard up."

"I couldn't do that!"

"But you could lie to Mom."

"Yeah, because she's family."

Marta said she understood perfectly, which meant they were both pretty screwed up in the head. Maggie said it was too late to start worrying about that now. The future was what mattered. For both of them. Had she ever considered giving LA a try? She could boost her acting career just as easily here as in New York.

"Have to wait until the play's done. It could run through spring," Marta said.

"What play?"

Marta told her about the understudy role.

"That's awesome!"

"Thanks!"

"But maybe afterwards?"

"Unless you're ready to come back here."

Guess we can't get by on our own.

Not in the long run.

"Good thing we found out when we did. Saves us the trouble next time," Maggie said.

"If there *is* a next time."

There won't be.

"Oh, and you'll never believe this. We ran into a lady who knows your work. Giselle. She wants to see more of it. You should call her."

"My stuff is still in Sullivan. I guess I could get some of it shipped down to her place."

"I thought maybe she could put you in touch with a gallery in LA."

"Yeah?"

"When you talk to her, just say you spaced mentioning that you were moving west."

"She thought you were me?"

"Yup."

"Oh, man!"

Maggie said that was one ruse that worked out. Then she asked how things were going with Luis. Marta said fine, they got along pretty well, had fun together, but probably weren't in love. She talked about the job at the vintage place which she'd decided to quit, even though rehearsals didn't start for a couple more weeks. Then she said she'd gotten caught shoplifting.

"Shit, where?"

"Where I was working."

"You stole from your own boss?"

"Yeah. Can't quit being the bad girl, I guess."

Maggie said maybe being the bad girl was an act, one she started performing when they were kids, just to set herself apart. Marta thought there might be some truth to that. Of course, Angie would never see it that way. Angie thought they were both losers, didn't she? Maggie said she sure as hell seemed to.

"You should have heard what she said to me at dinner," Maggie said.

"Yeah? Like what?"

"That everyone always lets me off the hook. That I never suffer consequences."

Which wasn't true at all. Hell, there she was, three thousand miles away with a guy who was teetering on the edge. Looking back on it, she probably never should have left New York in the first place, but that was ancient history now.

Marta said it was obvious that something inside her needed to push itself out. Once it did, life might make more sense.

"And you? When is your life going to make more sense?" Maggie asked.

"Maybe when we can hang out again."

And that gave Marta an idea. How about if she flew out there and helped Maggie get settled in a new place?

"That would be awesome!"

Then Marta said how strange it was.

That we haven't seen each other for so long?

Exactly.

They agreed to make plans. Maggie wanted time to break it to Josh carefully, citing herself as the problem. She'd say she wasn't ready for the kind of commitment he obviously wanted, that she appreciated what he'd done by bringing her west, and so on.

Marta asked if she were absolutely sure she wanted to move out, given the number of impulsive decisions she'd been making lately. Maggie said she was.

I wish I'd never done it.

The ruse? I know.

"I think from now on, I'll be me, and let you be you," Maggie said.

"That's from a song, isn't it?"

They laughed some more. Maggie said it was getting late, she needed to pick up a new outfit, and didn't want Josh getting all worried again. Marta would let her know when she was coming. She'd make a hotel reservation and line up a car. Maggie asked if she could do any of that for her.

"Nah, I'm on it."

Maggie said she was looking forward to seeing her. Marta said the same.

Okay, I love you.
I love you, too.

THE END

about the author

Anne Leigh Parrish is the author of six previously published books: *The Amendment*, a novel (Unsolicited Press, 2018); *Women Within*, a novel (Black Rose Writing, 2017); *By the Wayside*, stories (Unsolicited Press, 2017); *What Is Found, What Is Lost*, a novel (She Writes Press, 2014); *Our Love Could Light The World*, stories (She Writes Press, 2013); and *All The Roads That Lead From Home*, stories (Press 53, 2011). Her short stories have been published widely in literary venues. Her essays have appeared in *Book Riot*, *BookTrib*, *Writer's Digest*, and *Women Writers, Women's Books*.

about the press

Unsolicited Press was founded in 2012 and is based in Portland, Oregon. The small press publishes fiction, poetry, and creative nonfiction written by award-winning authors.

Learn more at www.unsolicitedpress.com